"Looks like I w

When her eyes laughed
only grinned. All around them, people were celebrating the touchdown, but Natalie was too caught up in her victory over him to notice. Tickled pink with herself, she had a grin as big as Texas on her face and couldn't seem to sit still. She might have been a thirty-three-year-old mother of twins, but she looked like a high school cheerleader. Max had never seen her so carefree, and regardless of how many times he reminded himself she was off-limits, he couldn't resist reaching for her and pulling her into his arms.

Then she stared up at him with stunned blue eyes, and Max groaned.

"It's a tradition," he said gruffly, nodding toward the kissing couples that surrounded them on all sides. "Everyone does it when we score."

Dear Reader,

When I came up with the story for *A Younger Man* and I was developing Natalie's children, I was watching *Desperate Housewives*. Bingo. Suddenly, Natalie had twin boys and they were a handful—sweet and loving and each of them all boy. I loved the idea of them being identical twins because I'm an identical twin. My sister and I could fool everyone…except our parents. All our friends wished that they had a twin, but we really longed to be triplets! Wouldn't that have been fun! In our next lifetime, watch out.

I hope I was able to show the boys' closeness in the story—there's no closer relationship on Earth. My sister and I still do a lot together. She lives right down the road from me. Growing up, we wondered if there would come a day when people would stop asking us if we were twins. It hasn't happened yet.

So for my sister Brenda and all the twins out there, this one's for you. Enjoy.

Linda Turner

A YOUNGER MAN

LINDA TURNER

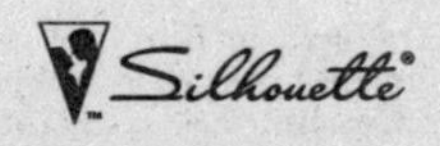

INTIMATE MOMENTS™
Published by Silhouette Books
America's Publisher of Contemporary Romance

ISBN-13: 978-0-373-27493-2
ISBN-10: 0-373-27493-9

A YOUNGER MAN

This edition published by arrangement with Harlequin Books S.A.

Visit Silhouette Books at www.eHarlequin.com

Printed in U.S.A.

Books by Linda Turner

Silhouette Intimate Moments

The Echo of Thunder #238
Crosscurrents #263
An Unsuspecting Heart #298
Flirting with Danger #316
Moonlight and Lace #354
The Love of Dugan Magee #448
**Gable's Lady* #523
**Cooper* #553
**Flynn* #572
**Kat* #590
Who's the Boss? #649
The Loner #673
Maddy Lawrence's Big Adventure #709
The Lady in Red #763
†*I'm Having Your Baby?!* #799
†*A Marriage-Minded Man?* #829
†*The Proposal* #847
†*Christmas Lone-Star Style* #895
***The Lady's Man* #931
***A Ranching Man* #992
***The Best Man* #1010
***Never Been Kissed* #1051
The Enemy's Daughter #1064
The Man Who Would Be King #1124
***Always a McBride* #1231
††*Deadly Exposure* #1304
††*Beneath the Surface* #1321
A Younger Man #1423

*The Wild West
†The Lone Star Social Club
**Those Marrying McBrides!
††Turning Points

Silhouette Desire

A Glimpse of Heaven #220
Wild Texas Rose #653
Philly and the Playboy #701
The Seducer #802
Heaven Can't Wait #929

Silhouette Special Edition

Shadows in the Night #350

Silhouette Books

Fortune's Children
The Wolf and the Dove

Montana Mavericks: Wed in Whitehorn
Nighthawk's Child

The Coltons
The Virgin Mistress

Silhouette Christmas Kisses 1996
"A Wild West Christmas"

A Fortune's Children Christmas 1998
"The Christmas Child"

Crowned Hearts 2002
"Royally Pregnant"

A Colton Family Christmas 2002
"Take No Prisoners"

Under Western Skies 2002
"Marriage on the Menu"

LINDA TURNER

began reading romances in high school and began writing them one night when she had nothing else to read. She's been writing ever since. Single and living in Texas, she travels every chance she gets, scouting locales for her books.

Prologue

"Listen up, everyone," the lead singer of the band called out as he and his fellow musicians finished performing one of the classic hits from 1988. "I've just been asked to announce that the buffet line is officially open. So those of you who've been trying to bribe your way into the kitchen can put your cash away. Let's eat!"

He didn't have to say it twice. Laughing and talking and catching up on the years that had passed since they'd all graduated from high school, the Liberty Hill High School Class of '88 gravitated en masse toward the buffet that had been set up on the far side of the VFW hall.

Moving to the back of the line with her friends, Natalie Bailey pointed out several of the men who had only been boys in 1988. "Look at the guys. Don't they look great! What have they been doing with themselves? They don't look like they've aged a day since high school."

"It's a rotten fact of life that men get better looking with age," Rachel said ruefully. "Women just get fat. How is that fair?"

"You're not fat," Natalie pointed out with twinkling eyes. "I, on the other hand..."

"Don't even think about going there," Abby warned. "You're a perfect size ten. How many mothers of twins can say that?"

"But I never lost that last five pounds of baby fat," she replied, looking down at herself with a wry grimace. "It doesn't seem to matter how many crunches I do or how many diets I try"

"So? It looks great on you," Lily said. "If you don't believe me, look around. You've been drawing looks all evening."

Natalie groaned aloud at the thought. "Please, spare me. I'm not looking for a man. All I want—"

"Is to go to college," her three friends said in unison, grinning.

Natalie had to laugh. "I guess I mentioned that already, huh?"

"Only six or seven times," Abby said with a chuckle. "So why aren't you?"

"Don't use the boys as an excuse," Rachel said before she could even open her mouth. "They're five now, aren't they? They're starting school. You should, too."

"I'd love to. But how do you suggest I pay for it? It takes everything I make just to get by—I don't even have the money to have my car fixed—it's leaking oil and I just keep putting more in and praying it'll last. Things would be different if Derek paid child support, but it takes money to go after him, and I don't have any because—"

"He doesn't pay child support," Abby finished for her.

"Exactly," she agreed. "Like it or not, I'm stuck."

"What a sleaze," Lily retorted. "I'm sorry, Nat. I know you loved him once, and he's the boys' father, but you worked to put that rat through college and law school. And what does he do? Turn around and find a way to shaft you again. Talk about a deadbeat!"

"He's the one who's missing out," Natalie pointed out. "He'll never have a relationship with his sons."

"One of these days, he'll live to regret that," Rachel said. "They're adorable."

Natalie grinned. "Sometimes they're like the twins on *Desperate Housewives,* but I wouldn't trade them for anything. Even if their father is the biggest loser that ever walked on two legs."

"Oh, no, you don't," Rachel retorted. "That's *my* ex! Derek may have walked out on you after you got pregnant with the boys, but at least you had your babies to console you. I spent years trying to get pregnant, and Jason never once told me that he'd had a vasectomy. Do you know how much I hate him for that?"

Natalie could only imagine. "It's not too late to have children, Rachel," she said quietly. "You're only thirty-six. You have plenty of time."

"Yes, she does," Abby said with a smile. "And you have plenty of time to go to school."

"I told you—I don't have the money."

"Get a grant. You're bound to qualify. And your grades were always great in high school. You were in the national honor society, weren't you? College will be a snap for you."

Natalie couldn't believe she was serious. "Are you

kidding? I can't remember the last time I had a chance to read a book. It must have been before the boys were born. That was five years ago!"

"Then you've got a lot of catching up to do," Abby said lightly.

She made it sound so simple. "What about my job? And the boys? Who's going to be there for them after school if I've got a class?"

"What about your mom? I thought she was thinking about moving to Eagle Creek to help you out."

"She was, but then she married Scot, and he wanted to travel. They're so happy. How could I ask them to give up traveling for me and the boys?"

"But you need help," Lily said, frowning. "You're completely on your own."

She shrugged, her smile little more than a grimace. "I have a friend who babysits the boys when I'm working at the restaurant. But that's not all day long."

"You'll work it out," Lily assured her. "Everyone who has kids finds a way to work it out. Just make sure you invite us to your graduation."

When her friends just grinned at her, Natalie raised a brow. "Oh, really? What about the three of you? You want me to go to school, but I don't see any of you making changes in your lives. I'll send you an invitation to my graduation when I get an invitation to Rachel's baby shower and Abby's wedding and a signed copy of Lily's first coffee-table book of her photos. What do you say to that?"

They all recognized a gauntlet had been thrown down. The question was…which one of them would pick it up first?

Chapter 1

"Look, Mommy," Tommy said happily, holding up the turtle he'd just carried in from the backyard. "I'm taking Pete with me to school!"

In the process of checking her sons' backpacks to make sure they would have everything they would need for their first day of school, Natalie glanced up in alarm. "What? Oh, no, you're not!"

"It's okay," Harry said as he followed his brother into the kitchen. Carrying his own turtle and unmindful of the dirty water dripping onto his clean shirt, he flashed a sweet, boyish grin at her. "The teacher won't care. Sean said everybody is supposed to bring something the first day for show and tell."

Swallowing a groan, Natalie didn't know if she wanted to laugh or cry. Sean Johnson, the next-door neighbor's son, was the bane of her existence. Nine going on thirty, he was constantly giving her sons advice that invariably led them into one mess after another.

"I'm sure Sean meant well," she told them as she quickly took the turtles from them and returned them to the small plastic pool they called home in the backyard. "You can take your turtles to school, but not today. First, you have to get permission from your teacher."

"She won't mind, Mom," Tommy assured her earnestly. "Sean said so."

"Just to be sure, we'll play it safe. Now, come on. I've got to get you two cleaned up or you're going to be late for school."

"Aw, Mom, not again! Do we have to?"

"We just changed shirts!"

They had, in fact, already changed *twice*, but she couldn't let them go to school looking as if they'd been playing in the mud. Bustling them into their room, she snatched their dirty shirts over their heads and had to laugh as they chatted like magpies.

She wasn't laughing thirty minutes later, however, as she hurriedly walked the boys to their classroom. "Can you stay with us, Mom? *Pleeeze?*"

"We don't want you to go to college," Tommy added, wrapping his arms around her legs. "You can go to school with us."

She saw the touch of fear in his eyes as well as Harry's, and forced an upbeat smile. "I'd love to, hotshot, but the principal won't let me. Your school is for boys and girls, not mommies. But you'll be okay—I promise. You're going to learn to read and add and subtract and do all sorts of things. Trust me…you're going to love it!"

They didn't look convinced, but then one of the little boys already in the classroom stepped forward and said, "Hey, are you guys twins? I'm a twin! See—there's my brother."

The boys absolutely loved being twins, and they were instantly fascinated. Turning to check out the other twins, they said in unison, "Wow!" Giving her a quick hug, they sprinted across the room to make friends.

Knowing they would never miss her, Natalie only took time to assure the teacher she would be back to pick the boys up when school was out, then rushed outside to her car. *Hurry.* The single word beat like a drum in her head. She had fifteen minutes to make it to class. She would have to fly.

It was a beautiful August day, and as she raced through the streets of Eagle, Colorado, all the lights turned green right on time. For a moment she thought she was going to make it. Then, just two miles from the campus of Mountain State University, her right rear tire blew with no warning. Startled, she gasped as the car swerved sharply to the right.

"Oh, no!" she cried, fighting to control it. "This can't be happening! I'm already late!"

The powers-that-be didn't care. The awkward thump of the flat echoed loudly as she steered her ten-year-old Honda over to the curb.

She wasn't a woman given to profanity, especially since she'd had her sons, but at that moment she could have cursed a blue streak. Class started in eight minutes. She was never going to make it.

"Well, damn!"

Another woman would have called her road service, then waited for a big strong man to change the flat for her. But she didn't have road service, and there was no big strong man in her life. Ever since Derek had decided he didn't want to be a father or a husband, she'd learned to do things herself. That included changing flats. Resigned, she turned off the motor and stepped to the back of the car to unlock the trunk and retrieve the jack. She didn't even worry about getting dirty—there was no point. It was a given she was going to get filthy.

Five minutes later she was struggling to loosen the lug nuts and not getting anywhere fast. Frustrated, she was considering giving the wheel a good swift blow with the lug wrench when a motorcycle suddenly pulled up behind her. A Good Samaritan at last, she thought with a sigh of relief. She was still going to be late for class, but she couldn't worry about that. She just hoped that whoever her rescuer was, he was big and strong. Because nothing short of a Hercules was going to loosen those darn nuts.

At any other time she might have been nervous if she'd been stranded on the side of the road with no one around to help her but a lone motorcycle rider. But she was on the main thoroughfare to the university, it was broad daylight, and it was the first day of the fall semester. Cars streamed by in never-ending numbers. Surely an ax murderer wouldn't be at work under such circumstances.

Rising to her feet to face her rescuer, a smile of gratitude already curling the corners of her mouth, she felt her breath hitch in her throat at the sight of him. She readily admitted that there was something about motorcyclists that had always fascinated her. Dressed in black leather, riding down the street on their growling steel-and-chrome bikes, they were like dark knights, bold and daring, in search of adventure. And if she thought there was even a chance her boys would grow up to ride motorcycles, she'd lock them both in their rooms until they were thirty-five!

That didn't mean, however, that she couldn't appreciate the man striding toward her. He'd taken off his helmet and left it on his bike, and she couldn't stop her heart from skipping a beat or two as she got a good look at him. Tall and lean, with thick golden-brown hair that was rebelliously long, he had a confident stride to his step and a glint of amusement in his blue eyes that was incredibly appealing. And he couldn't have been a day over twenty-two.

So? a voice drawled in her head. *He could be thirty-five and wonderful and you still wouldn't give him the time of day. You've sworn off men. Remember?*

She didn't deny it. When it came to love and romance, she was done, finis, finished. The only men in her life were her sons, and that's the way she intended to keep it. If she sometimes felt a pang of loneliness and longing in the dark of the night, then that was her little secret.

"Having trouble?" the knight in black leather asked her with a crooked smile. "Looks like you could use a hand."

"I just need the lug nuts loosened," she said. "I can do the rest myself."

His smile deepened into a grin. "A liberated woman. I like that. The way I see it, everyone should know how to change a flat and cook an omelet. It should be one of the essential skills they teach in school. Then you can always get where you're going and you won't go hungry."

Dropping down to one knee in front of the flat tire, he looked up at her with twinkling eyes. "You look like a woman who would know her way around a kitchen. What do you like to cook? French? Italian?"

She felt the warmth of his gaze all the way down to her toes, and for a moment, her mind went completely blank. Then his eyes crinkled with amusement and she realized she was staring at him as if she didn't have a brain in her head. Heat rushed into her cheeks, mortifying her. What was wrong with her? She was too old to blush!

"I'm sorry," she said stiffly. "I don't mean to be rude, but I'm really in a hurry. I've got to get to school."

Interest sparked in his eyes. "School? You go to Mountain State?"

She nodded, then grimaced wryly. "Well, I will if my professor doesn't kick me out before I even get to sit in on his first class."

"Oh, I doubt he'll do that," he replied as he easily loosened one lug nut, then another. "Most of the professors are pretty reasonable. What's your first class?"

"Archeology," she said, "with Professor Sullivan."

"Sullivan?" he said, arching a brow consideringly. "From what I've heard, he's a decent guy. Just tell him you had a flat on the way to school. I'm sure he'll cut you some slack."

"I've just waited so long to go to college, and I want to start out on the right foot. Not that the professor will probably even notice," she added. "I've heard that some of the classes are so large there's no way the teachers even know who all their students are."

"Oh, Sullivan will notice you," he assured her with a grin. "You're cute. And I heard he was partial to redheads."

Heat climbing in her cheeks, she narrowed her eyes at him. "Are you flirting with me?"

Not the least bit concerned by her warning tone, he winked at her. "Got it in one, sweetheart. How'm I doing?" When she just gave him a baleful look, he chuckled. "That good, huh? Give me time. I'm just warming up."

His eyes danced with laughter, and she had to admit that there'd been a time in her life when she might have been tempted. She'd always had a weakness for scamps, and there was no question that her handsome Samaritan had, no doubt, been using a smile and the glint in his eyes to get his way with women ever since he was old enough to crawl. But he had to be at least ten years younger than she was, and she was older and wiser than she'd once been.

Anxious to be on her way, she said lightly, "I really hate to shoot you down, but I've got to go. Thanks for loosening the lug nuts for me. I'll take it from here."

Not the least disturbed that she was giving him the brush-off, he only grinned. "No problem. I've got it." And not giving her time to argue further, he jacked up the back of her car and quickly replaced the flat with her spare. Two minutes later, he loaded the flat and jack in the trunk of her Honda, slammed the lid and turned to her with a smile. "You're all set to go."

"Thank you so much," she said with a sigh of relief. "You don't know how much I appreciate this."

"Get the flat fixed as quickly as you can," he told her as he opened her door for her and she quickly slipped into the driver's seat. "Your spare's pretty thin."

"I know. I've been meaning to get new tires, but you know how that goes." Smiling, she quickly started the car. "Thanks again for all your help. Gotta go."

"Hey, wait!" he said, startled, as she put the car in gear. "What's your number? Let's meet—"

Waving, she drove off.

"—for a drink," he called after her. She didn't even slow down. Ten seconds later she turned at the next corner and disappeared from view. Grinning, he grabbed his helmet and jumped on his bike. Ten seconds later he, too, turned at the next corner.

Her first class was in Old Main, and Natalie couldn't find a parking space anywhere. Softly cursing, she quickly cruised down the surrounding streets, keeping a eye out for the campus police and any space big enough to squeeze her car into. And with every tick of the clock on the dash, the knot in her stomach tightened.

When she finally found a parking place six blocks away, she was already late for class. Now it was only a question of how late. Quickly pulling into the small space between two pickups that were over their lines, she grabbed her backpack and sprinted for Old Main.

She was breathless by the time she reached her classroom. Hesitating outside in the hallway, she dreaded opening the door and walking in. Rushing in ten minutes after class started, the object of all eyes, was not the way she'd dreamed of starting college, but there was no help for it. Dragging in a calming breath, she straightened her shoulders and pulled open the door.

Just as she'd expected, all eyes swung her way. Heat climbed in her cheeks and she was only concerned with finding a seat and disappearing. But first she had to apologize to her professor for being so late. Forcing a weak smile, she directed her gaze to the man standing at the front of the classroom. "I'm so sorry—"

That was as far as she got. Her gaze locked with familiar

sparkling blue eyes that were full of mischief, and suddenly her heart was pounding in confusion. *This* was Maxwell Sullivan? A biker with a fast smile and a quick line who came to the aid of damsels in distress? He couldn't be! Maxwell Sullivan was not only a professor of archeology, but a writer who was a true-life Indiana Jones. He traveled all over the world, solving mysteries that were older than dirt, then came home and wrote bestselling novels about his adventures by weaving archeological facts into fiction. He couldn't possibly be her Good Samaritan! He was too young, too carefree, too cute to be a stodgy old professor.

"I'm sorry," she said huskily. "Excuse me. I must be in the wrong classroom."

"Not so fast," Maxwell Sullivan said easily as she turned to leave. "You're in the right place…or at least you are if you're Natalie Bailey. Everyone else answered roll."

Stunned, she just stared at him. "But you're supposed to be older!"

It wasn't until the rest of the class laughed that she realized she'd blurted out her thoughts. Mortified, she wanted to sink right through the floor. Forcing a weak smile, she said, "Excuse me while I take my foot out of my mouth. I just thought—"

"What everyone else in the class thought," he finished for her with an easy grin. "So, please, don't apologize. I'll be the first to admit I'm not your average professor."

"So just how old are you?" a cocky eighteen-year-old asked him from the front row. "Are you sure you have your Ph.D? You don't look old enough to shave, dude."

"You can thank my parents for that," Max retorted, chuckling. "I've got good genes. And yes, I do have my Ph.D. If you don't believe me—check me out. I didn't buy any of my degrees on the Internet."

"But you've got to be too young to be a professor," another student said with a frown. "How old were you when you graduated from high school? Nine?"

"Not quite," he laughed. "I was sixteen."

"Sixteen!"

"No way!"

Grinning at the uproar that created, he added, "I got my B.A. when I was nineteen."

The rest of her classmates found that hard to accept, but Natalie could well believe he'd finished college in three years. She'd read his books—they were complex and detailed and filled with fascinating historical facts. Knowing nothing else about him other than his published work, she'd never doubted that he was anything short of brilliant…which was why she'd been so eager to sign up for his class. She'd never dreamed he'd be a biker with peach fuzz on his cheeks.

Okay, so he wasn't *that* young. It was his quick, teasing smile that made him look like a teenager, she decided as her gaze moved to the sensuous lines of his mouth. Boyish dimples flashed with every smile, but it was the self-deprecating twinkle in his eye that charmed her. What woman could resist a man who didn't take himself seriously? How old *was* he? Frowning, she tried to do the math. If he graduated from college with his B.A. when he was nineteen, then spent the next four or five years finishing graduate school and his Ph.D., then he had to be at least…

"Twenty-eight," he said with a quirk of a smile as he looked her right in the eye and read her mind. "I've been teaching for five years."

From across the room, someone asked him when he'd gone on his first dig, but Natalie hardly heard his answer for the pounding of her heart. He gave the other students who asked questions the courtesy of his attention, but it seemed as if his gaze always returned to hers.

You're imagining it, she told herself. He's your professor, for heaven's sake! And a biker who's footloose and fancy-free. You're a mother with twins and the only one your boys can depend on to be there for them. The last thing you want or need is a man.

She couldn't argue with that. Her day started early and ended late, and, thanks to her deadbeat ex, she was not only the sole breadwinner, but also chief cook and bottlewasher, housekeeper, chauffeur, dragon slayer, crises solver, and entertainment director. She didn't have trouble sleeping at the end of the day—she just collapsed from exhaustion. Even if Derek hadn't totally put her off ever giving her heart to a man again, she didn't know how she would have fit one into the crazy days that were her life. There just wasn't time…especially now that she'd added college student to the many hats she wore.

She'd waited a long time for this day, she reminded herself grimly, as Maxwell Sullivan turned the conversation to the topics he would be covering over the course of the semester, the term paper that would count for twenty-five percent of their grade, and the dig they were all required to go on over the Thanksgiving holiday. The only reason she was here was to get an education.

Quickly grabbing a pen from her purse, she opened a spiral notebook and began taking notes. Diligently, she wrote down every word. She didn't have to look around to know that she was eighteen years older than the majority of the students, and she readily admitted that she was more than a little intimidated. How was she going to keep up? Most of her classmates had just graduated from high school a few months ago, and their study habits were as fresh in their minds as the memories of their senior prom. She, on the other hand, didn't even remember *how* to study. What, she wondered, trying not to panic, was she doing here?

Watching her from the corner of his eye as he discussed some of the well-known historical digs he'd been on, Max reminded himself that he wasn't the kind of teacher who allowed himself to become interested in his female students. Not only did the administration frown on it, but he didn't want or need the complication. So why the devil was Natalie Bailey so distracting? It wasn't as if she was trying to attract his attention. Most of the time her head was bent over her notes. She hardly looked up at all, and when she did, it was obvious that she was totally focused on his lecture. He should have been thankful for that. Instead he found himself wishing she'd look up and smile at him. What was going on here?

Losing his place in his lecture—something that rarely happened—he frowned and quickly got himself back on track…but not for long. He turned to pull down a map of ancient Egypt, and there she was again, right in his line of vision. He hadn't been lying earlier when he'd told her that her archeology professor was partial to redheads. He was—he readily admitted it. She'd twisted her dark-auburn curls up on her head, exposing the tempting lines of her throat, and he couldn't keep his eyes off her. She wasn't the kind of woman he would have called beautiful—with her quick flash of dimples, pert nose, and petite five-foot-two figure, she looked more like the girl next door.

But there was more to her than that. There was that stubborn chin that would challenge a man at every turn and the wariness that peeked out of her midnight-blue eyes. An interesting combination, he thought, intrigued. He'd seen her quick smile, the humor that danced in her eyes...and how quickly she stepped back from that. He would bet there'd been a time in her life when she'd been a lot more spontaneous than she allowed herself to be now. What had happened to change that? When had life taught her to be a more cautious soul? What was her story?

Suddenly realizing where his thoughts had wandered, he swore silently and did some mental backpedaling himself. What the devil was he doing? If she was unusually distracting, it was only because she was so different from the female students he usually dealt with, he reasoned. They were too young and flighty, too eager to fall in love and live happily ever after. There was nothing flighty about the conscientious Ms. Bailey. She had a maturity about her that the rest of her eighteen-year-old classmates lacked, and she had no idea how refreshing that was. How old was she? Thirty? Older? Was she married? Divorced? What had she been doing since high school?

Whatever it was, he sincerely doubted that she'd spent any time in college—otherwise, she would have known it wasn't necessary for her to write down every word he said. And that could present a problem for her, he realized, frowning. He was a tough teacher—he readily admitted it. His tests were fill-in-the-blank and essays and difficult for students fresh out of high school. Anyone who hadn't been in school in years would, no doubt, have a difficult time passing his class. If Natalie didn't want to find herself in trouble, she was really going to have to stay on top of things from day one.

Concerned—in spite of the fact that he demanded a lot of his students, he didn't enjoy it when they failed—he finished his lecture with an assignment. "Read the first two chapters before Wednesday," he said as the bell rang. "Oh, and Ms. Bailey, can you stay for a moment? I need to talk to you, if you have a minute."

He wasn't surprised when she hesitated. He'd flirted outrageously with her when he'd stopped to change her flat for her. He obviously had some fences to repair.

Silence fell like a stone when the last student filed out of the classroom, leaving the two of them alone. She still stood at her desk, facing him from halfway across the room. "I hope you realize I was only teasing earlier," he said. "At first I didn't realize you were one of my students. If I made you uncomfortable, I'm sorry. That certainly wasn't my intention."

Heat climbed into her cheeks, but she met his gaze squarely. "You really should have told me who you were."

He couldn't argue with that. The second she'd told him she was late for *his* class, he should have identified himself. And he certainly shouldn't have asked her out. That was a temporary loss of judgment. Aside from the fact that he didn't date his students, just last week, he'd sworn he was through with women. Everyone he'd dated in the past six months was looking for a husband, and he wasn't going there. Not after watching his father walk down the aisle, then into divorce court, more times than he could remember. From what he had seen, marriage only ruined the romance and made people who had once loved each other despise each other. He wanted no part of it.

So why was he so drawn to her? he wondered. He only had to remember the way she'd tried to give him the brush-off when he'd stopped to help her. He'd always liked smart, independent women who could take care of themselves. And even though he knew nothing about her except that she knew how to change a flat—once the lug nuts were out of the way—he didn't doubt for a moment that Natalie Bailey didn't need a man to lean on to get through life. That was the only reason he needed to avoid her like the plague.

"You were already upset about being late for class," he told her, dragging his attention back to the conversation. "I didn't want to upset you further by telling you who I was. I was afraid you'd be embarrassed."

That sounded good, but Natalie was the mother of twin boys and she knew a line of bull when she heard one. Her lips threatened to curl into a smile. "That sounds like something my sons would say."

So she had sons. He grinned. "You're not buying it, huh?"

"What do you think?"

"Damn. And I thought I was being so clever." His smile fading, he walked across the room and held out his hand to her. "Let's start over. I'm Maxwell Sullivan. It's nice to meet you. I hope you enjoy the class."

The simple gesture—and the sincerity in his direct blue gaze—charmed her as nothing else could, and the smile that she'd been trying to hold back tugged free. "I'm looking forward to it."

She placed her hand in his, only to frown in confusion when his fingers closed around hers. There was something so right about the feel of her hand in his. Almost as if he'd touched her a thousand times before, she thought, shaken. But how could that be? She'd never laid eyes on him before today. What was going on?

The thunder of her heartbeat loud in her ears, she eased her hand free and stubbornly, quietly, reminded herself why she was there. "I've waited a long time to go to college," she said huskily. "I just hope I can handle it."

"Actually, that's what I wanted to talk to you about," he replied. "Don't take this wrong, but you're obviously older than the rest of the class. How long has it been since you've been in school?"

She wasn't ashamed of her age. "Eighteen years," she said with a wry smile. "Better late than never."

"It's like riding a bicycle," he assured her. "You may be a little shaky at first, but it won't take you long to get back into the swing of things."

"I'm worried about the term paper," she admitted. "I don't even remember how to write a footnote."

"You're not alone," he said. "If you asked the rest of the class, they'd probably say the same thing, and they just graduated from high school last year. Don't worry—I've got a whole list of books that will help you with your paper. I'll bring it to class on Wednesday. If you need any other help, just let me know. Okay?"

His blue eyes were direct and sincere, and there was no sign of the flirtatious biker who'd asked her out when he'd stopped and changed her flat for her. Relieved, she appreciated his professionalism. But a few minutes later, as she thanked him and turned to leave, she couldn't forget the way her heart had jumped when his hand had closed around hers.

"Don't be an idiot," she muttered to herself as she hurried to her next class. "He's still a baby. So what if he looks like Lancelot on a motorcycle? Hello? He's your *teacher!* And you've got enough on your plate with school and the boys and your job—you don't need a man!"

Deliberately pushing the memory of Max Sullivan's twinkling eyes from her head, she was determined not to give the man a second thought the rest of the day. Unfortunately, he wasn't as easily dismissed from her mind. As she headed to her next class, she found herself comparing him to every man she passed on the street. They all came up short.

Chapter 2

Staring at his computer screen, Max read the only line he'd written in the past hour, then swore softly. It was stiff and awkward and hardly the work of a writer who'd made the *New York Times'* Bestseller List with his first two books. And to make matters worse, he couldn't think of a single way to improve what he'd written. He didn't mind admitting he was worried.

Starting the fall term was always stressful, he reminded himself. There were meetings, university functions he was required to attend, and this year the administration had added two more classes to his workload. And he had no one to blame but himself. Because of the success of his books and his rapport with the students, his classes were in hot demand. Normally he would have been flattered by all the attention, but he was on a short deadline with his next book and getting nowhere fast. He'd be okay once everything settled down.

"Yeah, right," he muttered to himself as he leaned back in his chair in disgust. "And if you believe that one, you might as well write a letter to Santa and ask *him* to give you a finished manuscript. At this rate that's the only way you're going to make your deadline."

The phone rang, and he welcomed the reprieve. Snatching it up, he growled, "Sullivan."

"Well, I guess I don't have to ask if you're having a good day," his father said dryly. "What's got your shorts in a knot? One of your girlfriends giving you trouble?"

"I don't have a girlfriend, Dad."

"Ah, so that's the problem. You should have told me. I could have made some calls for you."

Max swallowed a groan at the thought. He didn't doubt that there were any number of women his father could call—he'd been married eight damn times and had, no doubt, probably dated every woman in town over the age of thirty-five! Which was exactly why his old man was the last person he'd call for advice on women.

"Thanks, Dad, but meeting women isn't the problem. I can get my own dates." Absently glancing at the clock on the wall directly across from his desk, he frowned. "Hey, wait a minute. You and Joanna were scheduled to leave for Las Vegas this morning, weren't you?"

"We decided not to go."

"Not to go!" he repeated, surprised. "But you already have your tickets. And you love Vegas! The last time I went there with you, I had to pry you away from the tables with a crowbar. What's going on? Are you okay?"

For a long moment his father didn't say a word. And in the silence of his hesitation, Max knew what he was going to say before his next words ever left his mouth. "We're getting a divorce."

"Dammit, Dad!"

"There's no use getting upset about it," his father grumbled. "Some things just aren't meant to be."

"Yeah, and they all have a name," he retorted. "Susan, Karen, Bridgett, Laura… Shall I go on?"

"I don't regret a single one of my marriages," John Sullivan said stiffly. "I loved every one of my wives."

"You just couldn't stay married to them. I thought Joanna was the love of your life. Of course, that's what you said about Cathy and Tanya and—"

"I was hoping for a little sympathy. This isn't easy for me, you know. Just because this is my eighth divorce doesn't mean it doesn't hurt."

"I know that, Dad." He sighed, guilt tugging at him at his father's wounded tone. "I know how crazy you were about Joanna. What happened?"

"She thinks I'm having an affair."

"And are you?"

"Of course not!" he said indignantly. "I've never cheated on any of my wives. I would think you'd know that about me."

Now he'd hurt his feelings. Swearing under his breath, he reminded himself that his father really was hurting. "I'm sorry, Dad," he said quietly. "I didn't mean to imply that you weren't faithful. I just don't understand why you keep doing this to yourself."

"What? Getting married…or divorced?"

"Both! You're too old for this." He knew his father didn't want to hear anything negative when he was already down, but Max had held his tongue for too long. "The world's changed, Dad. It's not like it was when you and Mom were young. You don't have to marry every woman you want to sleep with."

"Watch it," John Sullivan warned. "You're starting to sound like a cynic."

"Because I don't put myself through the torture that you do?" he retorted. "C'mon, Dad! There's nothing wrong with enjoying a woman, then letting her go. You don't have to complicate your life by marrying her."

"You're talking about sex," his father said flatly.

Max didn't deny it. "You're damn straight. And what's wrong with that?"

"Because there's more to life than sex," the older man said indignantly.

Max winced. "There you go again—talking about love. It doesn't exist, Dad. Haven't you figured that out? That's why marriage doesn't work. You let your raging hormones convince you you've found your soul mate, and while you're under the influence, you make everything nice and legal. Then the magic wears off and you lose half of everything to a woman you no longer 'love.' You've got to stop this."

He was truly worried about his father, but he might as well have saved his breath. John Sullivan had always been an eternal optimist, and if eight failed marriages couldn't change that, than nothing else could. "You're the one who needs to stop the way you're living, son. What are you now…twenty-six?"

"Twenty-eight," he said dryly.

"Almost thirty," his father said. "And you've never had a serious relationship, never fallen in love. And that worries me. If you keep this up, you're going to miss out on what life is all about. And I don't want to hear that malarkey about love being nothing more than raging hormones. If you'd ever been in love, you would know that it's a hell of a lot more than that. It's finding someone you can share not just your bed with but your life. Aren't you lonely?"

"Oh, no, you don't," Max said quickly. "You're not going to turn this around and make it all about me. I'm perfectly happy with my life, thank you very much. Let's stick to the subject—you."

Far from offended, John Sullivan only laughed. "A bit touchy, are we? What's the matter? Did I hit a nerve?"

"Dad, I'm warning you!"

"Just think over what I said," he said, sobering. "Okay?"

"If you'll do the same," Max replied. "I mean it. I'm worried about you."

"I'll be fine," his father assured him gruffly. "I just need some time."

"Let's have dinner next week," he suggested, frowning. "We'll go to Pete's and have some ribs. I'll take you for your birthday."

"Hey, that sounds good. I can't remember the last time I went to Pete's."

Not surprised that he'd jumped at the offer—his father had been going to Pete's for ribs since before he was born—Max grinned. "I'll see you Wednesday, then. Are you still at the apartment?"

Just that easily the conversation returned to the divorce. John Sullivan's sigh carried easily across the phone line.

"Yeah, but it just doesn't seem the same without Joanna. She's moved in with her daughter."

"It'll take time, Dad," Max said quietly. "Try not to let it get you down."

As he hung up, however, Max knew his father was hurting. He was a sensitive man who didn't handle rejection—or divorce—well. He always moped around, stuck close to the house and generally felt sorry for himself for at least a month. Then—just when it seemed like he would never smile again—he would meet someone and the roller-coaster ride would start all over again.

If it would just end there, Max thought as he returned his attention to his writing, there would be nothing to worry about. But it was only a matter of time before his father planned his next proposal—he couldn't seem to help himself.

Just thinking about it made Max groan. Returning his attention to his writing, he tried to dismiss his father's troubles from his mind but without much success. When the phone rang again twenty minutes later, he hadn't written a single word.

Irritated with himself, he reached for the phone. "Yes?"

"Uh-oh, I don't like the sound of that. I take it you're still having problems."

At the sound of his editor's voice, a reluctant grin curled the corners of Max's mouth. "How'd you guess?"

"You sound just a little bit testy," Katherine Stevens replied. "Have you pulled all your hair out yet?"

"Not yet," he said, "but I'm considering it. How'd you know I needed to talk to you?"

"I'm psychic when it comes to my authors. What chapter are you on?"

He hesitated, but she would have to know sooner or later. “Two.”

Even though she didn’t say a word, he could almost hear her wince. Finally, quietly, she said, “You know you’re trying too hard, don’t you? You don’t need to put all this pressure on yourself. If you’d just let me reset the pub date, everything would be fine.”

“I can do this.”

“I don’t doubt it,” she agreed, “but the point is you don’t need to. Ed understands that our authors don’t live in a vacuum. Life happens. We have to be adjustable.”

Ed Quinn was the sole owner and publisher of St. John’s Press. Max had met him after his first book made the *Times* list, and he had to admit that Ed went out of his way to work with his authors. Max just hated to ask for extra time for writer’s block, of all things. He’d never had this kind of problem before, and he didn’t like it, dammit!

“Don’t make any changes in the pub date just yet,” he said gruffly. “I may still be able to make it.”

“You just need to lighten up,” she assured him.

“How? I’ve tried everything short of standing on my head.”

“Let’s go to dinner tomorrow night and talk about it.”

“Tomorrow? Are you in town?”

“I will be tomorrow,” she said with a chuckle. “Right now I’m in Denver for a conference. I thought I’d rent a car and drive up to see you tomorrow afternoon. If you’re free, of course.”

“Of course I’m free. Why don’t you meet me here at my office? When you come into town, turn right on University Avenue and it’ll take you straight to Old Main. There’s visitor parking out front. I’m in 204.”

"I should be there by five," she replied. "Send out the cavalry if I'm not. My sense of direction stinks."

"Don't worry." He laughed. "It's almost impossible to get lost between here and Denver. There's only one road and it goes straight to Eagle Creek."

"Trust me—you haven't seen me with a map."

Laughing, she hung up, and for a moment Max found himself grinning at his computer screen. Katherine was a saint—and a hell of a good editor. If anyone could walk him through writer's block—and he still wasn't convinced that was possible—it was Katherine Stevens. Lighten up, she'd said. It sounded easy, but as he studied the single line he'd written in Chapter Two, his stomach knotted with tension. So much for lightening up, he thought grimly.

When Natalie's alarm went off the next morning, she blindly slapped at the snooze button and found it without lifting her head from the pillow. It couldn't be six-thirty already, she thought groggily. She'd just gone to bed at...what? Three?

She groaned at the thought. No wonder she was exhausted! She'd been working on her homework for all her classes, trying to get ahead of the game before she found herself behind. It had seemed like a good idea at the time, but she'd never dreamed it would take so long just to read three different homework assignments and go over her class notes. And that was after only the first day of classes! How was she going to keep up the pace all semester when she had projects to do, papers to write, the boys to take care of, and she worked four days a week? She could forget snoozing five extra minutes in the morning, that was for sure. She didn't have time!

Jumping out of bed, she hurriedly dressed, then woke the boys. Then the fun began.

"I don't want to wear that. It itches!"

"That's my shirt! Mom! Tommy has my shirt!"

Playing peacemaker, aware of every tick of the clock, she separated them, found shirts that didn't itch and belonged to the right boy, then rushed to the kitchen to pop some waffles in the toaster. When the boys straggled in a few minutes later, she had everything ready. "As soon as you're finished, put your plates in the sink and go brush your teeth while I put on my makeup," she told them. "No playing around, guys. We can't be late again this morning."

Everything should have gone smoothly—she'd even poured the syrup, so all the boys had to do was sit down and eat. But she'd just smoothed foundation onto her cheeks when she heard a crash in the kitchen and one of the boys yelled, "Mom! Bongo ate my waffles and knocked over the trash can!"

"What?" Dropping her makeup, she rushed into the kitchen. "No, Bongo! Down!"

Too late. Bongo jumped up, planted his large, damp paws on her chest, and greeted her with a wet, sticky kiss. "Woof!"

"Oh, you bad dog! Down! Who let you in?" She shot a stern look at her five-year-olds, but she might as well have saved herself the trouble. They giggled in unison, and she couldn't hold her frown. "Scamps! What am I going to do with you?"

"Take us to McDonald's," Harry suggested, mischief dancing in his eyes.

"Pleeese, Mom," Tommy entreated, turning his mouth down into a sad little smile. "We didn't get breakfast. We're hungry."

"Why do I have the feeling I've just been scammed?" When they just grinned, she laughed and ruffled their hair. "Okay, we'll go through the drive-through—this time. Let me change."

She was five minutes behind schedule by the time she changed and got the boys and their backpacks loaded in the car. When she pulled into the McDonald's parking lot and zipped around to the drive-through, she knew it was going to be another one of those days when nothing went right. There were five cars ahead of her.

If she'd just had herself to worry about, she would have skipped breakfast, but the boys couldn't go all morning at school without something to eat. Resigned, she got in line.

Fifteen minutes later she pulled up in front of the boys' elementary school and couldn't help but notice what a difference a day made. Unlike yesterday, when they'd begged her to stay with them, this time, they hardly took time to kiss her goodbye before they grabbed their backpacks and burst from the car with huge grins on their identical faces. Their two new twin friends ran to meet them, and Natalie realized with amusement that she was all but forgotten.

With two hours to spare before she had to report for work, all she wanted to do was go to the university library and begin researching possible topics for her term paper for her archeology class. Unfortunately she still had a flat that had to be repaired, all because Derek was nowhere to be found. She hoped he was enjoying his life in the Caribbean with no responsibility, she thought grimly. She and his sons were doing just fine without him.

The old resentment stirred at the thought of his abandonment of them, but as she finally stepped into the university library, she was relieved to discover she wasn't nearly as angry as she'd once been. And there was only one reason for that—after all these years, she was finally in college.

Still unable to believe it, she hurried into the library with a light step and a smile on her face. When Max Sullivan had told the class about the term paper that was due at the end of the semester, her younger classmates had grumbled about the amount of work they would have to do, but she'd been waiting for eighteen years for the chance to do just such an assignment, and she couldn't have been happier. Finding a small alcove close to the archeological section, she went to work.

Lost in an ancient tomb filled with fascinating details about a dig in Peru, Natalie didn't even notice the other students who quietly passed her alcove. Then she felt the touch of eyes. Glancing up, she gasped in surprise. "Professor Sullivan!"

A pained look wrinkled his brow. "Please...call me Max. In case you hadn't noticed, I'm not hung up on titles."

When his mouth curled into that quick, engaging smile that always seemed to knock the air right out of her lungs, she couldn't seem to drag her gaze from the sensuous curve of his mouth. Lord, he was good-looking! If only he wasn't so young...

The thought shocked her. What was she doing? She didn't care if he was forty and as dependable as the sunrise. He was her teacher. And she wasn't looking for a man! How many times did she have to remind herself of that?

"Natalie?"

She blinked, and her gaze flew to his. She took one look at the amusement dancing in his eyes and realized too late that he obviously knew exactly what kind of effect he had on her and every other woman who had any estrogen in her veins. Mortified, she just barely held back a groan. What was it about him that had her acting like some kind of starstruck teenybopper? She had to stop this!

Cursing the hot color in her cheeks, she straightened her shoulders. "I beg your pardon, *Professor.* Did you say something? I was up late last night working on my homework and my brain's not working very well today."

"You've found my secret hiding place," he said, grinning. "Do you mind if I join you? Feel free to tell me to take a hike if you need the space to yourself. You were here first, and I don't want to intrude."

She should have sent him on his way. It certainly would have been the wise thing to do, considering the way her heart seemed to skip a beat every time her eyes met his. He knew exactly what she was doing by insisting on calling him *Professor,* and she had a sneaky feeling he was just biding his time. For no other reason than that, the last thing she should have done was share a table with him in a secluded nook of the library. But when she opened her mouth to tell him she worked better alone, she heard herself say instead, "Of course you're not intruding. I just didn't expect to see anyone I knew."

"I always come here when I need to jump-start my creativity," he said as he pulled out the chair directly across the table from her. With an animal grace that was incredibly sexy, he dropped into the chair and stretched out his long legs.

Underneath the table, his foot innocently brushed against hers. Just that quickly, the air in the alcove grew much more intimate. If he noticed that she'd gone as still as a post, he gave no notice. Instead he nodded at the book open before her on the table. "Are you working on your term paper already?"

"I can't afford to get behind," she said simply. "I have to be at work in an hour, but I thought I'd at least get started." Cocking her head at him, she frowned. "What about you? What did you mean...you come here to jump-start your creativity?"

He grimaced. "Writer's block."

"Are you serious?"

"Hopefully, it's not a permanent condition," he retorted in disgust. "Though it certainly seems like it. Every time I sit down to write, all I do is stare at the screen and get nowhere." Suddenly realizing how that sounded, he grinned crookedly. "Wah! Feel free to call me a crybaby. Sometimes, the truth hurts."

She had to laugh. "Well, now that you mention it..."

"No more whining," he promised her. "You're here to study and I'm just rambling on, bothering you. I'll shut up now."

"You're not bothering me," she said.

"Shhh," he whispered, grinning as he pointed to a sign on the wall. "No talking. Can't you read?"

When she gasped, then narrowed her eyes at him, he almost laughed. Damn, he liked her! Unable to resist the chance to find out more about her, he abandoned any idea of reading and sat back to openly study her.

"What are you doing?" she hissed, blushing.

Wicked mischief flashed in his eyes as he leaned forward and said in a whisper that forced her to lean forward, too. "Watching you. I was just wondering how everything's going. What other classes are you taking besides mine?"

He watched in delight as she narrowed her eyes at him again. "I thought you came here to read."

"No, I came to jump-start my creativity," he corrected her. "That's what I'm doing."

"Oh, really? And how are you doing that? All you're doing is asking me questions about school."

He smiled. "You don't have a clue how fascinating you are."

"I bet you say that to all the women you find yourself sharing this table with."

Uncaring of the sign asking for silence, he burst out laughing. "I like you, Mrs. Bailey."

"Like I said, Professor, I bet you say that to all the women—"

Chuckling, he didn't deny it. "Guilty as charged. Now that we've got that settled, what was that you were saying about your other classes?"

For a moment she gave him that look again, the one that made him want to laugh, then she laughed herself. "Okay. I don't know why you're so interested, but I'm also taking English lit and algebra. With your class, that's nine hours. I'd love to take more, but with the boys and my work schedule and everything, that's about all I can manage."

"I think it's incredible that you're able to take anything when you have children," he said honestly. "Do you have any time at the end of the day to just sit down and put your feet up and relax with your husband?"

Something flickered in her eyes, but she only said quietly, "The husband took a hike a long time ago, but yes, I do get to put my feet up once in a while."

So that was what had put the shadows in her eyes, he

thought. Obviously, there was more to the story, but he didn't intend to push. "If you find time to relax when you've got sons, then you must be better organized than my mom was when I was growing up," he said easily. "Most of the time she was running from daylight to midnight."

"Oh, I can handle that." She chuckled. "Algebra is another matter completely."

He grinned. "Not your thing, huh?"

"God, no! The only math I've done in the past eighteen years is balance my checkbook, and sometimes, I don't do that well. Give me your class any day. It's a piece of cake compared to algebra."

"Really? Maybe I need to toughen up the curriculum," he said dryly.

Only just then realizing what she'd said, she gasped, "Oh, no! I didn't mean—"

Laughing, he sat back to grin at her. "I was just kidding. The class is hard ènough as it is. So tell me what else you've been doing besides taking care of your kids, working and studying. Have you joined a sorority yet?"

"Yeah, right." She chuckled. "Somehow, I don't think I would fit in very well with the eighteen-year-olds."

"I think you'd fit in with just about anyone," he replied honestly. "What about football games? Dances? I know it's early in the semester, but you are planning to get involved in the social scene, aren't you?"

"Oh, no," she said, horrified at the very suggestion. "I'm thirty-six years old—"

"So?"

"I've got kids!"

His mouth twitched. "I know I sound like a broken record,

but...so? And don't say you won't fit in," he added quickly. "You've obviously waited a long time to go to college. It should be about more than studying, don't you think?"

He had a point, one that Natalie hadn't considered. She had waited years to go to college. Why shouldn't she enjoy it? Just because she was a little older and had children didn't mean she couldn't be a part of university life like the rest of the freshmen in her class.

"I'll think about it," she promised.

"Good." Glancing at the clock on the wall across from their alcove, he said, "I hate to break this up, but don't you have to get to work?"

Natalie took one look at the clock and gasped. "Oh, my God! Where did the time go? I've got to go!"

"Time flies when you're having fun," he called after her as she snatched up her things and ran for the door. "Have a good day!"

Never looking back, she waved and disappeared from sight. Chuckling, Max sat back with a smile on his face. As a quiet stillness settled over the small alcove, he should have turned his attention back to the reading he'd come to do. Instead all he could think of was that he'd never be able to sit in his favorite alcove again without thinking of Natalie.

Racing down Main Street, every tick of the clock echoing in her head, Natalie groaned when the traffic light thirty feet in front of her abruptly turned red. She had no choice but to hit the brakes. She was going to be late. Resigned, she knew she had no one to blame but herself. She'd lost track of the time talking to Max.

No, she corrected herself as she raced into the parking lot

of Finn's, the restaurant where she worked. She hadn't just lost track of time—she'd forgotten about it altogether. When Max turned his blue eyes on her and grinned, he made her forget her own name. Did he realize that? Just thinking about it mortified her.

When she pulled open the back door of the restaurant and stepped into the kitchen, she wasn't surprised when Sam Finnegan, her boss, immediately spied her. His office had a wall of windows that gave him a bird's-eye view of the kitchen, and it didn't matter how busy he was at his desk, he saw everyone who came and went.

Looking up from his paperwork, he drawled, "Well, as I live and breathe, if it isn't my star waitress. I was beginning to wonder if you were going to put in an appearance today. What's the matter? Couldn't tear yourself away from your sorority?"

Well used to her boss's caustic, teasing remarks, Natalie stepped into the open doorway of his office and said dryly, "I'm not the sorority type, Sam. You know that."

"So where you been?"

"I had to do some research at the library before work and I sort of lost track of time. I'm sorry."

"Yeah, yeah," he grumbled, tossing her one of the company aprons that all the waitresses wore. "I don't know why I'm surprised. You get your head stuck in a book and you're on another planet."

She couldn't deny it. Everyone who knew her knew she loved to read. She never went anywhere without a book in her purse. "Isn't it awful?" she said with a grin. "I've got a whole new library to explore. I'm loving it."

When he just sniffed and gave her his patented scowl, she wasn't surprised…or fooled. At first glance, Sam Finnegan appeared to be one of those men who didn't have a soft bone in his body. He was gruff and sarcastic, and no one in their right mind would ever mistake him for a teddy bear...until they got to know him.

When Derek had suddenly walked out on her and left her penniless when she was pregnant, Sam had turned out to be her knight in shining armor. He hadn't asked her why a woman who was big as a house needed a job or where the hell her husband was. He'd simply looked at her with those piercing brown eyes of his, told her he had an opening for a waitress, then asked her if she could start immediately. Then he sat her in a corner and had her do book work for him so she wouldn't be on her feet all day. When the boys were born, he gave her maternity leave and refused to let her return to work until her doctor gave the okay. That kind of generosity in the restaurant business was unheard of in a college town where there were always students looking for a job.

She'd accused him then of being a sweetheart of a man, and he'd flat-out denied it. But over the years he'd given himself away time and time again. Whenever the boys were sick or had a doctor's appointment or needed her for anything, he grumbled and complained...and let her off with pay. And when she'd approached him about going to college, he pretended to be totally against the idea, then he told her that he'd been thinking about changing her shift so that she worked every other day. He'd claimed that he was going to change everyone's hours—it would make the running of the restaurant more efficient—but he never changed anyone else's but hers.

"You know it's all your fault," she said lightly as she stepped further into his office and dropped into the chair in front of his desk. "If you hadn't changed my hours and made it possible for me to go to school twice a week, I never would have had access to the university library."

"Oh, no, you don't," he growled. "You're not blaming this on me. I had nothing to do with you going to college. All I did was change your shift. And I'm going to change everyone else's as soon as I have time to work out a new schedule."

If Natalie hadn't known him so well, she might have believed him. But she'd worked for him for over five years, and she knew from experience that when he decided to make changes around the place, he moved quickly. Once, he'd changed the entire menu and had the restaurant painted in a week. If he was going to change everyone's shifts, he would have already done it.

"Okay," she said, fighting a smile. "I guess I'm just a victim of coincidence and there's no one to thank."

"I guess so," he grumbled. "Of course, you're losing a lot of hours by missing two days of work every week. And I'm short-handed Saturday afternoon since Evelyn quit. I could really use some help if you're interested in putting in some extra hours."

Bent over his paperwork, he never looked up as he casually threw out the offer of more work. Watching him, torn between tears and laughter, Natalie could have kissed him. The rat! He didn't need extra help on Saturdays—Evelyn had quit two months ago and he'd said on more than one occasion that he hadn't really needed her, anyway! He was just trying to help her out financially.

If the world had been a perfect place, she would have sincerely thanked him for the offer and turned him down. She was spending too little time with her boys as it was, and she hated being away from them. But money was tight, and she had to make up the time and money she was losing wherever she could.

The boys would understand, she assured herself. And it wouldn't be forever…just until she finished college and got a teaching job. Then she would be home whenever the boys were out of school, and she would no longer have to feel guilty for leaving them.

"I would love to work Saturdays or any other time you need me when I'm not in class," she said huskily. "Thanks."

Not surprisingly, he only grunted, "Don't thank me. You're doing me a favor. Now get to work before I dock you for standing around shootin' the breeze."

"Yes, sir," she retorted, saluting smartly. "Anything you say, sir. I'll get right on it, sir."

Whirling, she stepped out of his office…just as he hit her in the back with a wadded up piece of paper. Grinning, she went to work.

Chapter 3

"Hi, sweetie. Did everything go all right at school?"

"Harry put a worm on the teacher's desk after recess," Tommy said proudly. "You should have heard her scream, Mom. She thought it was a snake."

Natalie groaned. She always called the boys during her break and checked with Susan Reed, their babysitter, to make sure everything was all right. Invariably, the boys had one outlandish tale after another to report. "I'm sure the entire school heard her," she said dryly. "Let me speak to your brother."

"Sure, Mom. Is he in trouble?"

"What do you think?" she replied. "Let me speak to him."

She didn't have to ask twice. Not wanting to get in trouble himself, he quickly handed the phone to his brother. "Hi, Mom," Harry said glumly.

"You got in trouble, didn't you?"

"Yes."

"Am I going to have to meet with your teacher?"

"She sent a note home."

Natalie could just imagine what it said. "We'll discuss this later," she told him grimly.

Thankful to get off so easily, he said quickly, "Luv ya, Mom," and hung up before she could ask to speak to Susan and get the real lowdown on what happened.

Her break over, she didn't have time to call Susan back, so she returned to work. When Derek had walked out on her, she'd readily admitted that the thought of raising boys by herself terrified her. She was an only child with no close male cousins, so boys had always been a mystery to her. How could she teach them to be boys?

Even now, thinking about her mindset before they were born made her want to laugh. Obviously, her sons needed no help being boys. They were wild and outrageous and a constant source of delight to her, despite worms and snakes and frogs and an endless array of clothes that would never come clean. Given the chance, she wouldn't have traded them for anything.

Wondering how she was going to discipline Harry without breaking into a smile, she headed back to her station, grabbing a couple of menus for the couple who'd just claimed one of her tables. She couldn't see the man, but the woman was drop-dead beautiful. Blond with a sophistication that was seldom seen in Eagle Creek, Colorado, she was simply dressed in a black knit top and white slacks, yet she still managed to draw every eye in the room.

Wondering if she could wear her hair in the same sleek style,

Natalie approached with a friendly smile. "Hello," she began. "My name is Natalie. I'll be your server for the evening—"

She always introduced herself to her customers, then told them the day's specials, but when her eyes fell on the woman's companion, the specials flew right out of her head. "Professor Sullivan!"

A slow grin curled the corners of Max's sensuous mouth as his dancing eyes met hers. "Mrs. Bailey! You know, it's funny the way we keep meeting this way. If I didn't know better, I'd swear you were following me."

"Actually, you're the one who turns up everywhere I am, Professor," she retorted, "so I believe that's my line."

"I beg your pardon." He chuckled. "You're right." Suddenly remembering his manners, he turned to his companion. "Katherine, this is Natalie. She's one of my most promising students."

"I don't know about promising," Natalie said ruefully, "but I'm certainly one of his oldest. It's nice to meet you, Katherine."

"You, too," she said easily. "I bet Max is a hard taskmaster."

She sent him a smile that told Natalie that this was no first date—they knew each other well and liked each other. And something twisted in Natalie's heart, something that felt an awful lot like disappointment. From the first moment she'd met him, she'd known that he was a man who enjoyed the company of women. And why shouldn't he? He was young and carefree and didn't answer to anyone.

So why was she suddenly so sad? she wondered. If she was in the market for a man—which, again, she wasn't—he was nothing like the kind of man she would pick, anyway.

She needed a family man, someone who was responsible and settled and ready to be a father to her boys. As much as she was attracted to Max Sullivan—and there was no point in denying it further—she didn't think he would be ready for fatherhood anytime soon.

"It's too early in the semester to tell," she replied. "I'll know more after the first test." Handing them each a menu, she took their drink orders, then added, "If you like fish, you might consider trying the grilled rainbow trout. It's fantastic."

Giving them time to study the menu, she hurried away to fill their drink orders, and in the quiet she left behind, Max looked up from his menu to find Katherine studying him with a glint of amusement in her brown eyes. Surprised, he lifted a dark brow at her. "What? Why are you looking at me like that?"

"She's very attractive."

"Mmm."

She grinned. "And older than most of your students."

"I believe she did mention that."

"You like her."

"I like all my students."

"Max! Stop that. You know what I mean."

He did know what she meant—and he wasn't going there. "I don't date my students, Katherine. You know that."

"I know you haven't in the past," she replied. "But you've never been interested in eighteen-year-olds. Natalie's different. What's her story?"

"None of your business—"

Natalie arrived then with their drinks, and he shot his editor a quick, quelling look. Ignoring him, Katherine sat back in her chair and looked up at Natalie with a friendly smile. "I don't get to meet Max's students very often. How long have you been working here?"

"Over five years," she replied. "I started here two months before my twin sons were born."

Surprised, Katherine said, "Your boss hired you when you were seven months pregnant?"

Natalie grinned. "He told me later he must have been out of his mind. He likes to think he's a tough guy."

"I know the type." Katherine chuckled. "My first boss was that way. He grumbled and scowled...and gave me a month off with pay when my mother was dying."

"Sam did the same thing for me when my sons were born. And I'd only worked for him for two months!" Five years later that still amazed her. Pulling out her order pad, she smiled. "So...have you decided what you'd like to eat?"

They both ordered the fish, and Natalie only took time to find out what dressing they wanted on their salad before she once again left them alone. She was hardly out of earshot before Katherine leaned across the table and said softly, "She's not wearing a ring. Has she mentioned a husband?"

"Dammit, Katherine, I told you—"

"Oh, hush," she scolded. "I'm just teasing you. So...is she married?"

He shouldn't have answered her, but he could tell from the glint in her eye that she wasn't going to let it go. "She's divorced. Okay? All I know is her husband left her a long time ago. Obviously, he was a jackass."

"See! You *are* interested! I knew it!" He started to object, but she held up her hand, stopping him. "You would be interested if she wasn't one of your students," she corrected, biting back a smile. "I suppose I should admire your scruples, but…"

"Don't say it!" he warned.

"I just don't think you should let that stop you. She's not a kid, and neither are you. What if she's your soul mate? What are you going to do? Just let her walk away? That's crazy!"

Staring at her in amazement, he said, "You're something else, you know it? You're an editor—you work with words. How many times do I have to say I'm not interested?"

"You can say it until the cows come home, but it's not going to mean a damn thing as long as you can't take your eyes off her," she retorted. "Admit it. You're fascinated with her."

When he just looked at her and didn't say a word, she chuckled. "C'mon, Max, don't be mad. I'm a sucker for romance—you know that. Indulge me."

When he rolled his eyes, she laughed and reached across the table to pat his hand. "Trust me, this is just what you need to shake you out of the slump you're in with your writing."

"There is no *this,*" he insisted. When her eyes just twinkled in understanding, he had to laugh. "I think I need a new editor."

As she waited on Max and Katherine for the rest of their meal, making sure they had everything they needed and that the food lived up to their expectations, Natalie couldn't help but envy Katherine. Max was teasing and attentive and made no effort to hide the fact that he thoroughly enjoyed Katherine's company. And for the first time since Derek had walked out on her, Natalie wished she had a man in her life.

Shocked by the thought, she told herself that it had been a long day and she was just tired and feeling sorry for herself.

But later, as she watched Max and Katherine walk out of the restaurant with eyes only for each other, the emotions tugging at her heart had nothing to do with tiredness.

And things didn't get any better over the course of the next week. She was lonely and more than a little restless. As she watched the young eighteen-year-old girls in her archeology class flirt outrageously with Max in an effort to get his attention, she felt all alone…and far older than her years. She found herself examining her life, the choices she had made, and she realized that nothing had turned out the way she'd expected. She'd always wanted a home and family and a husband she could go through life with. She had two out of the three, and most of the time, that was enough. She adored her sons and thanked God for them every day. And even though her home was a cottage and not a grand showplace, it was nice and, most important, all hers. Derek had signed it over to her in the divorce. It was the only decent thing he'd done to provide for his children.

She tried to convince herself she was content, but she couldn't count the nights when she lay awake in the dark, aching to have someone beside her. She was an independent woman, but she didn't thrive on her single status. In spite of the way her marriage had ended, she'd loved being in love, loved being married. Nothing had ever felt so natural. Yet she was alone. And she had a sinking feeling she always would be.

By Saturday the walls were closing in on her and she couldn't stand the thought of staying home to study. She had to work the dinner shift at the restaurant, but she had hours to kill before then, and the boys were just as anxious as she to get out of the house. Thumbing through the newspaper in search of a movie to take them to, she arched a brow at the headlines of the sports page. Eagles Take On Bobcats.

You've waited a long time to go to college. It should be about more than studying, don't you think?

Max's words echoed through her head, tempting her. Why not? she thought, smiling for the first time in what seemed like days. Going in search of the boys, she found them in the backyard, playing with Bongo. "Hey, guys, how would you like to go to a football game?"

They'd never been to a real football game before, and neither, for that matter, had she. As the three of them approached the football stadium with a steady stream of other fans, she had to admit that she was as excited as the boys. The game was scheduled to start in ten minutes, and the stadium seemed, from the outside, at least, to be already packed.

Quickly paying for their tickets, Natalie hurried them through the entrance gate just as the Rocky Mountain University marching band began playing the school fight song. A roar of approval went up from the crowd, and suddenly the old stadium that had been standing in that same spot since the 1920s was rocking.

Holding her sons' hands in each of hers, Natalie looked down at the boys and grinned when she saw their wide-eyed expressions. "Pretty cool, huh, guys?" she said with a grin. "C'mon. Let's find our seats."

She didn't have to tell them twice. Tugging her after them, they sprinted for the stairs.

Their tickets were for general admission, so they could sit anywhere that wasn't reserved. With the stadium nearly full, however, there just weren't that many available places to sit. Searching through the crowd, Natalie was beginning to think they might have to stand for the entire game when she suddenly spied a few seats in the sea of humanity to her right. "I think we just got lucky, boys. Hurry. There're some places right in front of the man in the yellow shirt."

There were people coming up the steps behind them, also looking for seats. Lightning quick, she pulled the boys after her into the crowd. "Excuse me. Excuse us, please. Thank you. I'm so sorry—"

Long seconds later they burst through the crowd to their seats just as the opposing team lined up across the width of the field for the kickoff. Their kicker ran toward the ball at a steady lope, then kicked it with all his might, sending it sailing toward the opposite end of the field. With a deafening roar of encouragement, the crowd surged to its feet and the fun began.

Grinning down at her sons, who couldn't see a thing except the adults standing in front of them, Natalie teased, "What are you guys doing down there? C'mon, stand up here next to me and tell me what you think."

Quickly they jumped up onto the metal bleachers that served as seats and stood on either side of her, broad grins of excitement splitting their identical faces. "Wow, this is cool! Look how little they look!"

"Can we go down on the field, Mom? We want to play. We can catch the ball like that!"

She laughed. "Your time's coming," she promised. "When you're older."

"Awh, Mom, you always say that!"

"We're big. We can do it now!"

Watching the expressions that flitted across their faces, she grinned and swept them both into a bear hug. "You guys are going to be awesome when you get to play, but for now, we've got to let the big boys play. Okay?"

They grumbled, but were quickly distracted when the crowd once again roared in approval and the band broke into the fight song. "Look, guys! See number 22? Oh, my goodness! He's going to score!"

Her eyes on the field, Natalie didn't see Max Sullivan making his way through the crowd in the row behind her. He, however, spied her almost immediately. "Natalie? Is that you?" When she whirled, shocked, he laughed. "I don't believe this! I didn't know you were coming to the game!"

"I didn't know you were. This is too weird!"

"Maybe fate's trying to tell us something," he suggested, grinning.

"Or maybe this is fate's idea of a joke…if you believe in that kind of thing."

"Maybe." His gaze dropped to the two identical young boys staring up at him with wide eyes. "You didn't tell me you had two boyfriends."

"We're not her boyfriends," Harry said, grinning. "She's our mom!"

"No kidding?" he said, pretending to be surprised. "She doesn't look old enough to be a mom. You must be…"

"Harry Bailey," he said proudly.

Struggling to hold back his own smile, Max said soberly, "It's nice to meet you, Harry Bailey. I'm Professor Sullivan, your mom's teacher." When he held out his hand for a shake, Harry's eyes widened to saucers as he carefully placed his small hand in Max's much bigger one.

On the other side of Natalie, Harry's twin said, "Wow! You're a teacher? How come you're not all mean looking like the teachers at our school?"

Max laughed. "Just lucky, I guess. And you are..."

"Tommy Bailey," he said with a grin, whipping out his hand for a shake. "We're twins!"

"You're kidding? Really? I would have never known."

Impressed with the ease with which he captivated the boys, Natalie lifted a delicately arched brow at him. "I didn't know you had kids."

"I don't."

"Really? Then you must have a lot of nieces and nephews. You're a natural."

"Actually, my parents were each married a number of times—" talk about an understatement! he thought wryly "—so I have a ton of stepsisters and brothers, and it seems like they're all determined to have enough kids for their own basketball team. The kids are all as sharp as tacks and keep me on my toes. They're doing a good job."

Just the idea of a dozen or more nieces and nephews talking circles around him made Natalie grin. "What'd they do? Trick you out of your car keys?"

"No, just a trip to a go-cart track for some laps at the speed of sound."

Natalie saw her sons' eyes go round and quickly warned, "Don't even think about going there, boys. Maybe when you're fifty-two."

"Awh, Mom!"

Max chuckled, then nodded toward the field. "Hey, guys, look! It's fourth down. I bet the coach calls a field goal."

"Surely not," Natalie argued, frowning at the drama unfolding on the field. "It's only fourth and two and we're on the twelve-yard line. We've got to go for it."

Surprised, Max lifted a dark brow. "You know football?"

She grinned. "Why, Professor, I would have never taken you for a chauvinist. Don't you know any women who like football?"

"No," he retorted wryly. "Do you?"

"Yes." She laughed. "My mother. She's a Dallas Cowboy fan. When I was little, we spent every Sunday afternoon in front of the TV, watching the Cowboys."

Impressed, he grinned. "So you know your stuff, do you?"

"Well, I'm no expert, but yeah, I know enough to understand what's going on."

"Good. Care to wager a little bet on the next play?"

For an answer, she grinned and held out her hand. "Make it easy on yourself."

"I never bet more than two dollars," he warned with twinkling eyes, then promptly closed his fingers around hers. "You're on."

All around them, the crowd went crazy as the teams ran back on the field after a quick time-out. Natalie could almost hear the pounding of her heart and told herself it was because she was caught up in the game and wanted the satisfaction of winning the bet. If she could still feel the warmth of Max's fingers around hers, she intended to keep that little bit of information to herself.

"Looks like I was right," Max said smugly, making no effort to hide his grin as he drew her attention back to the field. "We're kicking a field goal."

"What?" Snapping back to attention, she frowned down at the field as the Eagles lined up for a field goal. "I can't believe this! It's only the first quarter! Why's the coach playing it so safe?"

"Maybe he'd rather have three points than nothing," he replied. "Here we go. Have you got your money ready?"

"I think college football needs some women coaches," she sniffed. "A woman would have gone for it."

The words were hardly out of her mouth when the center hiked the ball to the quarterback, who was supposed to catch the ball and hold it steady on the kicking T so the kicker could kick it. Instead of placing the ball on the T, however, the quarterback jumped to his feet the second he caught the ball. A heartbeat later, he threw a pass to his favorite receiver, who sprinted into the end zone before the other team even realized that the home team had just faked a field goal.

Stunned, the crowd went wild. Laughing in delight, Natalie grabbed her sons and did a little dance. "Yeah! Touchdown! Did you see that pass, guys? Right in the breadbasket! Looks like I won the bet."

When her eyes laughed up into his, Max only grinned. All around them, people were celebrating the touchdown, but Natalie was too caught up in her victory over him to notice. Tickled pink with herself, she had a grin as big as Texas on her face and couldn't seem to stand still. Jumping up and down, pumping her fists, she had no idea how cute she was. The boys were as excited as she, but Max couldn't take his eyes off Natalie. She might have been a thirty-six-year-old mother of twins, but she looked like a high school cheerleader. Max had never seen her so carefree, and regardless of how many times he reminded himself she was his student and off limits, he couldn't resist her. Taking advantage of the fact that the boys were watching the band as it jumped into a frenzied rendition of the fight song, he gave into impulse and reached for her.

His lips touched hers, and almost immediately he realized his mistake. She was soft and sweet, and the taste of her went straight to his head. If they'd been anywhere but in a crowd of screaming people and in full view of her five-year-old sons, he would have pulled her close and lost himself in the taste and feel of her. Instead all he could do was step back before her sons noticed that their mother's teacher was on the verge of kissing the stuffing out of her.

When she stared up at him with stunned blue eyes, Max groaned. *Don't!* he wanted to tell her. If she kept looking at him like that, he was going to reach for her again, and then he really would be in trouble. "It's a tradition," he said gruffly, nodding toward the kissing couples that surrounded them on all sides. "Everyone does it when we score."

Dazed, her lips still tingling from his kiss, all Natalie could think of was the six touchdowns the team had scored last week. She'd missed that game, but she'd read about it in the newspaper. According to all predictions, this game was going to be even more of a runaway. Would Max kiss her every time the Eagles scored?

"Natalie? Are you okay? I didn't mean to offend you...."

"What? Oh, no...I—"

"I'm hungry, Mom! Can we have some popcorn?"

"I want a hotdog...with chili!"

"I'll get that," Max told her when she looked down at the boys like they were speaking a foreign language. When she blinked up at him in confusion, he grinned. "I owe you." When she just looked at him, he chuckled. "For the bet? Remember?"

She blushed. "Oh, no! I was just playing around."

"A bet's a bet," he insisted. "So, we need popcorn, a chili dog, and I'm getting a sausage on a stick. How about you? What do you want?"

She should have said she didn't need anything—somehow, the game was turning into a date, and she didn't even know how it had happened—but she was thirsty and didn't want to appear rude by turning him down, then getting something for herself later. "Just a cola. Do you need some help carrying everything?"

"No, I can get it. Stay here and enjoy the game."

As he made his way through the crowd toward the aisle on his left, Natalie stared blindly at the action still going on down on the field and tried to calm the wild pounding of her heart. Max had kissed her! Touching her fingers to her lips, she could still feel the warmth that had streaked all the way to her toes the second his mouth had brushed hers. It had only lasted mere seconds, yet with nothing more than that, he'd shaken her to the core. What had possessed him? What did he want from her? She wasn't one of his teenybopper freshmen students looking for a good time. Even at eighteen, that hadn't been her style. She hadn't slept around then and she didn't now. She had responsibilities…children. She didn't intend to forget that just because Max Sullivan had kissed her and made her go weak at the knees….

"Mom? You look kind of funny."

"Yeah, your cheeks are all red. Are you sick, Mom? Do you have a fever?"

Jumping up onto the bleachers so he was eye level with her, Harry placed his hand on her brow and frowned into her eyes. Startled out of her musing, Natalie blinked both sons into focus and blushed all over again. How could she explain to her five-year-old sons that she was in la-la land because her professor had kissed her for all of five seconds? They wouldn't understand, of course, and she couldn't say she blamed them. She didn't understand it herself!

"I'm fine," she assured them huskily, forcing a smile. "I think I just got a little too hot jumping around. It's warm today, isn't it? I should have worn something cooler."

She was wearing a thin, short-sleeved cotton blouse that should have been more than cool enough for the middle of September, but the boys were too young to notice that. Then the Eagle band broke into the school fight song, distracting them, and there were, thankfully no more questions about her "fever." Standing beside them, her gaze directed unseeingly at the field, Natalie could think of nothing but Max...and the kiss.

Caught up in her thoughts, she didn't notice that he'd returned until he suddenly joined her. Carrying a cardboard tray full of food, he grinned down at her. "What'd I miss?"

A dozen answers sprang to mind...the crazy need he stirred in her, the rush of her blood, the pounding of her heart every time he smiled at her. The last thing Max needed when it came to women, however, was encouragement. He was far too sure of himself as it was. "Just the kickoff," she said lightly. "Here, let me help you with that." She took the drink he'd bought for her, then handed the boys their food. "What do you say?" she asked them.

"Thank you, Professor Sullivan," they said in unison, flashing their twin dimples at him.

"Can you make another bet with Mommy so we can get some nachos later?" Tommy added. "We really like nachos."

"Tommy Bailey!" Natalie gasped, shocked. "You know better than that! Apologize right now!"

Chuckling, Max only reached over and ruffled Tommy's red head. "You got it, sport. But how do you know your mom's going to win the next bet?"

"Because Mom's really smart," he said simply, proudly. "She always wins when we bet."

"So you're a gambling woman," Max teased, interest sparking in his eyes. "I would have never guessed."

"We only bet on little things—like who can run the fastest or jump the highest," she said ruefully. "If these monkeys keep growing the way they are, it won't be long before they leave me standing in their dust."

Max could just see her running with her boys, encouraging them, daring them to be the best they could be. She was a good mother—and her sons clearly adored her. So where was her ex? he wondered. She'd said he'd taken a hike, but to where? Had the divorce been amicable or hostile? Did she still love him? If she did, then she wasn't as smart as he thought she was. The man had to be a fool. He'd walked away from a fascinating woman, and Max didn't have a clue how he'd done it. Because he wasn't even involved with her, and he was finding it harder and harder to keep his distance.

Down on the field, the opposing team marched steadily down the field. Normally Max would have been grumbling with the rest of the fans, but to his consternation, he discovered that he didn't care what the other team did. He just wanted the Eagles to make another touchdown so he could kiss Natalie again when the boys weren't looking.

You've got it bad, man, a voice in his head warned. *What happened to all that talk about not getting involved with one of your students? What was that? Just lip service because you hadn't met anyone you were interested in?*

Scowling, he swore under his breath. No, it wasn't just lip service. Natalie was different, dammit. Try as he might, he couldn't think of her as one of his students. She was older than he was, for heaven's sake—with kids! He'd never been involved with a woman with children—he'd never thought he'd wanted to. Not that he was *involved* with her, he quickly assured himself. He just liked her…a lot. There, he'd admitted it. Now he had to decide what he was going to do about it.

The final score was seven to three, with the home team winning their second straight game of the season. Less than pleased with the single touchdown the Eagles had scored, Max should have told Natalie he'd see her on Tuesday. Putting some distance between them would have been the smart thing to do. Instead, he heard himself suggesting, "Why don't we all go someplace for something to eat? You've got to be hungry," he told Natalie. "All you had earlier was a soda. And the boys just had a snack. What about pizza? We could go to Airport Pizza. The boys would love it."

He was right—the boys would love it. Airport Pizza had a real single-engine airplane hanging from the ceiling of a small hangar that its innovative owner had converted into a pizza parlor, and the food was supposed to be fantastic. But she and the boys wouldn't be trying it today. "I'm sorry," she said with a regretful smile. "I wish we could, but I have to work."

"Mom!"

At the boys' cry of objection, Max had to grin. "C'mon, guys, give your mom a break. She can't help it if she has to work. We'll go another time."

They weren't pleased, but the boys weren't whiners. "How about tomorrow?" Harry said brightly.

Max laughed and ruffled his hair. "Nice try, sport. We'll do it when you least expect it." Arching a challenging brow at Natalie, he grinned. "Right?"

Caught in the trap of his eyes, she had no choice but to gracefully give in. "Of course. It'll be fun."

"Where are you parked?"

"Over there," she said, pointing to the west end of the stadium. "How about you?"

He grinned wryly, nodding in the opposite direction. "East."

She should have been relieved. There wouldn't be any offer to walk her to her car, no drawn-out goodbye. She and the boys would go their way, and he would go his. And that was the way it should be. They hadn't gone to the game together—they'd just met by chance. So why did she feel as if she was walking away from a date? This couldn't be because of that silly kiss. There'd been nothing romantic about it—it was just a silly tradition. He'd probably already forgotten it. She had, she told herself.

Liar!

Heat climbing in her cheeks, she ignored the irritating little voice in her head and forced a smile that didn't come nearly as easy as she would have liked. "Well, I guess this is goodbye, then. Thanks for everything. The boys had a blast."

"I hope you did, too."

"It was fun," she said honestly. She didn't want to end the

day, didn't want to walk away. But she still had to find her car and deal with the traffic, then leave the boys at Susan's before she went to work. Regret tugging at her smile, she said, "I guess I'll see you in class on Tuesday."

Reluctantly she headed toward her car with the boys in tow. Her heart skipping every other beat, she didn't glance over her shoulder to see if Max was still standing where she'd left him. She didn't have to. She could feel the warmth of his gaze with every step she took.

Chapter 4

After she dropped the boys off at Susan's, Natalie arrived at work to find the restaurant packed with the after-game crowd. They were hungry and excited and boisterous, and because one of her co-workers didn't show up for work, she and the rest of the waitresses had to pick up the slack. For the next three hours, she rushed from one table to the next and never knew where the time went.

The craziness didn't end, however, with her shift. She had to pick up the boys, read them a story before putting them to bed, then start a load of laundry and her homework. By the time she went to bed, she was exhausted. The second she closed her eyes, however, the memory of Max's brief kiss at the football game teased her, taunting her with wistful feelings of what-if.

He was a man she could dream of, there was no doubt about it, and she readily admitted she was concerned. But over the course of the next few weeks, she didn't, thankfully, have time to fantasize about him often. There never seemed to be enough time in the day to get everything done. Tuesdays and Thursdays she was busy with her classes, and the rest of the week was occupied with work at the restaurant. And every evening when she and the boys finally got home, the routine was the same: she helped the kids with their schoolwork while she cooked dinner and started a load of clothes. There were baths to be taken, clean clothes to be folded and put away, dishes to be washed. Invariably, it was ten o'clock or later by the time she started her own homework. Most nights she fell asleep over her books.

She wasn't even halfway through the semester, and she was already exhausted. That should have worried her, but she took great pride in the fact that she was still, somehow, able to keep up with her classes. Her professors didn't make it easy for her. Especially Max. Aside from the term paper he'd assigned the first day of class, he required his students to read two chapters for every class. And they were long chapters.

How she kept up with everything, she didn't know. Still, she dreaded the first test in Max's class. He was tough, and she didn't doubt that his test would be equally tough—which was why she was a basket case the night before his test. She bought a pizza for supper, rented a Disney movie for the boys and settled down to study for the rest of the evening.

It should have been easy. She had everything around her she needed, the boys were enjoying the movie, and she was soon lost in her studies…until Harry suddenly made a quick trip to the bathroom. "Mom! I think you'd better come here."

Not taking her eyes from the notes she was studying, she

said absently, “What is it, sweetie? I’m trying to study. If you need toilet paper, it’s in the cabinet—”

“I don’t think that’s going to help,” he said ruefully. “There’s water all over the floor.”

Trying to memorize the pertinent details about a dig in the Valley of the Kings in Egypt, she was only half listening. Then his words registered. “What?”

Alarmed, she jumped up and hurried down the hall to the bathroom, gasping in horror when she saw that a pipe under the sink had burst and there was water everywhere. “Oh, my God! Boys, quick! Get some dirty towels from the laundry room. I’ve got to turn this water off!”

Lightning quick, the boys ran to the laundry room off the kitchen and returned seconds later with four big bath towels. Struggling to turn off the water valve under the sink, Natalie was already soaked. “This valve’s stuck,” she panted, trying to get some leverage on the slippery floor. “Damn, I can’t budge it!”

“Uh-oh,” Tommy said, wide-eyed. “You said the *D* word.”

“We’ve got to call Grandma and tell her,” Harry added. “You told us we could report you to grandma whenever you say a bad word.”

Her wet clothes clinging to her and water still gushing from the pipe, Natalie had to laugh. “I think even Grandma would expect me to cuss tonight, but you’re right. I did tell you you could call her. It’ll have to be later, though. We’ve got to get this water turned off and get to Home Depot before it closes.”

Thrilled by the unexpected excursion, the boys quickly changed out of their pajamas while she hurried outside to turn off the water at the shut-off valve by the front sidewalk.

Thankfully it wasn't frozen open, and within seconds all water to the house was completely turned off.

She should have been relieved—the crisis was, for the moment, anyway, under control. But she found little satisfaction in that when she hurried back inside and her eyes fell on her abandoned books at the kitchen table. So much for studying, she thought grimly. Resigned, she quickly changed into dry clothes and grabbed her purse. "C'mon, boys. Home Depot's waiting."

It never entered her head to call a plumber. She just didn't have the money for plumbers or electricians or a handyman. She'd installed her first faucet a week after Derek walked out on her, and she'd been doing small repairs around the house ever since. Normally she enjoyed it. That wasn't going to be the case tonight. Feeling time—and her chance to study—inexorably slipping away from her, she quickly found what she needed at the hardware store, then hurried home.

The boys wanted to stay up and help her, but it was already well past their bedtime, so they gave her little argument as she bundled them into bed. Still, it was nearly ten o'clock before she could start working on the bathroom, and another hour before she finished. By the time she finally returned to her studying, it was after eleven and she was exhausted. Resigned, she once again turned her attention to her notes on the dig in the Valley of the Kings.

She never knew when she fell asleep. The next morning she woke to find herself slumped over her books. Horrified, she jerked up, pushing her hair out of her face as she tried to focus on the clock on the wall across the kitchen from her.

Seven? "Oh, God!" She had to get the boys up, get them to school, get herself to Max's class for the test.

She paled at the thought. How late had she studied? Two? Three? She'd been so tired, and after a while, everything had all run together. She didn't even know if she had gone over all her notes—and there was no time now. Sick at the thought of failing her first test, she pushed back from the table and hurried down the hall to wake the boys.

Forty-five minutes later, she rushed into Max's classroom, panic tightening her throat. The rest of the class was already there, and she only had time to sink into an empty desk at the back of the room before Max began to hand out the test. Any hope she'd had of flipping through her notes before class started died a quick death. Ready or not, she'd run out of time.

She told herself she could still pass the test. She *had* studied, and even though it had been eighteen years since she'd taken a test—and that was in high school!—she wasn't a dummy. She could do this.

Then she read the first question…and her mind went blank.

Seated at his desk, observing the class, Max frowned as his eyes lingered on Natalie. Since he'd kissed her at the football game, he'd tried not to let his gaze wander her way too much in class, so that the rest of the students wouldn't notice his growing fascination with her. With every passing day, however, that became increasingly difficult. She was just so damn pretty, and trying to figure out what was going on in her head was always a challenge. She usually showed up for class with a spark of interest in her eyes and a smile on her face that he found impossible to resist. But the minute she stepped into the classroom, he'd seen that there was no spark in her eyes, no smile on her lips. He'd taken one look at her and he'd known something was very, very wrong.

She was pale, without an ounce of color in her face, and sat as still as stone, just staring at the test. She was obviously reading the questions, but she looked stricken.

What was going on? he wondered, concerned. If he didn't know better, he would swear she hadn't studied, which was ridiculous. Out of all his students in all his classes, she was the one he could always count on to be the most prepared for class. It had to be something else. Maybe one of the boys was sick.

Frowning at the thought, he almost asked her to step out into the hall for a moment so he could ask her what was going on, but he knew that was impossible. She would not appreciate being singled out. And whatever problem she was having, she hadn't come to him about it. Until she did, he had to treat her like any other student and let her take the test.

Watching the expressions on her face as she struggled to get through the test, however, was one of the most difficult things he'd ever witnessed. Why didn't she talk to him? Didn't she know she could come to him with whatever problem she was having? Even if he hadn't kissed her, even if there hadn't been an ounce of attraction between them, she could have come to him. All of his students knew that. So why hadn't she?

The hands of the clock on the back wall of the classroom dragged, but time didn't move as slowly for the rest of his students. One by one they finished the test, turned it in and made a hasty exit. With fifteen minutes left in the class, he and Natalie were the only ones left in the room. In the absolute silence that surrounded them, she never looked up, and Max had never been so frustrated in his life. *Talk to me!* The words echoed in his head, but he didn't say them. As her teacher, he couldn't.

When the bell finally rang, signaling the end of class, he sighed in relief. Finally! Now she would tell him what the hell was wrong.

But when she walked to the front of the room with quiet dignity to turn her test paper in, she didn't say a word. She just laid her paper with those of the other students and turned to leave.

"Natalie?"

"I have to go," she said huskily, and hurried out.

Swearing, Max picked up her test, hoping it would give him some answers to what was going on. But he took one look at it and was more confused than ever. She'd only answered a handful of the questions! Why? Natalie was a sharp, conscientious student. He'd never gotten the impression that she didn't understand the material. And she was so excited about finally going to college—there wasn't a doubt in his mind that she'd studied. Obviously, something else had to be going on. But what, dammit?

He wanted to go after her, to demand some answers, but there wasn't time. He had another class, and she was obviously in no mood to talk to him right now, anyway. Later, he promised himself. He would get answers, but he would have to wait until later.

But putting those questions—and Natalie—out of his head wasn't nearly as easy as he would have liked. After he handed out the test to his next class and began grading the previous class's papers, he found himself reaching for Natalie's test again. It took him all of ten seconds to grade it. Forty-two, he thought in frustration. How could such an intelligent woman make a forty-two? His jaw clenching back an oath, he wrote her grade in red at the top of her paper, then added a short note, recommending she schedule a conference with him. For now that was all he could do. Turning her paper facedown on the desk, he went on to the next test.

Later, Natalie didn't know how she got through the rest of her classes that day without falling completely apart. She'd waited forever—*eighteen* years!—to go to college, and what had she done? Flunked her very first test. Oh, she didn't know the exact grade she made, but she didn't need the number to know that she'd failed miserably. How could she not? She'd answered…what? Four…five questions? She winced, just thinking about it. Once he saw her test paper, Max would think she was a complete moron, and she couldn't blame him. She couldn't have done any worse if she hadn't studied at all.

And this wasn't high school, she thought glumly. She couldn't make up a failing test grade by doing extra credit or throwing out the lowest score at the end of the six weeks. There were only four tests all semester, and they all counted!

Worried if she'd even be able to pass Max's class now, she hardly slept that night. And her mood wasn't any better the next day. Getting dressed for work, she kept flirting with the idea of dropping archeology altogether. The only way she'd been able to afford to go to school was through grants and scholarships, and she would lose those if she failed.

But just the thought of not seeing Max again squeezed her heart. Okay, so he was her teacher and too young for her and there was absolutely no chance of anything serious developing between them, but she loved his class and she'd never been so drawn to a man in her life. How could she just drop his class? She'd never see him again.

Fighting the need to cry, she pulled herself together and reported to work with a determined smile on her face, but she might as well have saved herself the trouble. Sam took one look at her and scowled. "What's wrong now?"

"Nothing," she retorted, sweeping past him to store her purse in her locker in the back room. "I'm just tired."

"And I'm Mother Teresa. Is something wrong with the boys?"

"No."

"Your mother? Has she been calling you again, trying to get you to move back home?"

A reluctant smile curled the corners of her mouth. "She's been doing that since the day I moved here eighteen years ago. That's nothing new."

"Then what is new? And don't tell me 'nothing.' I'm your boss, remember? The guy who sees you day in and day out and knows you like a book? You always get that sad-puppy-dog look in your eyes whenever something goes wrong."

"Puppy-dog look?" she repeated, lifting a delicately arched brow at him. "Are you saying I look like a dog?"

"No, of course not! I just said—"

Fighting a smile, she adopted an injured look and sniffed, "You don't have to repeat it. I heard it the first time."

Far from impressed, he just gave her a steady look. "Are you going to tell me what's wrong or not?"

"I'm fine," she insisted, and deliberately changed the subject. "What station do you want me to take? Elizabeth looks like she could use some help today. She's the one who needs to go home."

"I told her the same thing," he retorted, glancing over at the six-months-pregnant Elizabeth with a frown. "She's just as stubborn as you are. I don't understand it. I'm surrounded by stubborn women! How did this happen? Is anybody listening? Does anybody care?"

Natalie had to laugh. "Of course we care. But you know yourself that this place wouldn't be nearly as interesting without us."

He couldn't argue with that. "Go help Elizabeth," he growled. "Hey," he called after her when she started to head toward station eight. "If you change your mind and want to talk, you know where I am."

She couldn't talk to him. After telling everyone for years how badly she wanted to go to college, she couldn't admit to anyone that she was now thinking about dropping out. "Thanks," she said huskily, and hurried to help Elizabeth.

She struggled to act as if nothing was wrong, but she was fighting a losing battle. Her eyes burned with the need to cry, and she found it nearly impossible to concentrate. She was usually an excellent waitress, even if she did say so herself. She always kept her orders straight—or she had until today. Time and again, she forgot who ordered what, but the customers were, thankfully, forgiving. So was Sam…until she mistakenly ordered a rib eye for a vegetarian at table six.

"You did *what?*" Sam growled when she set the steak back on the counter in front of the grill where he was cooking. "How could you confuse rib eye with broccoli rabe? What am I supposed to do with this?"

She winced. "I don't know…eat it, I guess. I'm sorry,

Sam. I don't know what happened. I guess I wasn't listening very closely. I was worried about—"

When she hesitated, he just rolled his eyes. "What's the big secret? Whatever it is, you know you can tell me. But don't," he added quickly when she opened her mouth to put him off again. "I don't need to know. My only concern is you and the boys. Are the three of you all right?"

"Define *all right.*"

"Natalie..."

She had to smile at his warning tone. "Just kidding. We're fine," she assured him. "*All* of us. Okay? I'm just having a meltdown over a decision I have to make. I'm sorry I brought it to work with me. I just can't seem to concentrate."

"Which is why you need to go home early and take care of whatever this decision is you have to make."

He meant well, but she couldn't do it. "I can't afford to, Sam. You know that. The boys are growing like weeds. It seems like they need new shoes every other week. I need all the tips I can get." When he gave her a pointed look, she had to laugh. It wasn't often that he used subtlety. "I know. I'm not going to get any tips if I don't get the orders straight. I'll work on it. I promise."

"Just don't run all my customers off, okay?" he retorted. "I need them to keep the place open."

"I'll do my best," she promised dryly.

She went back to work and, as promised, focused on keeping her orders straight. And for the most part, she was successful. If the smile she flashed her customers was more than a little strained and she didn't chat with them the way she usually did, she couldn't help it. She considered herself an optimist—she didn't usually let things get her down. But then again, the only other time she'd had to face the death of a dream was when Derek had walked out on her. Quitting college didn't equate with the death of her marriage, but it was close. She couldn't remember a time when she'd been so disappointed in herself.

By the time her shift ended and she punched out, she was exhausted. She'd hardly slept last night, and today had been an emotional roller coaster. She still didn't know what she was going to do about school, but she didn't have the energy to think about it anymore. She just wanted to pick up the boys at Susan's, go home and put her feet up for the rest of the evening. Tomorrow would be soon enough to decide what she was going to do.

But she was three blocks from the restaurant and heading for Susan's when her car suddenly started sounding strange. A split second later, the motor made a loud jarring clatter that seemed to shake the entire car. Her heart in her throat, she hit the brakes, instantly slowing down, but it was too late. The motor died right there in the middle of the street. Powerless, she could do nothing but guide the car over to the curb and coast to a stop. Just that quickly, silence fell like a shroud.

Horrified, she stared at the flashing red CHECK ENGINE light on the instrument panel and felt her heart sink. "Oh, no!" she groaned. "This can't be happening! Not now."

Frantic, she tried to restart the car, but she might as well have saved herself the trouble. When she turned the key, the only response was the click in the ignition. The motor did absolutely nothing.

Stricken, sick with worry, she wanted to kick herself. This was all her fault! She should have listened to Nick. Nick Lewis was not only her neighbor, but he knew enough about cars to change her oil for her and check her battery connections whenever her battery needed a charge. He didn't, however, do major repairs, though he could usually predict when she needed work done. And he'd warned her months ago that she needed a ring job, or she would be asking for some serious trouble.

She hadn't doubted him for a second, but how could she pay for car repairs when she didn't even have the money to buy the boys shoes? So she'd started saving every spare dollar she could, but then the refrigerator had gone out and all her savings had gone to that. She'd been left with no choice but to keep putting oil in her Honda every time she drove it. She'd thought she was buying herself some time, but time had, apparently, just run out.

And she still didn't have any money.

Sick at the thought, she released the hood latch, then stepped out of the car to lift the hood. Not that it did her any good, she thought grimly. She could add oil and water and check the belts and battery cables, but the motor itself was a mystery. It looked just as it always did—grimy and dirty. Had she killed it for good? There was only one way to find out. She had to have it towed to a garage. She didn't even want to think what it was going to cost. Resigned, she turned back in the direction of the restaurant and started walking.

Out for a ride on a motorcycle to clear his head and the writer's block that held his creativity in a vise, Max welcomed the rush of the wind in his face. As soon as he reached the outskirts of town, he was going to open up the throttle and fly. Maybe then he'd be able to write more than two sentences when he sat down in front of his computer again. If the fresh air didn't help, he didn't know what he was going to do. Maybe stand on his head and stack BBs. Anything to spark his creativity again.

Muttering a curse just at the thought of possibly having to reschedule his book, he didn't see the woman walking down the street toward him until he was almost even with her. And even then he was well past her before he recognized her. Natalie! What the hell was she doing out walking when it was almost dark? Then he saw her car parked half a block ahead of him with the hood up.

Surprised, he didn't even think. He just slowed down, checked his mirror, then whipped around in a quick U-turn. Gunning the throttle, he raced back to Natalie, passed her again, then made another U-turn. When he pulled up next to her, he was smiling as he pulled off his helmet. "You look like you could use a ride."

Stunned, she blinked in surprise. "What are you doing here?"

"I was just riding around, blowing the cobwebs out of my head," he replied with a grin. "You all right? What happened?"

"I think I killed my motor," she said with a grimace. "It's been leaking oil and I didn't have the money—" Suddenly breaking off abruptly, she sighed. "It's a miserable story. I don't think you want the details. Anyway, I was walking back to Sam's to use his phone to call a tow truck. "

"Where you going to take it?"

"I don't know," she said, wrinkling her nose. "Somewhere cheap, if there is such a thing."

"I may be able to help with that," he told her, and reached for his cell phone. Punching in a number from memory, he grinned when his call was answered. "Hey, Smitty, you old goat. Is your wrecker out on a call? Good. I've got a customer for you. No, it's not me—it's a friend. Her car broke down just down the road from you at the corner of Second and College. How long will it take you to get here? Then I guess we'll see you in a few minutes. Her blue Honda is parked on the west side of Second."

When he hung up, he turned to her with a smile. "You'll like Smitty. He's the best mechanic I've ever known, and he won't charge you an arm and a leg."

Natalie knew he meant well, and she appreciated that. But considering the current condition of her finances, anything over fifty dollars was an arm and a leg. The cost of towing alone was bound to be more than that, but what choice did she have? The car had to be fixed. "I just hope I haven't blown the motor," she said, worry gnawing at her stomach like battery acid. Looking down the road, she saw a huge black tow truck barreling toward them. "Your friend doesn't waste any time," she told Max, nodding down the road. "Here he comes."

The words were hardly out of her mouth when the tow truck pulled up with a flourish in front of her car and Smitty climbed down from the monster truck to greet them. Natalie took one look at him and blinked in surprise. When Max had said that he was a friend, she'd expected the other man to be close to Max in age. Instead, he was sixty if he was a day, with short curly gray hair and blue eyes that sparkled merrily. Before he said a word, Natalie liked him.

"What'd you do to this poor lady's car?" he teased Max. "Cut her off with that bike of yours?" Not giving him a chance to answer, he turned to Natalie with a grin and held out his hand. "I'm Smitty. Don't worry about a thing. If he made you have a wreck because of his crazy driving, we'll make him pay for the repairs."

"Max didn't do anything but call you," she said with a smile as she placed her hand in his for an easy shake. "I'm Natalie. And unfortunately, I'm the one who killed my car."

"Oh, I doubt it's that bad," he scoffed. "What happened?" When she told him how the motor was acting before it quit on her, then mentioned the ring job she should have gotten months ago, he didn't bat an eye. "Don't plan the funeral yet. Let me get it back to the shop and take a look under the hood. It may not be as bad as you think."

"I told her you were a crackerjack mechanic," Max told him with a teasing grin. "Does the word *pressure* mean anything to you?"

"Do I look worried?" Winking at Natalie, he added, "I'm good. What can I say?"

"That's why I called you," Max retorted. "I know you won't jack the bill up and fix anything but what's really broken."

Interrupting, Natalie delicately cleared her throat. "Speaking of the bill—"

"I won't stick it to you," Smitty assured her. "I'll call you tomorrow after I've had a chance to check everything out." He quickly got her phone number and address, then asked, "Do you need a ride home?"

"I'll see that she gets home," Max said dryly.

Amused at the quickness with which he answered, Smitty grinned. "Maybe you should ask her first if she likes motorcycles. Not everyone's as crazy about them as you are."

"Don't get started on bikes," Max warned teasingly. "Just because you're an old fogy and won't ride on anything that doesn't have four wheels doesn't mean Natalie's the same way. She's cool—"

Amused Natalie waved her hand between the two of them. "Hello? Just in case you guys didn't notice, I can speak for myself."

"Of course you can," Smitty said promptly. "Tell him you're not an old fogy just because you don't want to race down the road like Steve McQueen. And don't ask me who Steve McQueen is," he growled. "If you don't know, I'm not telling."

"I'm not one of Max's typical freshmen students," Natalie replied, chuckling. "I grew up watching *The Great Escape*, so yeah, I know who Steve McQueen is. I've just never ridden a motorcycle before."

Max frowned. "Does that mean you don't want to? You don't have to be afraid. I won't let anything happen to you."

With no effort whatsoever, Natalie could imagine him saying those same words in much more intimate circumstances. Heat spilled into her cheeks at the thought, but she met his gaze head-on. "Do you have another helmet?"

Nodding toward the helmet that was mounted on the back of his bike, he grinned. "I never go anywhere without one. Is that a yes?"

She hesitated, but she couldn't deny him any more than she could deny herself this one little adventure with him. "Don't make me regret it."

"You'll love it," he promised.

Turning to Smitty, she said ruefully, "It looks like I don't need a ride home, after all. But I will need a vehicle while my car's being fixed. Do you have any kind of loaner I could use? I have to take my sons to school, then go to work and school myself, and I don't know how I'm going to do that without wheels."

"No problem," he assured her easily. "I've got a VW bug I keep for just that reason. The garage opens at six. I can have one of my workers drop it off in the morning if you can bring him back to the shop afterward. Is six-thirty too early?"

Relieved, she started to smile, then hesitated. "I don't have a lot of money…."

"The loaner's free," he assured her. "My competitors think I'm crazy, but I don't think customers should have to pay for repairs and a rental, too. Okay?"

Natalie could have hugged him. "Okay! Thank you!"

A few minutes later Smitty drove off with her car trailing behind his wrecker, leaving her alone with Max. When he handed her his spare helmet, her heart thumped crazily. Too late, she questioned her sanity. Whatever possessed her to agree to this?

"You know, this might not be such a good idea after all," she said quickly. "I can call Susan…my babysitter. She'll come and get me and take me and the boys home and you don't have to bother. You've already done so much already…."

His mouth quirking into a grin, he lifted a brow at her. "You're not chickening out on me, are you?"

She wasn't falling for that one. "Nice try, Professor," she said dryly, "but it's not going to work. There's nothing wrong with a good healthy dose of fear."

He laughed. "Smart girl. If I promise not to bite, will you get on the bike?"

Still hesitating, she eyed the motorcycle with more than a little misgiving. But he was right—he wouldn't bite. And if she kept hemming and hawing, he was going to ask what she was really afraid of, and she wasn't going there. "I'm just nervous," she said, cursing the color that rose in her cheeks.

"I'll take every corner on two wheels," he assured her with a smile. "Here…let me help you with that."

He took the helmet from her and stepped toward her. His eyes met hers in the glare of the streetlight, and suddenly there wasn't enough air in her lungs. Carefully, gently, he helped her put on the helmet, then fastened the strap under her chin. "Okay?" he asked huskily as his fingers brushed against her throat.

She couldn't have said a word if her life had depended on it. The rush of her blood loud in her ears, she could only nod numbly.

"Good. Now, just climb on back and put your feet on the footrests."

Thankful that he let her get on the bike first, she did as he said, then found herself holding her breath as he climbed on in front of her. Almost immediately, the spicy scent of his cologne floated back to her, teasing her senses. Why did the man have to smell so good? she wondered, swallowing a groan. He was too close, too masculine, too tempting. Did he have a clue what he was doing to her?

He started the motor, and her heart jumped into her throat. "Wait!" she cried before he could pull away from the curb. "Where do I put my hands?"

"Anywhere you like!" He laughed, and gunned the throttle.

He didn't, however, take off like a bullet before she was ready. He waited until she'd carefully settled her hands at his waist. His gaze trained straight ahead, Max's smile faded.

How long had he been waiting to feel her hands on him? Did she know? Did she feel the heat that sparked between them? Would she think he had completely lost his mind if he turned around and kissed her senseless?

"Professor? Is something wrong?"

Dragging his attention back from the incredibly enticing fantasy that teased his senses, he thanked God she couldn't read his mind. "I just remembered I forgot to ask where you live."

"At 253 Canyon Loop," she said in his ear. "It's off of North Central."

"Out by Eagle Park, right? I know exactly where it is. Hang on."

That was all the warning she got. He took off with a roar, and, giving a startled shriek, she wrapped her arms tighter around his waist and pressed close against his back. She felt him laugh and found herself grinning as a laugh bubbled up like champagne inside her. The wind whipped at them, pulling at her clothes, and as Max took a corner that sent them leaning into the curve, she should have been terrified. Instead she'd never felt so alive in her life. Clinging to him as they raced down the street, she didn't want the ride to ever end.

All too soon, however, he pulled up with a flourish in front of her house and cut the motor. Her arms still around his waist, Natalie knew she was in serious trouble when she didn't want to let him go. What had he done to her? she wondered wildly as she reluctantly let go. He was too young, too wild, too carefree. That should have been enough to send her running for the hills. Instead she was horrified to admit that it was those very things about him that appealed to her the most.

What was so wrong with being attracted to a younger

man who wasn't weighted down with responsibility? a voice in her head demanded. *You haven't had any fun in a long time. Enjoy yourself!*

She wanted to—she hadn't realized how much until just that moment. But as tempted as she was to throw caution to the wind and explore the attraction that sparked between them, she couldn't forget her responsibilities. Her boys depended on her completely—they had no one else but her to see to their needs. How could a man like Max, who could do anything he wanted, go anywhere he wanted, without answering to anyone, understand that?

Regret pulled at her, but she had too much pride to let him see. So she hopped off his motorcycle and faced him with an easy smile. "Well, that was fun! You sure know how to show a girl a good time."

He laughed. "It was your first bike ride. I wanted to make it memorable."

"Trust me—it's not something I'll forget anytime soon." Her smile fading, she pulled off her helmet and held it out to him. "I don't know how to thank you for everything. It's hard to find a mechanic who's trustworthy."

"Smitty's a good man," he said as he placed the helmet on the back of his bike. "He'll do right by you."

The niceties taken care of, Natalie knew there was no reason to linger. "I guess I'd better go inside and call Susan to let her know what happened. She'll have to bring the boys home for me."

"Will she mind? I'd offer to get them one at a time on the bike, but I know you wouldn't go for that, and frankly neither would I. I don't have a helmet that small, and I'd just be afraid something would happen."

"Thank you for that," she replied. "I don't take chances with my kids. And Susan's as protective of the boys as I am. She won't mind bringing them home."

With that settled, there was nothing more to say. She started to turn to go into the house, only to stop. "Professor…about the test yesterday—"

"We'll talk about it in class tomorrow," he said huskily. "You've got enough on your plate tonight without worrying about that." Impulsively kissing her on the cheek, he turned her around and gave her a gentle push toward her front door. "Go inside, Natalie. While you still can."

Her heart pounding crazily, she didn't need to be told twice. Without a backward glance she hurried inside.

Chapter 5

Max considered himself an intelligent man. He was well-read, a seasoned traveler and, when the situation called for it, he could pull off sophistication. He could talk to just about anyone from hard-core bikers who lived to ride the open road on their Harleys to Arab guides in the desert to college presidents and politicians. He had his head on straight, his heart under lock and key, and the last time he'd made a fool of himself over a woman, he'd been sixteen. He'd fallen like a ton of bricks for Mary Jo Simmons, who hadn't, unfortunately, been impressed in the least with him. He'd written her poetry and sent her flowers every week for an entire summer, and all for naught. She'd still refused to go out with him and never even thanked him for the flowers. He hadn't lost sleep over a woman since.

Until now.

Long after he dropped Natalie off at her house, she haunted him. He could feel her arms around his waist, her breasts pressed against his back as they'd raced down the street, and he knew he'd never be able to ride his bike again without thinking of her. Deliberately pushing her from his thoughts, he grabbed his laptop and tried to lose himself in his writing. But he couldn't concentrate and spent the next hour writing and deleting scattered thoughts that made no sense. He finally gave up and went to bed, but the situation only went from bad to worse. The second he stretched out and closed his eyes, she was right there in his dreams, pressing close as she had on the back of his motorcycle, driving him crazy.

He didn't sleep worth a damn.

Needless to say, he was in a bear of a mood the next morning when he went to work, and he still couldn't get her out of his head. Had Smitty gotten the loaner to her on time this morning? She couldn't afford a cab to get the boys to school. Money was obviously tight—she had to be worried sick about her car. How was she going to pay for the repairs if she'd thrown a rod? She was a waitress, for heaven's sake!

She's not your problem, the voice of reason whispered in his ear. *She got by just fine before you came along. She'll get by now. The woman's a survivor.*

He knew that, but as he retrieved his mail and messages from his box and headed for his office, he couldn't stop worrying. Irritated with himself, he unlocked the door to his office and dropped his briefcase on his desk. Scowling, he quickly flipped through his mail. There was a note from the dean reminding him of a get-together at the end of the week with "friends" of the university; an archeological newsletter he subscribed to; and some DVDs he'd ordered of a dig in the mountains of Turkey. But the first thing he reached for was a letter from Mountain Adventure Tours, the tour group that was handling the arrangements for the dig he and his students were taking over the Thanksgiving holidays.

When he'd gotten the okay from the university, finally authorizing his first school-sponsored dig, he'd immediately contacted the tour company and hired them to handle the arrangements. He'd heard nothing but good things about the company, which was were located right in Eagle Creek. So far, the staff at Mountain Adventure had been very efficient. They'd promised to have the travel schedule to him by this week and they'd obviously delivered. Pleased, he couldn't wait to see what they'd come up with.

He tore open the envelope, but the letter he pulled out was not the travel schedule. Instead, it read:

Dear Professor Sullivan,
We regret to inform you that due to circumstances beyond the control of Mountain Adventure Tours, we have been advised by our accountants to file for bankruptcy. The company closed its doors for the last time on Wednesday, September 30th, and is no longer open for business. We regret any inconvenience this may have caused you and wish you luck booking your tour with another tour group.
Sincerely,
Mountain Adventure Tours

"What the hell!" Stunned, Max swore roundly. This had to be a mistake! They couldn't shut down! He'd already paid for the trip with his own money so he could get the best price for his students. They would reimburse him by next week, but that was beside the point. He wasn't going to let *them* take the hit for this. They couldn't afford this kind of loss. And he was the one who'd stupidly signed up with Mountain Adventure, not his students. He was the one who would have to pay the price.

Grimly reading the letter again, he swore out loud. A company didn't just find itself in bankruptcy without any prior warning. The owners must have suspected months ago that they were in trouble. They certainly must have known last month when they took his money that there was a very good possibility that they would be shutting their doors soon. And they hadn't said a word.

Furious, he reached for the phone and quickly punched in the number Mountain Adventure had so thoughtfully included on their letterhead. They weren't going to get away with this, he promised himself. But the call had barely gone through when a recorded voice announced, "We're sorry. The number you have dialed is no longer in service."

"Damn!" Slamming the phone down, he reached for the phone book and quickly looked up the numbers of Ted Reynolds and Debbie Johnson, the owners of Mountain Adventure. Over the course of the last month, he'd dealt with each of them on a number of occasions, and they'd seemed to be reputable businesspeople. There had to be a way to work this out.

But when he placed a call to each of their homes, the same recording played in his ear. "The number you have dialed is no longer in service."

Left with no choice, he called Joshua Walker, his lawyer.

* * *

Taking the boys to school in the VW Bug Smitty had lent her, Natalie was halfway to school when she realized that she'd forgotten her English lit homework, which had to be turned in later that afternoon. Swearing softly to herself—and thanking God the boys weren't there to call her on it—she whipped the car around the next corner and raced back to the house.

"It should be right here," she mumbled as she quickly riffled through the papers on her desk. "Where the heck…ha! Thank God!"

Whirling, she headed for the door and was about to walk out when the phone rang. She almost let the machine get it. She was running late, and she didn't have time to talk to anybody. But even as she pulled open the door, she hesitated. What if one of the boys had gotten hurt at school or something? She'd just dropped them off, but she knew from experience just how quickly they could get into trouble.

Concerned, she strode back into the kitchen and snatched up the phone. "Hello?"

"Mrs. Bailey? This is Smitty. I checked out your car the second I came in this morning…."

Natalie's stomach dropped like a rock. "Yes, of course. I was going to call you later today. I guess there's no point in putting it off. How bad is it?"

When he hesitated, she knew the news wasn't good. "That bad, huh? Don't try to sugarcoat it, Smitty. Just spit it out."

"You're looking at somewhere in the vicinity of a thousand dollars," he said grimly. "And that's after cutting costs to the bone. I tried every way I could think of to keep the tab down, but that *is* down. I wish I had better news, but…"

Sick to her stomach, she said huskily, "Please, don't apologize. When the car first started leaking oil, I shopped around to see how much the repairs were going to cost. No one gave me a price anywhere near as low as a thousand dollars, and the car was running then! So don't worry. I'm not offended. I know what a deal you're offering me. I just don't know what I'm going to do. The car's not worth that much."

"No, it's not," he said honestly. "But at least you know what you have. Can you buy another car for a thousand dollars that you won't have to put any money into? If you find something, I'll be happy to check it out for you at no charge."

"Oh, no, you don't have to do that."

"I know," he chuckled. "But you're a nice lady and you're a friend of Max's. And you've hit a rough patch. If I can help, I will."

Touched, she smiled. "Thank you. Max was right when he said you were a good man. Unfortunately, I don't know what I'm going to do yet—I need a couple of days. Would you mind if I kept the Bug for the rest of the day? I'll bring it in this afternoon."

"Keep it for a couple of days," he assured her. "I'm not using it right now. In the meantime, I'll keep my eyes open for something else. If I come across anything that I think might work for you, I'll give you a call."

"I'll be in touch," she promised, and hung up. Only then did tears sting her eyes. Dear God, what was she going to do?

Worry eating at her, she drove to school in a daze. Where was she going to get a thousand dollars? She had some savings, but it was her emergency slush fund, and with the boys getting into one scrap after another, she had to dip into it far more often than she wanted to. Even if she'd been willing to use it for a car, which she wasn't, it wasn't nearly enough. Which meant she had to get a loan.

Cringing at the thought of adding another monthly bill to the ones she was already just managing to pay, she walked into Max's classroom just as the bell rang. He was talking to a student at the front of the classroom, but when his eyes immediately met hers, she knew he'd been waiting for her. Forcing a weak smile, she slipped into the same desk she always sat in at the back of the classroom.

She'd been crying. Concerned, Max took a step toward her before he could stop himself, only to swear softly. She'd obviously been worrying about her car all night. He should have called her last night after he got home, should have reassured her that she didn't have to go through this alone. She had friends. She had him....

"Professor Sullivan?"

Jerking his attention back to the student who'd been asking him about the dig, he raised his voice so that the rest of the class could hear him. "Russ has a question about what you're going to need for the dig. We'll discuss it after I hand the tests back."

Those students who had been standing around talking, waiting for class to start, quickly took their seats, and he began handing the tests back. From the corner of his eye, he saw Natalie stiffen, but she didn't so much as flinch when he laid her paper on her desk. He watched her read the note recommending that she meet with him for a conference to discuss her failing grade. Then she folded the paper in two with fingers that weren't quite steady. He knew she had to feel like the weight of the world was coming down on her, first with her car, now with an F on her test, but he could hardly console her in front of the entire class. His expression grim, he handed out the rest of the papers to the other students.

Returning to the front of the class, he arched a dark brow. "Okay, so what's the consensus? Was it harder or easier than you expected?"

"Harder!"

Not the least apologetic, he grinned. "I warned you the first day of class that my tests weren't a cakewalk. I wouldn't be doing you any favors if I made it easy for you."

"Yeah, but you didn't say it was going to be all fill-in-the-blank and essay," a member of the football team complained from the back of the room. "If I flunk out, Coach is going to have my hide!"

"Actually," he corrected him, "I believe I did tell you about my tests the first day of school. I think you were napping at the time." When the rest of the class laughed, he gave the football player a pointed look. "You can do this. Your fate is in your hands. All you have to do is study instead of partying, and you won't flunk."

"But I'm a football player. Partying's what I'm best at!"

Max laughed. "No, flunking'll be what you're best at if you keep that attitude. Then where will you be when the pro scouts come to check out your teammates? Sitting in the stands with everybody else."

"That's what all my teachers say," he grumbled. "You guys just take all the fun out of college."

"Quit your crying," Max retorted. "You'll have plenty of fun on the dig. Speaking of which," he told the rest of the class, "there's been a problem with the tour group booking it. The long and short of it is, I'm taking care of the trip myself, so the dig will continue as planned. Which means you have until a week from Friday to turn in your money for the dig. If that's a problem, you need to let me know because the dig is a required part of the curriculum."

"What about the itinerary?" one of the students in the front row asked. "You said we'd get it today."

His expression grim, he admitted, "Since I'm not using the tour group, that's going to take longer than expected. I'll try to get it to you by the end of the week."

He'd have to work his tail off to do it that quickly, but he'd find a way. The dig would continue as planned—he'd already decided that. He was going to lose a ton of money, but there wasn't a lot he could do about it now. He'd put in a call to his attorney about Mountain Adventure Tours and the news hadn't been good. The company was in debt up to its ears and had, indeed, filed for bankruptcy protection. All assets were frozen, and once the courts got through with the company, the most Max could hope to recoup was pennies on the dollar.

Just thinking about it infuriated him, but he refused to cancel the dig. He'd had to fight to convince the university that taking the students on a dig was one of the most important parts of the archeology curriculum, and he wasn't giving it up just because he'd run into a little bit of bad luck. He could make the arrangements as easily as a tour group—he'd already checked out some rates. Time, however, was of the essence. The dig began the day after Thanksgiving, and it was already the first week in October.

"Now that we've got that settled, let's talk about the different Indian tribes that once roamed Colorado," he said, turning the subject to the topic of the day's lecture. "What can we expect to find on our dig?"

As one of the other students spoke up, Natalie hardly heard the discussion that followed. She'd forgotten about the dig! Now what was she supposed to do? She either had to pay Smitty the thousand dollars it would cost to repair her car or she would have to buy another vehicle. Either way, she was going to have to use what little she had in savings *and* get a loan just to have transportation again. Considering all that, how could she possibly justify spending more money for a dig she obviously couldn't afford?

Devastated, she could barely hold back tears. She'd been so excited about her archeology class, so psyched at the idea of actually going on a dig with the great Max Sullivan. And now that was out of the question. She'd learned a long time ago that it wasn't the things you did in life that you regretted—it was the things you didn't do. And this one was going to hurt for a long, long time.

She'd have to tell Max, of course. They had become friends over the course of the last month, and after he'd helped her so much with her car, the least she owed him was an explanation. She didn't doubt that he would try to talk her out of passing on it, but he couldn't. He'd just told the class that the dig had to be paid for by next week. She could work around the clock between now and then and she still wouldn't have enough money for the dig. Like it or not, she had to accept that. And Max did, too.

The rest of the class passed in a blur. Even though she knew there was no need to take notes since this was the last time she would sit in on one of Max's class, she couldn't stop herself. Max was such a great teacher. He obviously loved archeology, loved teaching. He was one of the most popular professors on campus, and it was easy to see why. He could take dry facts and transform them into a compelling story that transfixed the entire class.

Caught up in his lecture, Natalie didn't notice the passage of time. Then the bell rang, signaling not only the end of class, but of her time with Max. Pain squeezed her heart, but she refused to give in to tears. Instead she gathered her things together and rose to her feet as most of the rest of the class began filing out. Four other students lingered, however, collecting around Max at his desk like fans at a rock concert. They all had questions about their tests, and he quickly scheduled conferences for the following day.

By the time they left, his next class was starting to file in, and there was obviously no time to talk. "I was hoping we could talk now," she said quietly. "I forgot you had another class."

"What about this afternoon?" he replied. "Say around four? I don't know when your other classes are..."

"Four's fine. My last class ends at three-thirty."

"Good." He needed to start his next class and she should have left, but his eyes locked with hers, and neither of them noticed the other students filing into the classroom. "Are you all right?" he asked huskily. "I know you've got to be upset with the test and your car and everything. Just don't panic. Everything will work out."

She knew he meant well, but he just didn't understand her circumstances. And how could he? He wasn't a father and couldn't possibly know what it was like to be the sole supporter of twin sons. "It's just one of those little curves life throws you when you're not looking. I'll get past it."

Promising to meet him at his office at four, she hurried to her next class, but she might as well have skipped it. She couldn't concentrate. Disgusted with herself, she toyed with the idea of taking the rest of the day off and just going home, but she was already failing one class. She couldn't take any chances with the rest. So she pushed images of Max out of her head and fished her English homework out of her backpack and turned it in.

How she got through the rest of the day, she never knew. Time dragged. In between classes she worked out what she was going to say to Max at their meeting, but there was no easy way to say what she had to say. Then at four o'clock sharp, when she arrived at his office and found him inside on the phone, all she could think of was that after today she would be lucky if she ever saw him again. And it hurt. When had he begun to mean so much to her?

Quickly covering the phone with his hand, he said quietly, "I'll be right with you. Have a seat."

Still reeling from the realization that he had somehow become much more than a teacher to her, she dropped into the chair in front of his desk and didn't know if she wanted to laugh or cry. This was crazy! She couldn't be interested in Max. He was *eight* years younger than she was, and not the least bit interested in settling down! There had to be another explanation for her yo-yoing emotions. Maybe she was going through a midlife crises. That had to be it. It was the only logical explanation. So what if she was only thirty-six? Her life was in chaos right now, and her subconscious was obviously looking for a way to escape the stress. There was nothing wrong with daydreaming about a tall, good-looking man who was young and fun and had a career that was full of adventure. And just because she suddenly found herself fantasizing about running off on a dig with him and making love in the desert under a vast, inky sky full of stars didn't mean she had any intention of doing any such thing. She couldn't. She had responsibilities. She had children. She was a mom!

Caught up in her musings, she paid little attention to Max's phone conversation. Then she realized he was discussing the arrangements for the dig, and he was less than pleased with whatever figures he was getting. Scowling, he jotted down notes, then growled, "I think I can beat that price. I'll get back to you."

He hung up abruptly, muttering curses, then looked up to find her watching him. A rueful grin tugged at the corners of his mouth. "Sorry about that."

"No problem," she assured him.

He was obviously busy, and she should have immediately told him she was going to drop his class, then left him to his work. She certainly shouldn't have asked him anything about the phone conversation she'd overheard, especially since she wasn't going on the dig. But this was probably the last conversation she would ever have with him, and the fantasy that kept playing in her head wouldn't let her just say what she had come to say, then walk out. Not yet. She needed more time.

So she said instead, "I hope you didn't cut your phone call short because of me. Are you having problems with the travel arrangements for the dig?"

"Something like that," he said in disgust. "But we'll talk about that in a moment. First we need to discuss your test. What happened, Natalie? I know you know the material. In fact, you're one of the few students who's always prepared. Did you panic or what? I know it's been a long time since you've been in school—"

"It's not that," she said huskily. "I just didn't get a chance to finish studying. There was a problem at home."

"With one of the boys? What happened?"

"The boys are fine," she assured him. "A pipe broke when I was studying. There was water everywhere—"

"And you had to fix it, of course," he replied, frowning in concern. "So how long did it take you?"

"Hours," she said in disgust. "It was after midnight by the time I got back to my studying again, and I was so tired, I guess I just fell asleep."

"You should have told me before the test."

"Then I would have been making excuses, and I don't like doing that. If I'd been prepared and studied more ahead of time, the broken pipe wouldn't have made much difference."

"You still should have told me," he insisted. "I'm not unreasonable. I know life happens when you least expect it. I would have let you take the test the following day."

"It probably wouldn't have mattered," she admitted honestly. "The second I started reading the test, my mind went completely blank. That had nothing to do with the pipe breaking or studying as much as I needed to. I just froze. You couldn't have postponed the test for me for that."

She had a point. "No, but it's easy to understand why you shut down the way you did," he replied. "College is tough for eighteen-year-olds, and they haven't been out of school for eighteen years. You panicked. That doesn't mean you have to flunk. You can take the test again—I just can't give you a higher grade than a seventy."

"Are you serious?"

"Of course I'm serious," he said with a laugh. "I do it for

all my students on the first test. Some of my colleagues think I'm crazy, but this is a freshman course, and college is an adjustment, even for kids right out of high school. So I give anyone who fails the first test a break. After that, you're on your own. So when do you want to retake the test?"

He expected her to schedule the test for some time the following day. Instead, she said, "I'm not going to retake it. In fact, I'm going to drop the class. That's why I wanted to talk to you. After everything you've done, I couldn't just drop the class without saying a word."

Max couldn't have been more shocked if she'd told him she was going to join the army and leave the boys with friends while she went overseas to fight terrorists. Scowling, he growled, "This is a joke. Right?"

Dead serious, she shook her head.

Swearing, Max had never been so mad, so quickly, in his life. "Dammit, you can't do this! I know the test threw you for a loop, but you'll do better now that you know what to expect next time. You've just got to give yourself a chance. And if you still feel like you can't handle the material, I'll help you."

"I appreciate that," she said quietly. "And if that was the only problem, I'd take you up on that. But it gets worse. I can't go on the dig."

"Why not?" But even as he asked, he knew. "Smitty got back with you on the repairs on your car, didn't he? How bad is it?"

"A thousand dollars," she said flatly. "*If* I decide to get it repaired. It's not even worth that much, so it seems dumb to spend the money on it."

"You're thinking about buying another car?"

"I think it would be the smart thing to do, but that's going to cost me even more. Whatever I do, I'm going to have to use what savings I've got and get a loan for the rest." She'd never been one to whine about her personal life, and she never talked about her finances, but the words just came tumbling out. "I hate doing this! I love your class and I've been looking forward to the dig from the moment I first heard about it. But I don't get any child support from my ex-husband. When something goes wrong, I'm the one who has to find a way to fix it."

He winced. "I can't begin to imagine what that must be like for you."

"It's tough," she said honestly. "When I enrolled in your class, I knew I'd have to watch every penny in order to go on the dig, but I thought I had it covered. I never dreamed I'd have to use it all for the car."

When he'd made the dig a requirement in order to pass, he'd known there would be students who would, for one unexpected reason or another, be unable to go on the trip and would, consequently, have to drop the class. He'd convinced himself that he was prepared for that. But that was before he'd met Natalie, before he'd become friends with her, before he'd kissed her. Something squeezed his heart at the thought of her dropping out of his class, and for no other reason than that, he should have told her how much he enjoyed having her in class and how sorry he was to lose her. It would have been the smart thing to do, but at that particular moment, he didn't give a damn about playing it smart. He wasn't ready to tell her goodbye.

"I understand money's tight," he told her. "That doesn't mean you can't go—"

"Of course it does! How am I going to pay for it?"

"The university has agreed to let me hire a student assistant to help with the trip," he fibbed. "It's a lot of work. I hadn't hired anyone so far because I turned the arrangements over to a tour group. That, unfortunately, isn't working out, so I'm going to need an assistant, after all. I thought you might like to apply for the job."

Another woman might have jumped at the opportunity, but Natalie was far more cautious than that. Examining him through narrowed eyes, she studied him suspiciously. "Let me get this straight. I tell you I don't have the money to go on the dig, and just like that—" she snapped her fingers "—you offer me a job out of the blue. Why does this smell fishy to me?"

"I don't know," he retorted, making no effort to hold back a grin. "Maybe you're just a bit suspicious, and for the life of me, I don't know why. I'm just trying to do you a good deed, and all I get is grief."

"You're laying it on a little thick," she said dryly. "Is there really a job or are you just making this up?"

She'd caught him red-handed, but he had no intention of telling her that. She'd turn him down flat if she thought he might be creating a job just for her, and he couldn't say he'd blame her. She was a proud woman who obviously didn't like to ask for help. But she wasn't asking—he was offering—and he really did need an assistant.

The more he thought about it, in fact, the better he liked the idea. She wasn't like the rest of his students—she was an adult, not a kid, and she knew how to manage money and her home. If she could take care of twin boys and all that that involved with no help from a husband, she was more than capable of helping him with all the details of a dig. And in exchange for her assistance, he could help her. Not only would she be able to go on the dig, she wouldn't have to drop his class, and the salary he paid her would help pay for the repairs to her car.

It was a win-win situation for both of them, he reasoned. What difference did it make if the job wasn't funded by the university? Now that he'd come up with the idea, he was sure he could convince the dean to pay for an assistant in the future. In the meantime, he'd pay for it himself this year, and Natalie would never have to know the difference.

"I've never been more serious in my life," he said honestly. "I never should have brought in a tour group. It's turned out to be a disaster." He told her about the letter he received from the tour group informing him that they had filed for bankruptcy. "According to my attorney, I might as well kiss that money goodbye—I'll be lucky if I get a hundred dollars of it back through the courts."

"Oh, no!"

He shrugged. "There's no use crying over spilt milk now. I trusted the wrong people. All I can do is regroup and start over again. I'm sure there are some honest tour groups out there, but I can't afford to risk any more money. So I've decided to take care of the arrangements myself. That's where you come in. If you're interested."

Interested? she thought incredulously. Was he kidding? Of course she was interested. This was the answer to her prayers! "What do you need me to do?"

"Everything," he said promptly. "We have six weeks to put this all together. I'm talking everything—transportation, tents, food, equipment—and it's going to take two of us to do it. You've already got a lot on your plate with the boys and your other classes and your waitressing job. Do you even have time for this? I guess I should have asked that first. If you don't, I understand, of course."

Time wasn't a commodity that she had a lot of, but the same could be said of money. And this was an opportunity she couldn't pass up. "Oh, no," she assured him. "I can do this! It's not forever, just until Thanksgiving. And I don't have to drop your class! When can I start?"

He laughed. "How about right now?"

Since she'd made arrangements to pick the boys up at Susan's at seven, Natalie had planned to use the time after her meeting with Max to study at the university library. Instead, she spent it with Max in his office, working on a list of everything he needed her to check out for him. It was quite a daunting list.

"I know it's a lot, but it's not that bad." He laughed when she looked it over and lifted a skeptical eyebrow at him. "Between the two of us, we'll get it done."

"Yeah. Maybe by Christmas—of next year!"

Far from worried, he said, "We're going to do fine. I know time is short, but so is money, thanks to Mountain Adventure Tours. So we're going to do some serious comparison shopping before we buy anything. While you get started on the supplies and see what kind of discounts you can get us, I'll check out transportation costs. It'd be great if we could rent a bus with a driver, but that may be too pricey."

"Then what's the other option?"

"Renting a fleet of vans," he replied promptly. "The problem with that is that then some of the students have to drive, which means I have to check their driving records. And there's insurance, of course, which is going to add to the cost."

"But aren't three classes going?" she said with a frown. "Wouldn't renting two buses be cheaper than an entire fleet of vans?"

"You would think so, but the cost of each bus also includes paying for a driver for the entire length of the trip."

"But the buses would probably have more room for the gear."

He grinned. "You don't have to sell me on the idea—I'm all for it. Unfortunately, it all comes down to dollars and cents."

"What about the tents? Do you want to buy or rent? If you buy, you've got to have some place to store them after the dig. But then you wouldn't have to rent tents again next year, which could save you a lot of money—if you don't have to pay a lot of money to store them. I'll look into both options and see which works out to be the cheapest."

"Good idea," he said with a grin. "I knew you'd be good at this."

"I've been pinching pennies for years," she said ruefully. "I'm glad it finally paid off."

"You're not the only one. This morning, when I found out the tour group was shutting down, I was not a happy camper. In fact, I was infuriated. Thank God, the day's ending better than it started."

Rising to his feet, he stepped over to a small refrigerator in the corner of his office. "How about something to eat? I've got some deli meats and cheeses I keep on hand in case I get hungry. Do you like Cajun roast beef? Smoked turkey? I've got some provolone, too. Are you hungry? I'm starving!"

She should have said she had to get the boys, but he caught her flat-footed. "Now that you mention it, yeah. I've been so worried about the car and flunking your test— Oh, God, I have to take it over, don't I?"

"You'll do fine," he assured her. "All you have to do is pass it—which I know you will—and you'll make a seventy. Come in tomorrow before you go to work and get it over with." Turning from the refrigerator to set the deli meats and cheeses in the middle of his desk, he shot her a crooked grin. "You don't know how relieved I am that you're helping me with the dig. I was afraid I was going to have to cancel it. What time do you have to get the boys?"

"Seven."

"Good. Then you've got time to eat. There are some crackers and paper plates in the cabinet behind you. What do you want to drink? Cola or bottled water?"

"Water."

He pulled two bottles of water from the refrigerator as she retrieved the crackers and plates from the cabinet. Ten seconds later she found herself sitting across from him, sharing a meal. It was a mistake, of course—the more time she spent with him, one on one, the more she found herself dreaming about the man. And now she was working with him! She'd obviously lost her mind, but she had to admit that it was an intoxicating, enticing insanity. When he smiled at her, when his eyes met hers and she felt the touch of his gaze, her heart lurched every time. He made her feel special, beautiful, as if she was the only woman in the world he was interested in.

Don't go there! a voice in her head growled. *It'll be years before a man like Max Sullivan settles down, and you know it.*

She couldn't argue with that. But what was wrong with enjoying the time she had with him? she reasoned. As long as she had no expectations and kept her heart under lock and key, she would be fine. Okay, so her pulse was racing and their impromptu picnic felt like a date. What was wrong with that? It had been a long time since she'd been breathless over a man. She intended to enjoy it even though nothing was ever going to come of it.

"You know, this reminds me of the picnics my third stepmother liked to have at the drop of a hat," he said as he helped himself to some Cajun roast beef. "She carried a picnic basket in the trunk of her car everywhere she went."

In the process of opening her bottle of water, Natalie raised a brow. "Did you say *third* stepmother?"

"Third or fourth," he said with a shrug, grinning. "I don't quite remember."

"Your father was married four times?"

He laughed. "I wish! Actually, he and number eight are in the process of divorcing right now. I've resigned myself to the fact that it's only a matter of time before there's a number nine."

Amazed, she could only stare at him. "Are you serious?"

He grinned. "I know it's wild, but that's my father. The eternal optimist. He's loved every woman he ever married. Unfortunately, none of his marriages last longer than two or three years."

"And he still keeps getting married?"

"Like I said, he's an eternal optimist. Every time he falls in love, he's convinced he's found his soul mate."

"What number was your mother—if you don't mind me asking?"

"She was his first. I was three when they divorced, three and a half when I got my first stepmother."

She winced. "That had to be rough."

He shrugged. "Sometimes. I had to say goodbye to a lot

of stepbrothers and sisters, but I can't complain about the women Dad married. They were great. I've just never understood why Dad felt like he had to get married to be happy. That's crazy! He could still have relationships—he just doesn't have to keep buying wedding rings."

He didn't have to say the words for her to hear what he was really saying. He wasn't like his father and had no intention of making the same mistakes he had. Marriage was not for him.

Chapter 6

Given the chance, Max would have spent the rest of the evening talking and laughing with her, but they were both aware of the passage of time as seven o'clock drew closer. When she glanced at the clock on the wall for the third time in as many minutes, he smiled ruefully. "You have to get the boys, don't you? C'mon. I'll walk you to your car."

"Oh, you don't have to do that! I just parked in the lot down the street."

"It'll be dark soon," he said, rising to his feet to put the remains of their meal away and collect his briefcase. "You shouldn't be walking in the dark by yourself."

It wouldn't be dark for at least another thirty minutes, and they both knew it. And even if it had been pitch-black, the university police patrolled the campus at all hours of the day and night. Short of bringing in personal bodyguards for every student, the place couldn't have been much safer. Max didn't care—he was walking her to her car—end of discussion.

She wasn't a woman who was used to being either pampered or protected. That was painfully obvious to Max as she hesitated, frowning. "I hate for you to go out of your way. Where are you parked?"

"Behind the building in the teacher lot," he replied. "Will you stop worrying? It's not like you're taking me halfway across the campus. I just need to know you're safe. Humor me, okay?"

Put that way, she couldn't refuse him. "Okay. But only if you let me give you a ride back to your bike."

"Are you always this stubborn?"

"When I have to be," she retorted. "Now that we know where we stand, let's go." And without another word, she sailed out the door, leaving Max to follow with a broad grin on his face.

It was dark outside, but not because of an early sunset. A storm had moved in over the mountains, and thick black clouds were gathering overhead. The scent of rain was in the air, and on the western horizon, lightning flashed. Seconds later, thunder rumbled like an old man clearing his throat.

Lifting her face to the wind, Natalie drew in a deep breath and let it out in a sigh. "Don't you just love the way a storm clears the air? When I was a kid, my mother would always catch me on the back patio, right before a storm hit, watching the wind whip the trees around. It was like being in *The Wizard of Oz.*"

Amusement glinted in his blue eyes. "So you were trying to get to Oz, where you?"

"Actually, I just wanted the ruby-red slippers," she confessed with a chuckle. "My poor mother. I think she was terrified I was going to get hit by a falling tree or something. She kept threatening to lock me in my room, then when that didn't work, she bought me a pair of red shoes."

"And?" he asked when she paused. "Don't just leave me hanging. Was that enough to keep you inside?"

Her blue eyes dancing, she arched a brow at him. "What do you think?"

"I think you feel about storms the same way I feel about my bike," he replied. "There's nothing like the feel of the wind blowing through your hair."

"I'll take the storm," she retorted, grinning. "Flying around corners on two wheels is a lot more excitement than I can stand."

"Chicken," he teased. "And here I thought you had a spirit of adventure."

"I did. Then I had kids. Storms are the only vice I allow myself now."

The words were hardly out of her mouth when a gentle rain began. Surprised, they both looked up…just as the skies opened up.

The car, thankfully, was only a half a block away. Shrieking with laughter, Natalie sprinted for the car and thanked God Smitty had loaned her a vehicle with keyless entry. She was still ten feet from the Bug when she hit the unlock button. The headlights flashed in greeting. Sprinting, she jerked open the driver's door and fell inside. She didn't realize Max was one step behind her until the passenger door was snatched open and he tumbled in beside her.

Outside, lightning flashed like exploding fireworks, and rain hammered at the roof of the car. Soaked to the skin, Natalie took one look at Max and giggled. "You look like a drowned rat!"

"In case you hadn't noticed, you're not so dry yourself, Shirley Temple," he retorted with a grin as he plucked a tendril of hair from her shoulder and held it up before her eyes. Dripping rainwater, it curled in a tight red ringlet. "See?"

Max knew any number of women who would have gasped in horror and immediately tried to repair the damage any way possible. Not Natalie. She only laughed. "It's the family curse. I've learned to live with it."

"I think it's cute," he said. "I bet you were a cute little girl."

"Please," she groaned. "Let's not go there. Every time I turned around, it seemed like my mother was taking me to an audition for a part in the community theater. She was convinced I was the next Annie."

Surprised, he blinked. "I didn't know you could sing."

"I can't."

"Oh, God, that must have been awful." He chuckled. "How bad were you?"

"My dog howls whenever I even hum. What does that tell you?"

He grinned. "You're making that up."

"Ask the boys when you see them again," she told him. "From the moment they were old enough to talk, they begged me not to sing 'Happy Birthday' to them. They said it hurt their ears."

"Yeah, right."

"No, I'm serious!"

Unable to take his eyes off her, Max was totally captivated and didn't, for the life of him, understand why. She was nothing like the women he'd dated in the past. She didn't dress to catch a man's eye or make herself up to look like some kind of glamour queen. Totally unconcerned with her dripping hair and wet clothes, she smiled up at him as if she didn't have a care in the world. And just that easily, she made him ache.

He told himself to not even think about touching her. He might as well have ordered himself not to breathe. Lifting his hand to her face, he gently traced a raindrop that slid slowly down her cheek to the corner of her mouth. Beneath his fingers, he felt her go still, and in the sudden silence that fell between them, he could have sworn he heard the pounding of her heart.

"Your skin is so soft," he murmured.

Her breath hitched in her throat. "Max…"

In the growing darkness, his eyes heated as they met hers. "Do you know how long I've been waiting for you to call me by my name, Mrs. Bailey?"

Surprised, she smiled right into his eyes. "Was it worth the wait?"

"Oh, yes," he rasped softly. And with a murmur that was her name, he pulled her into his arms.

Thunder boomed like dropping bombs as his mouth covered hers, but World War III could have been going on outside the car and she never would have noticed. There was only Max…the taste of him, the feel of him, the hot, tempting hunger of him. All this time, she thought, dazed. He wasn't the only one who'd been waiting. Ever since the football game, she'd been waiting for him to kiss her again, and she hadn't even known it. Until now. Until her blood was pumping and her heart was pounding and all she wanted to do was melt into his kiss and never come up for air.

Did he know what he did to her? she wondered. Did he know that he stirred something in her that she'd never felt before? Something that was so intense, so *right,* that it shook her to the bone and terrified her at one and the same time? How had she let this happen? There was no question that he was a wonderful man…attractive, intelligent, fun loving. But the last thing he wanted was a wife and twin stepsons slowing him down.

The thought stopped her cold. Abruptly coming to her senses, she pulled back. "I can't do this. I—"

"Can't do what?"

"This!" she said, gesturing helplessly between the two of them. "Kiss you! Let you kiss me! You're my teacher. And my boss!" Suddenly struck by a thought, she frowned suspiciously. "Why did you hire me to help you? There are other students who are smarter than I am. Why didn't you ask one of them to help you?"

"Because I know you're the best one for the job," he said simply. "You'll get twice as much done in half as much time as the other students." Studying her with searching eyes, he frowned. "What's this really about? If you think I hired you—and kissed you—because I've got some kind of ulterior motive, you can think again. I told you why I hired you, and I meant it. I kissed you because I find you incredibly attractive. One has nothing to do with the other."

He thought she was *incredibly attractive?* Stunned, she didn't know what to say. It had been eons since anyone had shown an interest in her. It was a heady feeling that she was afraid to trust. Was he serious? Or just giving into a basic instinct? And how did she feel? Incredibly attractive just might cover the storm of emotions whirling in her, but then again, maybe it was all just physical.

Confused, not very sure of herself, she said huskily, "I'm sorry. I didn't mean to accuse you—"

He stopped her apology with a quick press of his fingers against her mouth. "Stop," he growled softly. "You had legitimate concerns. You don't have to apologize. It's been a stressful day and you have to get the kids. I'll see you tomorrow. Okay?"

"Wait! I was going to give you a ride to your bike!"

"You have to get the boys," he reminded her. "I don't mind walking."

"But—"

Grinning, he silenced her with a quick kiss. Then, before she could do anything but draw in a quick breath, he was gone. Light-headed, her heart knocking a crazy rhythm against her ribs, she lifted her fingers to her mouth…and smiled.

Max had never had any difficulty keeping his professional and private lives separate. But then again, he couldn't remember the last woman who'd captivated him as much as Natalie did. And he'd come right out and told her. What in the world possessed him? Over the course of the next week, she was all business when she showed up at his office for work, as was he.

It didn't matter—he still couldn't get her out of his head. She retook her test and was thrilled with the seventy he had to give her, even though she only missed one question on the entire test. Her eyes sparkled with interest in class, and when she was able to negotiate a good price for something they needed for the dig, she couldn't have been more thrilled if she'd won the lottery. Her smile lit up her face and all he could think of was how much he wanted to kiss her again.

He didn't, though. He already thought about her too much, wanted her too much, and kissing her again, touching her again, holding her, would only make him want her more. The problem was...he'd set himself a nearly impossible task. The light enticing scent of her perfume intoxicated him. And then there was the sound of her laughter. It stroked him like a caress and haunted his dreams. What was a man supposed to do with a woman like that? Kiss her, of course! But he couldn't—except in the privacy of his own thoughts, and he found little satisfaction in that. Still, he was dealing with it.

When she didn't show up for class a week after she started working for him, he was surprised. She hadn't missed class once all semester. Surely her car hadn't gone again, he thought with a frown. Smitty had fixed it, and just yesterday she'd told him it was running better than it had in years. So where was she? She hadn't mentioned anything about needing the day off, but that didn't mean anything. One of the boys could have had an unexpected problem at school or a doctor's appointment that she'd forgotten to tell him about.

Not that she had to report her every move to him, he reminded himself as he began his lecture for the day. She was entitled to her privacy. He was just her boss, her friend, her wannabe lover.

In the middle of his lecture, he almost stopped dead in midsentence. When had he started thinking about making love to her? What was he thinking? A kiss or two was one thing. Becoming her lover was something else altogether. She wasn't a woman who would make love with a man lightly. She would want promises, commitment. Alarm bells clanged in his head just at the thought.

Troubled, he continued his lecture without pausing, but he

knew he wasn't his usual animated self. And the day went downhill from there. After his third—and last—class of the day, he didn't know who he was more disgusted with—himself, for wanting a woman he shouldn't have wanted, or Natalie, for being so distracting. He had a lot of thinking to do, and he didn't know how he was going to do that when Natalie was supposed to be there at four to work.

He needn't have worried. When he arrived at his office after his last class and listened to his messages, hers was the first voice he heard. "Hi, Max. This is Natalie. I hate to give you such short notice, but I'm not going to be able to work today or tomorrow. Tommy's got some kind of stomach bug. That's why I missed class this morning. I think it's one of those nasty twenty-four-hour things, but I'll keep him home again tomorrow just to make sure he's completely over it. So I guess I'll see you on Wednesday. Sorry."

His answering machine played the next message, but he hardly heard it. Maybe he should call her and make sure Tommy didn't have anything more serious than a bug, he thought with a frown. It couldn't be easy for her, taking care of the boys by herself all the time, but it had to be particularly difficult when one or both of them were sick. She never got a break. He'd help her if she'd let him. After everything she'd done for him with the dig, it was the least he could do.

You're paying her, a voice in his head reminded him dryly.

Okay, so what if he was? he reasoned. They were friends. What was the point of having friends if you couldn't help them out once in a while?

But even as he picked up the phone to call her, he hung up. No, he thought grimly. She'd sounded as if she had things under control. If she needed help, surely she knew she could call him.

She didn't call, however. And she didn't show up for class two days later. More concerned than ever, Max called her between his first and second class, but the answering machine clicked on almost immediately. That worried him even more. Was she all right? Had something horrible happened to the boys? What the hell was going on?

Frustrated, he almost gave his second class a walk so he could drive over to her house and check on her, but he stopped short of that. What if he was overreacting? Just because one of the boys had been sick didn't mean he still was. Something else could have come up. And he had a responsibility to his class. He couldn't just turn his back on his students and run over to Natalie's like some kind of knight on a crazy rescue mission just because she *might* be in trouble. He'd have to wait until after class.

Still, he couldn't shake the feeling that she was in trouble. The next hour and a half crawled by, and he didn't help matters by constantly checking his watch. When the bell finally rang, he was out the door almost as fast as his students. He took time only to slap a note on his office door, announcing that he was canceling office hours for the rest of the day. He rushed out to his bike, and five minutes later he was racing around the corner and heading for Natalie's.

Her car was in the driveway, but the house looked deserted. The blinds were drawn, and when he knocked on the door, no one answered. Pressing an ear to the door, he listened carefully but heard nothing. More worried than ever, he banged loudly enough to wake the dead. "Natalie? Are you in there? It's Max. Are you okay?"

His only answer was silence.

Scowling, he banged on the door with his fist. He knew

she was in there—she had to be! "Natalie? I'm worried sick about you. If you don't open up in ten seconds, I'm calling the police! Do you hear me?"

With no warning the dead bolt clicked open. "Finally! I've been worried sick about you—"

That was as far as he got. The door opened a crack, only to reveal Tommy and Harry confronting him with twin frowns of suspicion. Surprised, he looked past them, but there was no sign of Natalie. "Hey, guys," he said with a forced lightness he was far from feeling. "Remember me? I sat with you at the football game a couple of weeks ago."

"You're Mommy's teacher."

"The professor."

"That's right." Relieved, he looked past them into the small entry hall. "I've been worried about your mom. She hasn't been to class all week. Is she all right? Where is she?"

"She's sick."

"She threw up. A lot!"

Max shouldn't have found the situation the least bit amusing because it wasn't. But Harry—or was it Tommy?—seemed quite impressed with his mother's illness. Fighting a smile, Max said, "She sounds really sick. Maybe I should come in and check on her just to make sure she's all right."

"No!"

"Mommy said no one can come in the house!"

"But she might need my help," he pointed out. "How long has she been sick? Has she called the doctor? C'mon, guys, you need to let me see her. Your mother will understand—"

Harry's jaw set stubbornly. "Mommy said—"

"No means no," his brother finished for him, frowning.

"And Mommy means it. You don't want to get us in trouble, do you?"

"No, of course not!" he said, shocked. "I'm just worried about your mother. I think *she's* the one in trouble. She won't be mad if you let me check on her. I promise. I'll tell her I talked you into it."

Not budging so much as a fraction of an inch, they scowled at him with twin expressions of distrust. Torn between frustration and reluctant admiration, he sighed. Now what was he supposed to do? He could push past them, but they wouldn't forgive him for that, and he couldn't say he'd blame them. They were respecting their mother's instructions, and they wouldn't think much of him if he interfered with that.

"Okay" He sighed, resigned. "I understand why you can't let me in. You still need to let your mom known I'm here—just in case she wants me to take her to the doctor. I'll wait here while you go tell her."

For a long moment, he didn't think they would even do that. They hesitated, distrust clear in their eyes as they frowned at him. Then their gazes met, and without saying a word, they came to a decision. "You can't come in until Mommy says it's okay," the twin blocking the door warned.

"I won't budge an inch," Max assured him, fighting a smile. "I promise."

Before either boy could go in search of Natalie, however, she stepped into the entrance hall, looking as pale as death. Sweeping her tumbled hair back from her face, she frowned at him in confusion. "Max? What are you doing here?"

"He wanted us to let him in," one of the boys said quickly.

"Even when we told him you said no," the other twin added. "Did we do the right thing, Mommy?"

A weak smile curled the edges of her mouth as her sons moved protectively to her side. "Absolutely, sweetheart."

"I was worried about you," Max told her huskily, scowling as his gaze moved over her. "You look awful."

Awful, in fact, didn't begin to describe her. There were dark circles under her eyes, her face was white as a sheet, and she must have lost ten pounds in the last week. She looked like one good wind would blow her away, and it was all he could do not to cross to her and sweep her up into his arms.

For no other reason than that, he should have gotten the hell out of there. She stirred protective feelings in him that he hadn't even known he had, and it should have taken nothing more than that to make him avoid her like the plague. But he couldn't make himself walk away. Not when she was so sick.

Frustrated with himself, concerned for her, he scowled. "Have any of your friends been by to help you? What about Susan? She babysits the boys, right? Does she know you're sick? She must have come by to check on you. Surely she wouldn't let you go through this all by yourself."

"I wouldn't let her help," she replied. "She's got kids of her own. I couldn't take a chance on giving it to them."

"You should have called me. I was worried sick when I called and no one answered the phone."

"Mommy told us to unplug the phone so she could sleep," one of the twins volunteered. "We forgot to plug it back up."

He looked so apologetic that Max had to smile. "That's okay, sport. I guess you guys were pretty busy taking care of your mom. You must be ready for a break. How about a pizza? Why don't you go get your jackets on and we'll go get one at Airport Pizza? I still owe you one. Remember?

Since we didn't go after the football game, I promised to take you one day soon. Today's your lucky day…if it's okay with your mom, of course."

Their eyes sparkling with excitement, they glanced up at Natalie hopefully. "Can we, Mom? Can we?"

"We'll be good! Please?"

She hesitated, and for a moment Max thought she was going to say no. "I wouldn't offer if I didn't want to," he told her.

"Don't say no, Mom!

"You can sleep while we're gone. We'll turn the TV off before we leave, and it'll be real quiet!"

Hesitating, she knew she should have said no. He'd made it more than clear that he wasn't the kind of man who wanted the responsibility of a wife and family, so to continue any kind of relationship with him when she was so attracted to him was pure madness. But her defenses were down, she was sick as a dog, and when her eyes met his, all she wanted to do was let him take care of her. Just this once, she told herself. What would it hurt?

"All right." She sighed. "Take the Honda. The keys are on the hook by the back door. And mind your manners," she warned the boys, only to laugh when they launched themselves at her and gave her two fierce hugs. "No playing tricks on Professor Sullivan. He might not appreciate the twin thing."

"Yes, ma'am," they said in unison. "No tricks. We promise."

Watching them, Max grinned. They'd obviously made that same promise many times before, and it sounded good. But they both had sparks of mischief in their eyes, and he could just imagine what he was in for. "I can handle them," he promised Natalie. "What about you? Can I get you anything? Soup? Something at the grocery store? A potpie or something?"

Right before his eyes, her smile faded and she turned a light shade of green. "I don't think so," she said faintly, pressing a hand to her throat. "Food sounds…I don't even want to think about it."

She swayed on her feet, and in two steps Max reached her. Sweeping her up in his arms, he growled, "Okay. Back to bed for you. Where's your bedroom?"

"Down the hall," she said faintly, closing her eyes on a groan. "But I can walk."

"So can I, and right now I'll do it for both of us. Show me the way, boys."

He didn't have tell them twice. They ran down the hall and had the covers pulled back on her antique iron bed before Max carried her through the doorway. He had only an impression of pale-yellow walls, frilly curtains and bedding, before he gently laid her on the bed.

The green tint had faded from her face, leaving her as pale as the sheets, and all he wanted to do was gather her up in his arms and hold her close. Later, that need would haunt his sleep. Laying his palm against her forehead, he frowned. "You're hot. How long have you had a fever? Have you taken any aspirin?"

"A half hour ago," she said with a sigh as he pulled the covers over her and she sank deeper into her pillow. "It'll kick in in a minute. I just need to rest. I'm so tired."

Standing on the other side of the bed, the boys gazed at her solemnly as she closed her eyes and drifted into sleep. From the sudden glint in both their eyes, he knew they were both going to start crying at any second, and that horrified him. "She's going to be okay, guys," he promised them quietly as he quickly hustled them out of the room and shut the door. "She just needs to rest. While she's sleeping, why don't we go to the grocery store and see if we can find something she might want to eat when she's feeling better? Then we'll get the pizza. How does that sound?"

For a second he thought they were going to refuse. They glanced back over their shoulders at the door to Natalie's room and hesitated. Then Harry—or was it Tommy—looked up at him with the grin of a con artist. "Can we have extra cheese if we go quietly?"

"And lots and lots of pepperoni?" his brother added. "I love pepperoni!"

"No! We always get pepperoni. I want sausage and ham!"

Amused, Max grinned. So they didn't have red hair for nothing. What had he gotten himself into? "C'mon, guys, don't fight. You can both get your own personal pizza. How's that? We'll even get dessert. How about banana splits? We'll buy the stuff at the store and make them ourselves. Okay?"

He didn't have to ask them twice. "Race you to the car," they both challenged and sprinted down the hall to the living room.

"I get the front seat!"

"No! I do."

Grabbing the keys from the hook by the back door, Max caught up with them at the car, where they both had a death grip on the passenger side door and were trying to muscle the other one out of position. Fighting a grin, Max struggled to summon up a frown of disapproval. "No one gets the front seat but me. And I guess the banana splits are going to have to wait until another day."

Alarmed, they both stopped in mid push, and to their

credit—and Natalie's—they didn't make excuses. Instead, they had the grace to apologize.

"We're sorry."

"We won't do it again. Scout's honor!"

Surprised, Max lifted a dark brow at them. "You're Scouts? No kidding? So was I."

They couldn't have looked more surprised if he'd told them he had a two-headed dog. "You were not! Really?"

"Did you ever go to camp? Mom says we might get to go next summer."

"You'll love it," he assured them, grinning. "We used to have spitball fights when the counselors weren't around. It was great!"

The words were hardly out of his mouth when he saw interest spark in their eyes, and too late he realized that Natalie might not appreciate him sharing that kind of information with them. But they were boys, for heaven's sake. And if a spitball fight was the worst thing they ever did, then she could consider herself lucky. Growing up, he'd gotten into a lot more trouble than that. That, however, was something he didn't intend to share with them, he thought. Natalie would kill him if he put any more ideas in their heads.

By the time he pulled into Natalie's driveway an hour later, the boys were chatting with him like old friends. They helped him carry everything from pizzas to ice cream to three different varieties of canned soup and potpies into the kitchen, and they were so excited, they could hardly contain themselves. When Natalie discovered what he'd bought, she would, no doubt, accuse him of spoiling them all, but what was wrong with that? She obviously lived on a strict budget—she had to since her ex was a deadbeat—so that didn't allow her the chance to indulge the boys very much. What would it hurt to buy them a treat? They were good kids. He didn't think he could have taken as good care of his mom if she'd gotten sick when he was in kindergarten. They deserved a little reward.

"Okay, guys, how about a movie?" he said after putting the ice cream and pot pies in the freezer of the refrigerator.

"The Lion King!" they cried in unison.

"Works for me," he said with a grin. Spying the DVD player on the top shelf of the entertainment center, he frowned. "Does your mom let you put the movies in yourself or does she do it?"

"No, we can do it," Tommy assured him.

Working as a team, the boys plopped their pizzas on the coffee table and pulled a footstool over to the entertainment center. In five seconds flat Tommy had the movie in and Harry worked the remote control. The second the movie came on, the boys were totally engrossed. Never taking their eyes from the television screen, they reached blindly for their pizzas and sank down onto the living room rug to watch their movie.

That was easy enough, Max thought with a grin, and headed back to the kitchen. Not surprisingly, it was a mess. The sink was overflowing with dishes, the trashcan was in desperate need of being emptied, and the counters and kitchen table were loaded down with more dirty dishes, empty food containers that wouldn't fit in the trash and clean pots from the dishwasher that hadn't been put away. The place couldn't have looked much worse if it'd been hit by a tornado.

Taking it all in in a single glance, Max had no difficulty imaging what it must have been like for Natalie when the boys were sick. She obviously hadn't had time to put the dishes away, let alone clean, before she, herself, came down with the same stomach bug. If the boys were half as sick as she was, it was no wonder the place was a disaster area.

When she was feeling better, Max knew she would be mortified that he'd seen her house in such condition, but it couldn't be helped. And if she was anything like his mother, the last thing she'd want an outsider to do was come in and clean her house—which was why he had no intention of telling her what he intended to do until after the fact. Rolling up his sleeves, he unloaded the dishwasher and went to work.

Forty minutes later the dishes were done and the trash had been consigned to the garbage can in the garage. The boys were still glued to the television and thoroughly enjoying their movie, so he hurried down the hall to Natalie's room to see how she was doing. Not wanting to wake her if she was sleeping, he silently turned the knob and peeked inside. She was, as he'd hoped, still sleeping, but the nap she took was far from a restful one. The covers were tossed, her pillow had fallen to the floor, and as he watched her she moaned in her sleep. In three long strides, he was beside her.

"Natalie? Sweetheart?"

She only moaned again and turned toward him in her sleep. Concerned, he gently laid his hand on her forehead. She was burning up.

Chapter 7

Somewhere in the far-off reaches of sleep, Natalie felt his hand on her forehead, tenderly stroking her. But it was the worry in his husky voice that called to her. Frowning, she struggled to respond, but the sleep that held her in its grip was thick and heavy and hot and didn't want to let her go.

"Natalie? Can you hear me, sweetheart? Wake up."

Did he know what he asked of her? she thought groggily. Ten-pound weights seemed to be sitting on her eyelids, but somehow she managed to force them open. Almost immediately she realized her mistake. Even with that slight movement her stomach grumbled threateningly. With a groan she slammed her eyes shut. "I can't," she whispered hoarsely. "I feel awful."

"I know, honey, but you're burning up with fever. Are you sure you took some aspirin at three?"

"The boys were watching *Scooby-Doo*," she said, frowning as she tried to remember. "It comes on at three."

"And it's five-thirty now."

Confused, she blinked. "Five-thirty! But I just lay down. Where are the boys? I need to see about supper—"

"The boys are fine," he assured her. "They each have their own pizza and they're sitting in front of the TV watching *The Lion King*. You're the one I'm worried about. We're going to have to do something about your fever. Think you could manage a cool bath? It'll help bring the fever down."

She knew he was right, but tears welled in her eyes just at the thought of getting out of bed. She couldn't remember the last time she'd been this sick, and she hated it.

"Don't cry, sweetheart," he murmured, gently wiping away the tears that spilled from her eyes. "You're not fighting this alone anymore. Okay?"

"I just feel so rotten," she said, sniffing. "And you shouldn't even be here. This is an awful bug. If you get this because of me, I'm going to feel terrible."

Far from concerned, he only grinned. "Don't worry about me. My mother says I've got the constitution of a horse. I get exposed to everything from viruses to the latest strand of the flu going around the campus, and I still somehow manage to escape the worst of them. I'll be fine. You're the one I'm worried about."

Squeezing her hand, he rose to his feet. "I'll take care of everything—you just lie there and let me take care of you. I'll start the water running in the tub, then help you into the bathroom. Where are your clean nightgowns?"

She should have insisted that he'd done enough for her, but the steady look he gave her warned her he wasn't going to take no for an answer. And he didn't have a clue how much that touched her. It had been so long since she'd had someone in her life she could lean on—she'd forgotten how wonderful it could feel.

"In the top drawer of my dresser," she told him with a watery smile. "I can get it—"

"Don't even think about it," he growled. "I've got everything under control."

Not giving her a chance to argue further, he stepped over to her dresser, grabbed a clean nightgown and underwear and strode into the bathroom to start the water running in the tub. When he stepped back into the bedroom a few minutes later, he walked over to the bed and studied her consideringly. "I can carry you or help you into the bathroom. Either way, I'm afraid your stomach's not going to like it."

She grimaced. "I think you're right. But it'll be worth it for a bath. Here goes nothing."

Easing her feet to the floor, she held out her hands to let him help her up. Her stomach lurched, and for a moment she was afraid she was going to toss her cookies, as the boys said, right then and there. Her hands tightened in Max's, and with a soft moan, she leaned her head against his chest and closed her eyes as she waited for her stomach to settle. "I'll be okay," she said weakly. "Just give me a few minutes."

"Take all the time you need," he told her gruffly, and released her hands to wrap his arms around her.

His touch was so gentle, so tender, she suddenly found herself fighting tears. She'd thought she knew who he was, the kind of man he was, but she'd never dreamed he could be so caring. Every other man she knew would have cut and run at the mere mention of a stomach bug, but he'd made it clear that not only was he not going anywhere, he was going to be there for her as long as she needed him. If she hadn't been so sick, she would have kissed him for that.

When she sighed, he tightened his arms carefully around her. "Feeling better?" he asked huskily.

She nodded, then forced herself to pull free. "Here goes nothing."

Pale, her stomach gurgling the entire way, she cautiously made her way to the bathroom. Max was right behind her, hovering close, but she made it without mishap. "Can you do this on your own?" he asked as she sank down onto a small wicker bench next to the old-fashioned clawfoot tub. "I can help if you need me to."

For the first time in what seemed like a month, she laughed. "I'm sure you would, but I can take it from here."

"Damn," he swore, grinning. "You can't blame a guy for trying."

"Not at all," she said with a chuckle. "Now if you'll excuse me…"

She started to shut the door, but he quickly stepped forward and kissed her. "I'll be right here waiting for you. Call if you need help."

Max was waiting for her when she stepped out of the bathroom twenty minutes later, just as he'd promised. "That was fast," he said as he laid his palm across her brow. "Your temperature's gone down. Good. How's the stomach?"

"Still there," she admitted with a grimace. "But better, thank God."

He moved to help her to the bed, but she'd only taken a

single step before she stopped dead in her tracks as she got her first good look at her bedroom.

Over the course of the last week, her room had become a disaster area. She'd been so tired from taking care of the boys when they were sick that she hadn't had the energy to do anything but let her clothes fall where they may at night when she got ready for bed. She'd kept promising herself that she was going to pick everything up, but just as the boys had gotten better, she'd become sick herself.

The boys had done their best to take care of her, but they were kids, and they hadn't cared less that the entire house was a disaster area. They'd brought her juice and soup and snacks to tempt her appetite, then left the dirty dishes on her nightstand or dresser. And she'd been too miserably sick to care.

Max, however, had noticed—and done something about it. While she was in the bathroom, he'd not only picked everything up, he'd changed the sheets on her bed. Then he'd turned back the covers, fluffed the pillows in their clean pillowcases, and drawn the shades, turning her bedroom into an inviting hideaway. She took one look at her favorite sheets, and just that quickly her eyes flooded with tears. "Oh, Max!"

"Hey, what's this?" he growled, smiling into her eyes as he caught an errant tear with his thumb. "I thought you'd be happy that I picked up."

"I am," she sniffed. "I just wasn't expecting…men aren't supposed to know to do these things. Derek certainly never did. When I was pregnant with the boys, he didn't care if I was tired or had morning sickness. When he came home from work, he expected me to have dinner on the table."

Privately Max thought the man was a jackass. She'd been seven months pregnant with his sons, for God's sake! And what had he done? Walked away like they didn't exist, like she didn't exist! How? How could a man do that? Even if he'd fallen out of love with Natalie, she was still the mother of his children. If for no other reason than that, he owed her respect and support. Instead, he'd just abandoned her.

Just the thought of all the heartache her ex had put her through infuriated Max, but that wasn't his fight, he reminded himself. He would, however, give the man a piece of his mind if he ever got the chance.

In the meantime Natalie was his only concern. "My mother and grandmother are both incredibly caring women," he told her. "My grandmother used to say that nothing felt better than a bath and clean sheets when you were sick. Obviously, you agree with her."

"Oh, yes," she said as she sank down onto the edge of the bed and ran her hand over the soft sheets. "This feels wonderful. Thank you."

When she smiled at him like that, she could have asked for diamonds from the far side of the moon and he would have found a way to get them for her. "It was my pleasure," he told her gruffly. "Can I get you anything else? You must be hungry…."

"No," she began, only to yawn. "I'm sorry," she said, yawning again. "I'm just so tired."

"Then I'll bring you something to eat in a while," he promised, and pulled the covers up over her. "Go to sleep, sweetheart. I'll check in on you later."

He surprised her with a kiss on the cheek, and before she could find her voice again, he was gone. Disappointed, she wanted to call him back, but she just didn't have the energy. She yawned again and pushed her pillow into a more comfortable position. Seconds later she fell asleep, only to discover that Max hadn't gone far. He was right there in her dreams.

The rest of the day passed in a blur. Natalie woke several times to find Max sitting on the side of the bed, watching her in concern, but she only summoned a weak smile and drifted back to sleep. Later that afternoon her fever broke, thank God, and her stomach settled down, but it had been years since she'd had a chance to sleep, really sleep, and she was on the verge of exhaustion.

Still, she felt guilty for putting the responsibility of the boys off on Max. She tried to get up, but Max was there almost immediately to stop her. He assured her he didn't mind taking care of the boys—the three of them were getting along fine—and the only thing she had to worry about was not rushing her recovery. Too weak to fight him, she did as he said and slept.

When she finally woke up, she was rested…and starving. How long had she been out of commission? She glanced at the clock on her nightstand and gasped. Three o'clock? It couldn't be! It had been after four when Max had changed the sheets for her while she took a bath. That meant she'd slept around the clock!

Stunned, she tried to convince herself that she was mistaken, but she knew she wasn't. She'd been so tired, she must have just died away. And while she'd been playing Sleeping Beauty, Max had had the responsibility of her children. And that horrified her. Jumping up, she grabbed her robe. Was he still there? Still taking care of the boys? Had he spent the night?

Her heart knocking against her ribs, she stepped out of her room and paused, listening. The television was on in the living room, but the rest of the house was as quiet as a tomb. Where was everyone? Frowning, she quietly headed down the hall and stopped in surprise at the entrance to the living room. The boys were seated on the floor in front of the television, quietly coloring in what appeared to be new coloring books. But it was the sight of Max asleep on the couch that touched her heart. He was sprawled on his stomach, with his head half-buried under one of the couch pillows, and his feet hanging off the end. He looked dead to the world.

Later, she didn't know how long she would have stood there, watching him sleep, if she'd had the chance. But she must have made some kind of sound because suddenly, the boys glanced up sharply and spied her in the doorway. In the time it took to blink, they launched themselves at her.

"Mom! You're awake!"

"You slept all day and night! We thought you died!"

Laughing, she staggered slightly under their fierce hugs. "No, I'm not dead. You know I wouldn't go off and leave you guys. I was just really, really sick."

"You look a hundred percent better."

Max's quiet comment startled her, and she glanced back at the couch to find that he'd rolled to a sitting position and was watching her with sleepy eyes. Her heart lurched at the sight of him. No man had a right to look so sexy the second he woke up. His hair was tousled and spilling over his brow, his jaw rough and unshaven. And all she wanted to do was touch him.

Heat climbing in her cheeks, she said, "I feel a lot better, thank God."

"Max took us to the video store, Mom!"

"Look at all the movies we rented!"

At least ten movies were spread out on the coffee table, and Natalie only had to glance at them to see that they were all children's movies. "That was very sweet of you," she told Max. "I don't know how to thank you."

"No thanks necessary," he said with a grin as he pushed to his feet. "The boys and I had a great time, didn't we, guys? They beat the socks off of me at Go Fish."

"He was terrible, Mom!"

"We beat him ten times in a row!"

"Okay," Max admitted, chuckling, "so it's been a while since I played Go Fish. I was a little rusty. I didn't do so badly once I got back in the groove. So who's hungry for breakfast?"

"I am!"

"Me, too!"

"But it's three o'clock in the afternoon," she protested. "Surely you've already eaten breakfast."

"We were waiting for you," Harry said, looking up at her with a wide grin as he hugged her. "Max said we could have chocolate chip pancakes!"

"Oh, well, we can't pass that up," she said lightly.

"I'll have you know I know my way around the kitchen," he told her, grinning. "Ask the boys. I made everything they like while you were sick, including mac and cheese."

"Only, he puts hot dogs in his, Mom!" Tommy said, impressed. "We had it for supper and breakfast."

"Really?"

When she arched a brow at Max, he only grinned boyishly. "I was trying to take their minds off you. They were worried. And they like hot dogs."

"I'm not quite sure where hot dogs and chocolate chips fit on the food pyramid," she said with a chuckle, "but I don't guess they're any worse for you than anything else."

That was all the encouragement Max needed. He quickly whipped up some pancakes, and Natalie had to admit they were good. "I'm impressed," she told him, smiling. "I didn't know you liked to cook."

"I don't know if I would go so far as to say I can actually cook," he replied ruefully. "It doesn't take a lot of skill to throw chocolate chips into a pancake mix..."

"Or hot dogs into a box of macaroni and cheese," she teased.

"No, that was nothing more than pure genius," he corrected her, "and you know it."

"Maybe," she agreed with twinkling eyes. "A couple of five-year-olds were certainly impressed."

"I aim to please,"

He'd done that and more. The boys cleaned their plates, then asked for seconds and finished off the last of the pancakes. Watching them as they carried their plates to the sink, Max said quietly, "You've done a heck of a job with your boys, Natalie. They're good kids."

A soft smile curled the corners of her mouth. "I got lucky," she said simply.

"It's more than that," he insisted as the boys ran outside to play in the backyard. "Kids aren't well mannered and respectful by chance. And they're certainly not secure and confident and funny unless their mother is doing everything right. I enjoyed watching over them for you."

"I don't know what I would have done without you," she

said honestly. "When I first got sick, I thought I could handle it by myself, but then I just got sicker and sicker. It was awful."

"You were lucky you kept the boys home from school once they were feeling better. You could have been in serious trouble if you'd been here all by yourself."

"I hadn't planned to keep them home," she said wryly as she rose from the kitchen table to carry her plate and his to the sink. "I was just too sick to get them up in the morning for school."

"Next time, call me," he told her, joining her at the sink to put the dishes in the dishwasher. "You don't have to go through something like this alone. Okay?"

Tears misted her eyes. "Okay," she said thickly. "Thank you."

She stepped forward to give him a quick hug, and at the first feel of her arms around him, Max swallowed a groan. This, he told himself, was not smart. She was on the mend, well on her way back to being her old self, and all he could think about was kissing her. And it was all her fault.

If she hadn't gotten sick, if he hadn't spent the last few days taking care of her, he might have found it easier to remember that they were friends...*just* friends. But he'd changed her sheets for her, helped her to that bathroom, wiped her face with a cool cloth after she'd been sick, cooked for her, made himself at home in her home. Right or wrong, there was an intimacy between them that neither of them could ignore—he could see it in her eyes every time he looked at her—and he wanted to kiss her, dammit!

But after all they'd shared, he wasn't sure he could stop with just a kiss. And she was still weak from being sick, and the boys were just outside in the backyard. They could come inside at any moment.

That, more than anything, sobered him. He liked the little squirts. And he didn't doubt for a minute that they liked him. That didn't mean they wanted him kissing their mother. Frustrated, he told himself this was why he didn't get involved with women with children. Not that the reminder did him any good at this point. He *was* involved, and he didn't even know how it had happened.

Troubled, in need of some serious time to himself to think, he returned her hug, then eased out of her arms to study her with a frown. "You should spend the remainder of the day resting, you know. You don't want to jump back into things too quickly."

"I'm just going to lie on the couch and catch up on my reading," she told him. "What about you? You must have things to do…."

She'd just given him the perfect opening, and he knew he was in trouble when he felt guilty for using it. Irritated with himself, he nodded. "I need to get home, but I want your promise that you'll call me if you need me. I can be here in ten minutes."

"I'll be fine," she assured him. When he just looked at her, patiently waiting, she sighed, a reluctant grin curling the corners of her mouth. "Okay, okay. I promise."

Satisfied, he gave in to temptation and kissed her…but only on the cheek. "If you don't feel like working on the arrangements for the dig tomorrow, don't worry about it. We can get started on Tuesday."

"Oh, no, tomorrow will be fine."

"Then, I'll see you then," he said gruffly, and stepped outside to tell the boys goodbye.

Standing at the kitchen window, Natalie watched him tease the boys, then ruffle their hair before leaving though the side gate by the garage. Seconds later she heard his motorcycle roar down the street. She'd never heard a lonelier sound in her life.

Shaking off the sudden melancholy that threatened to settle over her, she refused to even consider the possibility that she was missing him already. She couldn't miss what she didn't have. He was a friend, a teacher, nothing more. Life was back to normal.

It didn't, however, feel that way as she approached his office late the following afternoon to work on the arrangements for the dig. Butterflies swarmed in her stomach, and a smile of anticipation tugged at the corners of her mouth. Images teased her…Max sprawled on her living room couch sleeping, while her sons played quietly on the floor in front of him; his hand tenderly pressed against her brow as he checked to see if she had a fever, the strength of his arms as he carried her to bed when she was too sick to get there under her own power.

Don't go there! her common sense warned sharply. *Don't start thinking you're falling in love with the man. You're just still caught up in the memories from the weekend. Once you change gears and go back to the relationship you had before you got sick, you'll be fine.*

But how did she forget?

She didn't have an answer for that. Her only option was to act is if he'd never touched her, never kissed her, never raced through the night with her on the back of his motorcycle. Yeah, right.

Dragging in a deep breath, she prayed she could be all business as she knocked sharply on his door, but she might as well have saved herself the effort. There was no answer. Surprised, she frowned. She'd told him she would work today. Where was he?

Chewing her bottom lip, she couldn't believe he wasn't there. The dig was just weeks away, and the arrangements they still had to make were daunting. They couldn't afford to lose any more time, especially since she hadn't been able to work at all last week. If she just had her notes, she could work at home. But his notes were in his office and he was nowhere to be found.

Frustrated, she impulsively tried the doorknob…and gasped when it turned in her hand.

"Aha! Caught you in the act!"

Startled, she nearly jumped out of her skin, then turned around. "Max! Don't do that!"

When she scowled at him, he only chuckled. "Don't do what? *You* were the one breaking in."

"It's not breaking in when the door's not locked," she retorted sassily as she preceded him into his office. "I was afraid you weren't coming back today."

"I made a quick trip to the grocery store for some coffee." Stepping around her, he moved to the small table in the corner that held a small microwave and coffeemaker. "How are you feeling? You look better."

His gaze moved over her, setting her heart thumping, and just that easily her vow to keep things strictly business between them was on the verge of going up in smoke. "I feel better, thank you." Determinedly bringing the conversation back to her purpose for being there, she added, "I lost a lot of time on making the arrangements for the dig, though."

"I worked on it most of the afternoon," he said, "but there's still a lot to do. Let me put some coffee on, and we'll get started."

Thankful that there was no time for anything but the task at hand, Natalie went over her notes, refreshing her memory about what still had to be done while he got the coffee going. They both then went to work, and the rest of the afternoon seemed to fly by. If her eyes fell on him every time she looked up and she found herself watching him whenever she dropped her guard, he didn't notice, thankfully. Still she was convinced she could keep things strictly business between them…until he brought up the boys.

"What are the munchkins up to today?" he asked as they took a short coffee break. "I don't know if I told you, but they impressed the hell out of me when they wouldn't let me in the door even though they were worried about you. They're very protective of you. And incredibly energetic," he added with a grin. "How do you keep up with them?"

She chuckled. "Most of the time I'm two steps behind them."

"I'm glad to hear it—I thought I was just getting old. Every time I thought they were winding down and I could take my eyes off them for a second or two, I'd turn around and they'd be in the kitchen, trying to cook you something special—or in the bathroom bathing the dog or brushing his teeth! And they said you said it was okay."

"Well, the vet did recommend that we brush his teeth."

"Really? And did he tell you to make sure Bongo flossed, too?"

Shocked, she laughed. "Oh, no, they didn't!"

"Oh, yes, they did. And trust me, Bongo wasn't happy about it. I didn't think I was ever going to get that floss out of his teeth."

Struggling between laughter and horror, she gasped, "Oh, God, he didn't bite you, did he? He won't even let the vet look at his teeth."

"I bet he would if he had a mouthful of dental floss," he retorted dryly. "He didn't give me a bit of trouble. In fact, he even licked me when I pulled out the last of it."

He looked so disgusted, Natalie couldn't hold back a peal of laughter. "I'm sorry," she choked when he gave her a baleful look. "I had no idea any of this was even going on. You should have told me."

"When you were barfing your guts up? I don't think so."

Touched, she grinned. "You're so thoughtful. Does your mother know what a good son she raised?"

His blue eyes twinkling, he shrugged. "Maybe."

"Trust me—mothers know their sons. I bet she knows all your secrets."

What could his mother tell her? Natalie wondered. She could just imagine. Oh, she wouldn't know about the women he'd been involved with—that he would keep private. But she would know who he'd dated in high school, his hopes and dreams, what kind of mischief he'd gotten into when he was Harry and Tommy's age. With no trouble whatsoever, Natalie could just picture him at five, the sparkle in his blue eyes and his boyish grin a sure sign that he was up to something. If he ever had a son of his own, he would probably look just like him.

Suddenly realizing where her thoughts had wandered, she stiffened, swallowing a quick curse. There she went again, fantasizing about the man when she'd sworn she wouldn't! How could she continue to work one on one with him when she couldn't even control her thoughts? If she didn't do something soon, she was going to make a complete fool of herself.

"I have to go," she said suddenly.

"Now? I thought you'd be able to stay until at least six."

"I...I can't. Something's come up with Susan and she can't keep the boys late anymore," she fibbed. "So if you don't mind, I thought I might start working from home."

"You're not going to be able to come into the office anymore?" he asked sharply.

She'd surprised him, and from the scowl suddenly knitting his brows, not in a pleasant way. Her heart fluttered, and for a second she wanted to believe he wasn't happy with the change in their arrangement because he enjoyed her company and didn't want to lose the time they had together. But that was just her foolish heart trying to get her in trouble again.

"Oh, I can come in," she assured him quickly, "but only when the boys are in school." He wouldn't be able to meet then, of course, because he had classes, which is exactly why she suggested it. What other choice did she have? Anytime she was within twenty feet of the man, she lost all sense of self-preservation. She had to do something!

"I should be ready to start buying supplies in a couple of days, anyway," she added. "We can keep in touch through e-mail—and the phone, of course. I know this is inconvenient and not part of our deal, but I don't have another sitter, and the boys can't be home alone. There's nothing else I can do right now."

Still frowning, Max didn't agree. There had to be *something* she could do, dammit! He didn't want to lose her. He tried to tell himself it was because he enjoyed working with her and was going to miss the one-on-one time they had together, but he knew he was lying to himself. It was more than that. A hell of a lot more. She'd somehow gotten under his skin, and for the life of him, he didn't know how. She wasn't even his type!

So why was he fighting this? he wondered suddenly, frowning. Maybe it would be better if she worked at home from now on. They'd spent a lot of time together while she was sick and had gotten a hell of a lot closer than he'd intended. A little space might be a good thing. Maybe then he'd remember all the reasons why he should be avoiding her like the plague.

"It's all right," he assured her. "There's no reason why you can't do most of this at home—I don't know why I didn't think of it. We do need to get together again before finalizing everything, though. And don't worry about the boys—you can bring them with you or I can meet you at your house. We can decide that later. Okay?"

"You don't know how much I appreciate this," she told him as she gathered up her notes. "I'll be in touch."

Long after she'd gone, Max sat at his desk, trying to work. The silence that engulfed him, however, was a distraction he hadn't expected. Frowning, he put a CD in the small boom box that sat on a shelf behind his desk, but it didn't help. His gaze kept drifting to the table he'd come to think of as Natalie's desk. It looked empty without her and her notes.

"Idiot," he growled. "You're acting like a lovesick fool."

Which was ridiculous, he decided. He wasn't in love, never had been and didn't intend to be. A fair number of women had tried to change his mind over the years, but all he'd had to do was think of his father—and all his ex-wives—and he'd had no trouble standing his ground.

This time, though, he *was* tempted to let his guard down and see what would happen, and that scared the hell out of him. What the devil was wrong with him? Maybe he'd been working too hard. He was too serious. He couldn't even remember the last time he'd been for a ride on his bike just to blow the cobwebs out of his head. He was just too damn busy.

So make some changes, the rebel in his head whispered. *Get the hell out of here and go for a ride!*

He didn't have to tell himself twice. The thought had hardly registered before he was shutting down his computer. Grabbing his helmet, he hurried outside to his bike.

He would have sworn he had no particular destination in mind, but before he even realized where he was going, he found himself turning down the street where his father lived. He laughed shortly, amused by the workings of his subconscious. What was this? A not-so-subtle reminder that he didn't want to fall into the trap that his father had? Okay, he got it!

He should have turned around, right then and there, and gone for a ride in the country, like he'd planned, but before he could, he saw his father's car coming down the street. Caught! There was nothing he could do. John Sullivan saw him almost immediately.

"This is a surprise," his father said with a grin as he pulled into the driveway and stepped from the car. "What are you doing here?"

"Heck if I know." He chuckled. "I was just out for a drive, and the next thing I knew, I was turning down your street.

Have you had dinner? Why don't we go to that new steak place over on Kansas Avenue?"

Regret flashed in his eyes. "I'd love to, but Becky's inside cooking dinner."

Max stiffened. *"Becky?"*

If his father heard his sharp tone, he didn't pay any attention to it. An all-too-familiar smile transformed John Sullivan's face into that of a man in love. "Didn't I tell you about Becky? I met her at the grocery store. Her cart ran into mine, and the next thing I knew, I was asking her out."

"Awh, Dad!"

"She's the most incredible woman," he said, smiling broadly. "Why don't you stay and join us for dinner? I'm sure there's enough, and I want you two to get to know each other."

Put on the spot, Max hesitated. How did he tell his father he wasn't really interested in meeting her? After all, what was the point? If she was anything like the rest of the women his father had fallen in love with over the past ten years or so, she would be pretty and flighty and not much older than Max, himself. And she would stay only long enough to realize that she didn't want to be married to an old man, after all.

He was, in fact, surprised that the unknown Becky was not only still around, but cooking. Max couldn't remember the name of the last woman his father had dated who had any domestic skills whatsoever.

"I hate to intrude, Dad," he said finally, frowning. "If Becky's gone to the trouble of cooking dinner for you, she's not going to want company."

"Are you kidding me? She cooks dinner for me every

night, and she's been harassing the hell out of me to meet you. She refuses to even consider marrying me until you meet her and give your blessing."

Far from impressed, Max winced. "You're getting married? Did you mention the *P* word? Does she know she's going to have to sign a prenup?"

His father only laughed. "Oh, she knows, all right. She's the one who suggested it! I'm telling you, son, you've got to meet her. I've never met another woman like her in my life."

Max didn't put a lot of stock in his father's opinion of women—how many times had he chosen the wrong one? Seven…eight times? And those were the ones he'd married! Max couldn't even count the others he'd just dated, but there was no point in even mentioning them. His father was in love…*again*…and this time, as in the past, he'd convinced himself it was forever. For his sake, Max hoped he was right, though he wasn't holding his breath. After all, what were the odds?

In the meantime, he had no choice but to stay for dinner and meet Becky. His father was engaged, and he expected him to be happy for him. Forcing a smile, Max said, "She sounds great. Of course I'll stay for dinner. If you two are talking about marriage, I need to get to know her. "

Pleased, his father slapped him on the back. "That's great! C'mon in. I'll introduce you."

Chapter 8

When Max walked into his house three hours later, loneliness clawed at him, shocking him. He loved his own space, loved the quiet solitude of his own home. When he felt the need for company, he had a host of people he could hang out with, including biker friends, women friends, colleagues. His schedule was busy, his outside interests were varied, and he just didn't have time to get lonely. So what the devil was going on?

He never should have stayed for dinner with his father and Becky, he decided. He'd expected Becky to be like all the other women his father had married after he'd divorced his mother: too young, too ditzy and looking for a man to take care of her so she didn't have to work. Instead, she'd turned out to be just a few years younger than his father, a chemistry teacher at the local high school and more than capable of taking care of herself. What had impressed him the most, however, was that she seemed to be genuinely in love with his father and protective of him. She didn't want him to make another mistake, refusing, in spite of his insistence, to rush into marriage. And, as his father had claimed, she was determined that if and when they married, there would be a prenuptial agreement so they would both be protected in the event of a divorce.

She was up-front and honest, and Max had to admit that he liked her. She seemed to love his father even more than he loved her, and every time their eyes met, her whole face lit up. Max considered himself an excellent judge of character, and he'd immediately recognized the schemers for exactly who and what they were. If Becky was an opportunist looking for the chance to take advantage of his father, then she needed to be in Hollywood because she was good—damn good.

And she'd given him a hell of a lot to think about. He had work to do—another test to put together—but instead of sitting down at his home-office computer in the spare bedroom, he grabbed a beer from the refrigerator and went out onto the patio. It was a beautiful night, clear and cool, with a full moon. He hardly noticed. Had his father finally found the right woman and a love that would withstand the test of time? It was too early to tell, but Max had to admit it certainly looked that way, and that shook him to the core. He readily admitted he was jaded when it came to soul mates and happily-ever-afters. How could he not be, when it took two hands to count his stepmothers? But what if he was wrong? What if true love actually existed? Was there a woman somewhere out there in the vast reaches of the universe he could trust enough to love?

Images of Natalie flashed in his head, images that teased and seduced and made him ache somewhere in the region of his heart. Stiffening, he told himself he wasn't in love with her. They were just friends, nothing more. If he wanted to pick up the phone and call her, even though he'd just seen her that afternoon, it was only because he was still reeling from the news that his father was in love…again. He just needed to talk to someone.

Was that the way it started with his father and Becky? Just thinking about it made his stomach knot.

Pulling into the parking lot of a discount surplus store on Wednesday afternoon, Natalie should have been proud of herself for sticking to her guns and putting some distance between herself and Max. She knew she'd done the right thing. There would be no more impromptu picnics at his desk, no more quiet conversations about hopes and dreams, no more moments when they were alone and their eyes met and she remembered all too easily what it felt like to be in his arms. They were back on track, back to the teacher/student, boss/employee relationship they never should have strayed from, and all was right with the world.

But as she walked up and down the aisles of the cavernous warehouse, her steps echoing eerily, she'd never felt so miserably lonely. Tears threatened, and with a muttered curse, she quickly blinked them back. She had to stop this! She wasn't usually a crybaby—she never had been, not even when Derek had walked out and she'd discovered that he'd been cheating on her for months. So why was she crying now? Max hadn't done anything to her. *She* was the one who had decided this was necessary, not him. This was what she'd wanted, what she needed to protect her heart. So why was she so unhappy?

"May I help you, ma'am?"

Looking up from her thoughts, she wasn't surprised to find a clerk studying her warily. She'd been wandering up and down the aisles for the past fifteen minutes, looking at absolutely nothing. "I'm sorry," she told him, smiling weakly. "I seem to be in a fog. Do you have any tents? I called yesterday and was told a new shipment was coming in today. Has it arrived yet?"

"It just came in this morning," he replied. "I believe there's a display on aisle three. If you'll follow me..."

She started to tell him that she could find it, but as he headed for the display without waiting to see if she followed, she realized that she'd already been down aisle three a number of times. And she hadn't even seen the tents!

"We have pup tents, nylon and canvas, and everything from two-man up to ten," the clerk told her as she joined him in front of the display. "What exactly were you looking for?"

"Nylon," she said promptly. "And something large enough to hold four people."

Studying her consideringly, he frowned. "Is this something you want to set up in your backyard for your kids or are you going camping? What do you need it for?"

"A dig with the university up on Black Mountain."

"Are you packing it in yourself or is there someone to help you?"

"Actually, there are fifty of us going, and so we'll all be carrying our share of the load," she replied. "We'll be hiking about three miles to the dig site."

"Have you considered buying two-man tents instead of

four-man?" he asked with a frown. "If price is a factor, two two-man are going to be more expensive than one four-man. If there's room in the budget, though, I'd go with the smaller tents. It's not that much difference in price, and there are other things to consider…like weight. A three-mile hike doesn't sound very far, but it's going to seem like an eternity when you're weighted down with heavy equipment. The lighter your load, the happier everyone's going to be."

Natalie couldn't argue with that. "I agree, but if I go with the smaller tents, I'm going to need twice as many." Skeptically, she eyed the supply he had on the shelf. "You don't have nearly enough, and you just got a shipment in."

"We have another warehouse," he assured her. "I'll check the inventory on the computer. Even if I don't have all twenty-five, I can get them. How soon do you need them?"

"By Thanksgiving," she retorted. "Can you work that fast?"

"I'm sure we can. Let me check the inventory and then we'll know what we're dealing with. Is there anything else you need that I can check at the same time?"

For an answer she held up the list of supplies Max had decided they would need for the dig. When his eyes widened in surprise, she smiled. "I know—it's a lot to get together on such short notice, but there was a last-minute problem with the tour group, so Professor Sullivan decided to do this on his own."

The clerk whistled softly. "That's a lot of work."

"And we've only got a short time to get it done." Nodding at the list, she said, "Assuming you have everything in stock—or you can get it in time for the dig—I need to know what kind of price you can give me. I've already gotten bids from several other outfitters. If you can give me a price that beats theirs, you'll get the order. Do you work on commission?"

He smiled slightly. "Actually, I do. Give me a few minutes and let me see what I can do."

"Take your time," she replied. "I haven't been here before so I'll just be wandering around the store."

"I'll find you," he promised, and hurried to the office to check the store's inventory on the computer.

She expected it to take the salesclerk at least thirty minutes to check everything and get back with her, but fifteen minutes later he found her looking at sleeping bags. Max was providing the tents for the class, but everyone had to bring their own sleeping bag and she didn't have one. She needed something cheap.

"There you are," the clerk said with a smile. "Okay, I'm all done, and I think you're going to be pleased. We have everything you need."

"And the price?"

When he gave her a price that was significantly lower than Natalie had expected, she almost laughed aloud. The other bids weren't even in the same ballpark. Max was going to be so pleased.

Still, she didn't jump at it…not yet. "Can you deliver?"

"Within city limits?"

"To a storage unit by the university," she replied. "We'll need everything delivered by next Saturday."

"That shouldn't be a problem. So…do we have a deal?"

On more than one occasion, Max had told her she didn't need his approval to buy anything—he trusted her judgment—and if she came across a good buy, not to hesitate. Grinning, she held out her hand. "Sounds like a deal to me."

* * *

"I bought everything."

"Everything?"

So excited she could hardly contain herself, Natalie laughed. She'd called Max the second she stepped out of the surplus supply store. "Well, not the food, of course. We have to wait until the Monday before Thanksgiving for that, but all the camping equipment, including the tents, will be delivered to the storage unit on Saturday."

"You're kidding! You must have found a hell of a deal. The last time we talked, you hadn't even found anything within budget."

"Oh, this is in the budget," she assured him dryly, and told him the price.

For a moment, his only response was stunned silence. Then he started to laugh. "Damn, woman, you're good! Did I happen to mention when I hired you that I'd pay you a bonus if you could bring the trip in under budget?"

Natalie grinned, wishing she could see his face. "Actually, you failed to make that clear, but that's okay. I'll still hold you to it."

"Don't worry," he assured her. "It's going to be a pleasure to pay you. How in the world did you pull this off?"

"One of the women I work with at the restaurant told me about a surplus store on the east side of town, over by the train station. She didn't remember the name of it and I couldn't find anything in the yellow pages, so I decided to drive over there and check it out. I hope you don't mind that I didn't call you first," she added, frowning. "And when the clerk gave his bid, I didn't know if it was a mistake or not, but I didn't want to give him time to change his mind."

"Are you kidding? Of course I don't mind! I would have done the same thing. This is fantastic!"

"I also made an executive decision," she admitted. "The clerk pointed out that the two-man tents are lighter than the four man, and since we were hiking to the dig site, the lighter we can make the hike, the better. If that's a problem, it's not too late to change the order…"

"The two-mans are fine," he assured her. "I should have thought of that myself. Did you buy an extra one in case we have an odd man out?"

"I already took care of it."

"You did a great job." he said, pleased. "This is going to be a great dig, and it's all because of you, Natalie. I don't know how I could have pulled any of this off without your help. Thank you."

"No thanks are necessary," she said huskily. "I'm just glad I could help."

Long after she hung up, Natalie couldn't stop smiling. Then she remembered that she had another test in Max's class tomorrow. After the fiasco of the last one, she had to pass this one. Otherwise, it was all over. Just thinking about it made her stomach clench.

The next morning dawned cold and wet and miserable. Given the chance, Natalie would have pulled the covers over her head and gone back to sleep. Unfortunately, that wasn't an option. She'd studied until she couldn't keep her eyes open any longer, and now it was time to face the music. She tried to convince herself that she was well prepared, that this time she could answer any question Max threw at her and the rest of the class. In the back of her mind, however, was the niggling fear that she would panic again and make a complete fool of herself.

Restless, too nervous to even think about breakfast, she hustled the boys through breakfast, warmed up the car while they were brushing their teeth and dropped them off at their school cafeteria a full half hour before she normally did. Max's class didn't start for another forty-five minutes, but she headed for the university, anyway. She'd spend the time going over her notes one more time.

His classroom was, not surprisingly, deserted when she walked in a short time later. Thankful to have the place to herself, she took her usual seat at the back of the room, pulled out her notes and started to study. But the classroom was too quiet, her mind too jumbled with all the facts she'd crammed into it over the past few days, and she could feel herself start to come unraveled. Horrified, she slammed her notebook shut and pushed to her feet. She knew the material—at least, she had last night. Now it seemed to be all jumbled in her head. Drawing in a deep breath, she released it slowly. She had to calm down!

When Max walked in ten minutes later, she was pacing restlessly. Surprised, he stopped short at the sight of her. "You're early."

"I've been up since five," she admitted with a grimace.

"You're panicking."

She didn't deny it. "I can't afford to flunk another test."

"You didn't flunk the last one."

"After I took it over," she reminded him. "I can't do that on every test!"

"No," he agreed, smiling. "But you won't need to. Will you chill out? You're going to do fine."

"That's easy for you to say. You know what's on the test!"

"So do you!" He laughed. "This isn't an ambush. At one point or another, I went over everything on the test in class." Grinning, he raised a dark brow. "Did you do this in high school every time you had a test?"

"No, of course not."

"Then why are you now?"

Put that way, she realized he was right. What was she doing? "I guess because I never thought I'd get to go to college. When Derek and I got married, we had an understanding that I would work and put him through college, then it would be my turn. But then he decided to go to law school, and after that I got pregnant with the boys. When he took off before they were born, I thought that was it. I was never going to get a chance to go to college."

"But you obviously did."

"True. But now that I am, I guess I'm afraid that I'm too old, that I can't cut it, that I can't keep up with the eighteen-year-olds. So I try harder."

"All the eighteen-year-olds are interested in is having a date for Friday night," he said dryly. "You know that, don't you?"

Still pacing, she stopped short, blushing, and laughed. "Of course! I didn't mean—"

"That you were looking for a date for Friday night? Damn! And here I was, all set to ask you out!"

"Max!"

"Natalie!" he mimicked, grinning. "I'm—"

Serious, he almost said, but he never got the chance. Before he could say another word, he heard a sound at the door and looked over just in time to see another student walk into the classroom. When she stopped short, her eyes wide with surprise, it was obvious she'd overheard him ask Natalie out.

"Good morning," he said easily, swallowing a curse. He wanted more time with Natalie, dammit! What was wrong with that? Since she'd started working on the dig from her house, he only saw her during class, and that wasn't nearly enough. "It's a rotten morning, isn't it?" he told the student. What was her name? Jennifer? Debbie? "We must have gotten an inch and a half of rain last night."

"We're in a flash-flood watch," Natalie added quietly as she stepped around him and slipped into her desk. "The weatherman's predicting another inch of rain before noon."

Just then another student walked in, then another, each shaking water from their hair, and Max was resigned to the fact that there would be no more private conversations with Natalie for the moment. If they hadn't been interrupted, would she have agreed to go out with him? He'd been fighting the need to ask her out for weeks, and why, for God's sake? Okay, so she was his student. She was thirty-six years old, married and divorced, and she knew her own mind. Of course, she hadn't said yes, but he'd been on the other end of the kisses they'd shared, and she wasn't indifferent. And neither was he. At some point in the future, he was going to have to decide what he intended to do about that, but for now, he just wanted to take her to a movie or out to dinner or both. What was wrong with that?

The bell rang, jerking him back to the matter at hand. "Okay, boys and girls," he said as everyone took their seats, "it's party time. Clear off your desks and let's get started."

Silence fell like a rock as he handed out the tests, and within seconds every student was bent over the test. Seated at his desk, Max kept an eagle eye for cheaters, but Natalie's class was a good one, and so far he hadn't had any problems with them. Relaxing somewhat, he shifted his gaze to Natalie and let out a silent sigh of relief. Unlike the previous test, when she'd sat and stared at it blankly, she was writing furiously.

Just barely keeping the panic at bay, Natalie moved from one question to the next with a frown, expecting her brain to fog over at any second. But when she finally reached the last question and read it, the answer sprang to mind almost immediately. Not sure if she wanted to laugh or cry, she quickly wrote it down, then hesitated. She had time to go back over the test and check her answers, but she readily admitted that she was afraid to. If she second-guessed herself, she could screw up the entire test.

Study Long, You Study Wrong.

She smiled as one of her grandmother's favorite sayings echoed in her ears. When she was a child and played dominoes with her grandmother, she'd always teased her whenever she hesitated, trying to decide what to do. Go with your gut, her grandmother had told her, and that was what she intended to do. She knew she'd passed the test—the question was, How well? With only a seventy on the last test, she needed a high A to bring up her average. She liked to think that she'd done that, but she couldn't be sure, and that was what worried her. She'd gotten grants and scholarships to go to college, and she needed to finish the fall semester with at least an eighty average to qualify for the grants she would need for next semester. She couldn't do that if she continued to make Cs in Max's class.

Worried, she started to read her answers over again, only to stop. No! she thought, scowling. Right or wrong, she was finished. She'd know on Tuesday if she passed. Gathering her things together, she made the long walk to where Max sat at his desk at the front of the room. He didn't say a word as she handed him her paper, but she could see the question in his eyes. How had she done? Her answer as silent as his question, she only shrugged, smiled slightly and walked out. The next five days were going to be incredibly long.

His eyes on her slim back as she disappeared out the door, Max would have liked nothing more than to grade her test right then and there. But he was determined not to show favoritism, so he neatly stacked it with the other papers that had already been turned in, then turned his attention back to the students who were still taking the test.

Thirty minutes later the last student walked out of the classroom. Max glanced at the clock on the wall and frowned as the bell rang. He should have placed the test papers from Natalie's class in his briefcase, then taken a break while he waited for the next class, which began in ten minutes. He usually graded tests at the end of the day, after everyone had taken it, but he didn't want a break, and just this once he didn't care if he was playing favorites. He had to know if Natalie passed. Flipping through the stack of test papers until he found hers, he quickly began to grade it.

After her last class, Natalie holed up in the university library and began working on her homework. She had an English paper to work on, a test in biology on Tuesday, and the term paper for archeology, which had to be completed before she went on the dig, because it was due immediately afterward. And the clock was ticking. So she settled in her favorite little nook, spread open her books and went to work.

Concentrating, however, wasn't easy. Her thoughts kept

drifting to her archeology test…and Max. With no effort whatsoever, she could still feel his hands gently kneading the tension from her shoulders, still feel the way her breath had caught in her throat when he'd asked her out. Had he meant it? Did she want him to mean it?

Suddenly realizing where her thoughts had wandered, she swore softly and reminded herself that she had a lot of work to do and she'd have to leave soon to pick up the boys. It didn't help. Max couldn't have distracted her more if he'd been right across the table from her.

An hour passed and she got very little done. Disgusted with herself, she finally packed up her things and headed for Susan's house to get the boys. She'd planned to buy a pizza for the kids, rent a video, then spend the rest of the evening at the kitchen table, working on her homework. But it had been a while since she and the boys had done anything together. Homework would have to wait, she decided. There was a new Disney movie at the theater and the boys had been begging her to take them. Tonight was their lucky night.

"Okay, guys," she said as they reached the house and carried their backpacks inside, "you need to put your things away and change into some clean clothes."

Interest sparking in his blue eyes, Tommy said, "We've got clean clothes on, Mom. We just put them on this morning."

"That was nearly twelve hours ago," she pointed out with a grin, "and you both look like you've been rolling around on the playground. Go change into something presentable, please. You can't go to Mr. Toad's looking like a couple of slobs."

"Mr. Toad's! Really?"

She nodded, trying not to smile. "And I don't think we could possibly go to the movies when you're so dirty—"

They launched themselves at her, screaming in delight, and the three of them fell onto the couch in a tangle of arms and legs. Laughing, Natalie hugged them fiercely. "Did I happen to mention how much I love you guys?"

"You're the bestest, Mom!"

"Better than Johnny Dunkin's mom," Harry agreed. "She can walk on her hands!"

"No kidding?" She chuckled, impressed.

"She does it all the time, just flips right over and walks down the sidewalk on her hands. It's really cool."

The doorbell rang then, surprising the three of them, but before Natalie could struggle up from the couch, the boys were racing to the front door.

"I'll get it!"

"No, I will! You got it last time."

"No, I'll get it, boys. You need to go change—"

Too late, the boys pulled open the door…and found themselves face-to-face with Max. With a whoop of delight, they grabbed his hands and pulled him inside.

"We're going to the movies and Mr. Toad's! Wanna come with us?"

"Please, Max! We're going to have frog nuggets and ice cream and everything!"

Grinning, Max hesitated. "I dunno, guys. It sounds like you got a date with your mom. I don't want to horn in on that."

"Mom doesn't care. Do you, Mom?"

Caught in the trap of three pairs of male eyes, Natalie had to laugh. Did she care? Of course not! She would love for him to go with them, more than she had any intention of admitting. Was that why he was here? To take up where they had left off when he'd asked her out before the test? Her heart skipped a beat at the thought.

"Of course I don't mind if Max goes," she told the boys, marveling at her easy tone. "But he might be busy, guys. We haven't even asked him why he's here."

When she lifted an inquiring brow at Max, he grinned. "I thought you might like to know that you made a ninety-five on your test."

"Are you serious? A ninety-five!"

He nodded. "I thought you and the boys might want to celebrate. A movie and Mr. Toad's sounds good to me."

"You might want to ask what the movie is," she advised with twinkling eyes.

"I hope it's the new Disney movie," he replied with a straight face. "I saw the commercial on TV the other day—it looks great."

"Yeah!"

"See, Mom, he wants to go!"

So excited they could hardly stand still, the boys ran to their room to change. Natalie never took her eyes from Max. "You're good," she said in admiration. "They believed you."

"Why wouldn't they?" he retorted, his blue eyes twinkling with mischief. "I wasn't lying. I do like Disney movies. *The Lion King*'s my favorite. I bet you liked *Beauty and the Beast.* You seem the type who would love a good romance."

Color stealing into her cheeks, she couldn't deny it. "Like I said, you're good."

The boys returned then, wearing identical red and white shirts and jeans. They'd taken time to brush their hair and wash the dirt off their faces and they looked absolutely adorable. Her heart melting with love at the sight of them, Natalie grinned. "Well, if it isn't the two best-looking men I know. Maybe I should go change. I feel downright scruffy next to you guys."

"Wear your red dress, Mom," Harry piped up. "Then we'll match."

"I'll wear my red sweater instead," she promised. "I'll be right back."

As she quickly changed, she told herself she was just getting into the spirit of the evening, but she knew it was more than that. She had a date with Max and her sons...sort of. Or did he have a date with her and the boys? Either way she looked at it, she and Max were going to dinner and a movie...and just thinking about it made her knees weak. Had she lost her mind? she wondered. She must have. How many times had she told herself since she met Max that she wasn't looking for a man? And here she was, going out with him.

"It's not a real date," she told herself in the mirror as she quickly changed into black jeans and her favorite red sweater. "There's nothing romantic about it. It's just dinner and a Disney movie with a friend, for heaven's sake. And the boys will be there."

But when she returned to the living room after she'd brushed her hair and checked her makeup, it wasn't friendship that she saw in Max's eyes when his gaze met hers. It was heat...the kind that stole her breath and warmed her blood and set her heart tripping over itself. The boys were raring to go and bolted out the front door, but she couldn't seem to move.

"Ready?" he asked huskily, and held out his hand.

She couldn't remember the last time she wanted to hold a man's hand so badly. But she was afraid, afraid to go there again, afraid to step off a cliff into something that seemed doomed to fail. She tried to remind herself it was just dinner and a movie, not a walk down the aisle, but her heart wasn't listening. She wasn't ready for this. "Max…"

"Nothing's going to happen this evening that you need to worry about," he told her quietly. "We're just going to have some fun. Okay?"

She had no reason to trust a man—the only one she'd ever loved had stabbed her in the heart and walked away—but Max wasn't Derek. He might be a flirt and a tease and seem to have no interest in settling down, but he'd never given her any reason to think that she couldn't trust his word. "Okay." She sighed, and stepped forward to place her hand in his.

It was a mistake of course—she knew it the second his fingers closed around hers. Just that easily he made her feel as if she was no longer alone. And that was something she hadn't felt for a very long time. It was intoxicating, seductive, wonderful. For no other reason than that, she should have pulled her hand free. Instead her fingers tightened ever so slightly around his. With a grin he pulled her out the door after the boys.

The boys were starving, so they went to dinner first, but Natalie barely tasted her food. She was in a daze and it was all Max's fault. As the boys chatted happily, Max played footsie with her under the table. When she gave him a pointed look, he only winked at her and playfully flirted with her ankles. With heat spilling into her cheeks, she didn't know if she wanted to laugh or throw something at him.

"Behave yourself," she hissed as the waiter brought the bill.

She might as well have saved her breath. He snatched up the bill before she could, paid it on the way out, then laced his fingers with hers as the boys raced ahead to the car. "You should have let me pay," she told him, fighting a smile as he swung their joined hands between them as if they were first-graders.

"We're celebrating your test score," he said simply. "My treat."

She could have pointed out that she and the boys had planned to go out, anyway, but he was a charmingly stubborn man and he was obviously determined to have his way. Giving in, she smiled. "I can see I'm not going to win this one, so all I can say is thank you. The boys are so excited, I don't know how they're going to sit still for the movie."

"Are you kidding? They talked about nothing else but the movie all during dinner. I was the same way when I was a kid and the first *Star Wars* movie came out. My dad took me to see it, and I didn't move a muscle the entire movie. When it was over, we got back in line and watched it all over again. Trust me, the boys are going to be the same way. They won't even know you and I are there when the lights go out."

Not surprisingly, he was right about that. Seated side by side on Natalie's right as the lights dimmed, they were riveted from the second the first promo flashed onto the screen. Grinning in the dark, she leaned toward Max, who sat next to her on the left. "Look at them," she whispered. "I don't think they're even breathing."

"I told you," he said in her ear, and just that easily, he melted every muscle in her body by pressing a soft, lingering kiss to the side of her neck.

Caught off guard, she swallowed a moan. "Max!" That was all she could manage…just his name on a soft sigh that didn't carry to anyone's ears but his. "You've got to stop this."

Smiling in the darkness, he backed off, but only to take her hand again. His fingers twined with hers, he ran his thumb over the back of her hand in slow circles, teasing her, making it impossible for her to concentrate on anything but his touch. Like the rest of the audience, her eyes were riveted on the screen, but from the first scene, she lost track of what the movie was about. And she couldn't find the strength to care.

When the final credits rolled at the end, Max grinned wickedly. "How'd you like the movie?"

She gave him a baleful look. "What movie?"

He laughed and jumped up to pull her to her feet. "Hey, boys, what'd you think?"

"Let's watch it again!" they said in unison.

"Oh, no, you don't." Natalie chuckled. "It's already way past your bedtime. It's time to go home."

They grumbled but went along peacefully enough, and long before they reached home, they fell asleep in the back seat. Pulling into her driveway, Natalie cut the engine and smiled ruefully at Max. "I knew this would happen. They always fall asleep in the car, and then get all grumpy when I have to wake them up."

"So don't wake them. I'll get them. You get the door."

She started to object—they were heavy little munchkins when they were deadweight—but he'd already climbed out of the car and was unbuckling Harry. Hurrying to the front door, she'd hardly pushed it open before he stepped through it, carrying Harry as tenderly as if he was his own son.

"I'll be right back," he growled, and headed down the hall to the boys' bedroom. Minutes later, he was back for Tommy.

Natalie expected him to leave then, but he stayed to help her undress the boys and stuff them into their pajamas. "I can't believe they didn't wake up," he told her as he followed her into the living room after she'd tucked both boys in and kissed them good-night. "World War III could have started in there and they wouldn't have heard a thing."

"Probably not," she agreed, chuckling. "They've always been like that."

"So how do you wake them up in the morning for school?"

"Bongo," she retorted. "He jumps into their beds with them and licks them until they wake up giggling."

"Aha. They're going to have great memories when they grow up."

"I hope so," she said softly, wistfully. "It's good memories that get you through the rough times in life." Dragging her thoughts from flashbacks of her own childhood, she suddenly realized that the boys hadn't thanked him for their night out. "The boys forgot to thank you. That's my fault. I should have reminded them. I don't know why I didn't. I guess I was…"

When she hesitated, his blue eyes danced with mischief. "Is the word you're looking for *distracted?*"

Heat spilled into her cheeks. "No!"

Grinning, he swore softly. "Damn. And I thought I was doing so well. I guess I'll just have to try harder."

And before she could guess his intentions, he reached for her.

Chapter 9

How long had it been since he'd kissed her? Max wondered as he lost himself in the intoxicating heat of her mouth. Days? Weeks? It seemed like an eternity. How could he have forgotten how right she felt in his arms...or how she tied him in knots when she pressed close and kissed him back with a hunger that matched his own? Sweet. Merciful heavens, she was sweet! And when she wrapped her arms around his neck and raised up on her tiptoes to take the kiss deeper, all he could think about was sweeping her up in his arms and carrying her to bed.

But the boys were just down the hall and he couldn't take a chance that they would walk in on them.

Groaning at the thought, he knew he had to get out of there. And he would, he promised himself. Any minute now he was going to come to his senses and walk out the door. He just needed one more kiss for the road.

But one kiss led to another, then another, and the couch was only two steps away....

Suddenly realizing where his thoughts had wandered, he stiffened. Dammit, he couldn't do this! Frustrated, he set her away, only to groan when she swayed back toward him. He'd never encountered this problem before and he didn't have a clue what to do about it. How did people with children make love?

"I've got to go," he rasped, giving in to the need to give her one last quick kiss. "I'll see you Monday when you come in to work on the dig."

Her blood roaring in her ears, her body aching, Natalie started to call him back as he walked out the door, but she came to her senses just in time. No, she told herself sternly. She had to get control of this...fascination...she had with the man. Okay, so they'd had a great time together tonight, and it was obvious the boys really liked him. And kids were great judges of character, she told herself. If Max was just pretending to like them, they would know. And so would she. Her mother's radar was always right on the money when it came to someone taking advantage of her sons, and there hadn't been so much as a bleep on the radar screen where Max was concerned.

Okay, so he was good with kids. That didn't mean he wanted to take on the job of daddy for the next thirteen years or so. And she and the boys were a package deal. If he wasn't interested in having an instant family, then he'd spent the last few minutes kissing the wrong woman. All she had to do was just remember that, and she'd be able to hang on to her heart. If she was lucky.

Clinging to that thought, she made her rounds through the house, just as she did every night, picking up toys and shoes and socks, then making sure windows and doors were securely locked before she made her way to bed. It had been a busy day and she was tired. She should have crashed the second her head hit the pillow. Unfortunately, she wasn't able to put Max out of her head as easily as she'd hoped. She dreamed of him all night long.

Across town Max wasn't faring any better. After he woke up reaching for her for the fifth time, he swore, and reluctantly accepted the fact that he could forget about sleeping—it wasn't going to happen. When had he given the woman permission to haunt not only his waking hours but his sleep, too? Irritated with himself, he rolled out of bed. Granted, he had no one to blame but himself—he never should have kissed her. But he was only human, dammit! And all she had to do was breathe to drive him crazy.

Booting up his computer, he decided that if he couldn't sleep, he might as well work on his book. But as his fingers settled on the keyboard and he reread what he had last written, he found it almost impossible to concentrate. He kept remembering the kisses he and Natalie had shared, how right she'd felt in his arms, how much he wanted to make love to her.

Suddenly realizing he'd been staring into space for at least ten minutes, he sat up straighter and forced himself to focus on his writing. He hadn't been able to write much since the tour group had notified him that they were declaring bankruptcy, so whatever time he could spend working on his book was too precious to waste. He needed to finish chapter four by the end of the weekend, and he was barely on page three. Focus! he told himself fiercely. All he had to do was focus.

He might as well have told himself to levitate. His thoughts were still scattered, and it took him over an hour to write a single paragraph. He tried to find some satisfaction in the fact that he was at least making progress, regardless of how limited it was, but then he read over what he'd written. A first-grader could have done better. Disgusted, he deleted the paragraph and tried again. Then again. And again.

It was nearly three in the morning when he finally accepted the fact that he was just spinning his wheels. Shutting down shop, he gave up and went to bed, and this time he slept.

He was back at his computer by seven and getting nowhere fast. Still, he forced himself to sit there for another two hours. His patience short, he finally gave up. Sometime in the not too distant future, he was going to have to call Katherine and let her know that he was still struggling with writer's block. She was a great editor and would, no doubt, sympathize with his plight, but she couldn't wait forever for his manuscript. If he didn't get it to her soon, she would have no choice but to change his publication date, and that was something neither of them wanted.

Sitting at his computer, staring at the screen for hours on end, however, was not the way to solve his block. In fact, trying to force creativity only made things worse. The only way to really deal with it was to get completely away from his writing for a while. Assuring himself that he wouldn't be gone long, he strapped a cooler and his rod and reel on the back of his bike and went for a ride.

At the most he planned to be gone for only a couple of hours, but the open road called to him and he headed up into the mountains. He didn't have a particular destination in mind, and he crossed any number of streams where he could have stopped to fish, but conditions weren't quite right. Either there were people already there or there was no access to the water or something about the location just didn't appeal to him. He headed farther north, turning onto smaller and smaller roads, not even sure what he was looking for.

Then, suddenly, there it was, a small stream that was deep and slow moving and nestled under large pines that looked as if they'd stood there for centuries. A small pull-off on the far side of the bridge spanning the creek gave access but was almost completely hidden from view until Max was past it. Braking, he circled back and pulled in among the trees. The place was deserted, which wasn't surprising. He hadn't seen another soul since he'd turned onto the narrow road that didn't seem to go anywhere except deeper into the mountains.

Pleased, he cut the engine to his motorcycle and pulled off his helmet. Silence engulfed him and was broken only by the whisper of the wind through the upper branches of the towering pines. This was what he'd been looking for, he thought as he drew in a deep breath and released it slowly…the quiet solitude of his own existence. Grabbing his fishing rod and the cooler from the back of his motorcycle, he made his way through the trees to the stream. Seconds later the only sound was the plop of his lure hitting the water.

The sun was already lost behind the mountains when he headed for home hours later. More relaxed than he'd been in a long time, he toyed with the idea of getting a room for the night somewhere nearby, but he'd already taken off more time than he should have. The dig began in five days, and even though Natalie had taken care of most of the camping equipment they would need, there was still a lot to do. Thanks to his unscheduled fishing trip, he'd be working right up until they left, packing equipment and supplies, making sure nothing was left behind. He still, however, didn't regret playing hooky for the day. For a while, at least, he would manage to put everything out of his head except fishing.

That ended when he stopped for dinner at a small café fifty miles from home. The place was little more than a hole in the wall, but the parking lot was full, so he figured the food had to be good. There was only one available table, and that was crowded into a small space next to the swinging door that led to the kitchen, but he was starving and the smells coming from there were fantastic. Pulling out a chair, he reached for the menu that was wedged between the napkin holder and salt and pepper shakers.

"You must not be from around here. Nobody ever orders from the menu."

Glancing up, he found himself confronting a waitress in a formfitting uniform who couldn't be a day over eighteen. Grinning at him sassily, she was short and cute and had flirt written all over her.

Sitting back in his chair, Max raised a dark brow. "Then why have a menu?"

"The old folks passing through town need them," she confided, winking at him. "They like to know what they're getting. You should try the hot wings. You look like the kind of man who would appreciate something hot and spicy."

Studying her through narrowed eyes, Max had always appreciated a flirt. Normally he would have flirted right back, but before he could even think of a comeback, images of Natalie stirred in his head…the surprise in her eyes when he'd kissed her at the football game, the love that lit up her whole face when she laughed at something the boys did, the tenderness of her touch when she tucked them in at night. And regardless of how cute the girl standing before him was, or how sexy she was in her snug little uniform, when he compared her to Natalie, she just didn't measure up. She was too young, too immature, too obvious.

Stunned by the direction of his thoughts, he scowled. Since when had a cute, sexy woman turned him off?

"Actually, I just want a cheeseburger and an order of fries," he said coolly. "I'm not really into hot and spicy."

Something that looked an awful lot like irritation flashed in her eyes, but she just gave him a tight smile and jotted down his order. "Anything to drink? Milk?"

Max bit back a laugh. Oh, yeah, she was irritated. Judging from the looks of her, she didn't get turned down very often. "Make it iced tea," he retorted.

"Whatever you say." She sniffed as she turned away and pushed through the swinging door to the kitchen.

When his food was delivered to his table a short while later, Max needed to take only one bite to know why the place was packed. At any other time he would have appreciated that. But his thoughts kept drifting to Natalie. It had been years since he'd let a woman get under his skin. How the hell had she managed it? And more important, what was he going to do about it?

"Is something wrong with the burger?"

Glancing up from his thoughts, he frowned at the sassy little waitress, who had obviously decided to give him another chance. "No," he retorted. "I guess I'm just not very hungry, after all. Just bring me the bill."

"How about dessert? That might tempt your appetite."

A half smile curled the corner of his mouth. He had to give her credit—she just didn't give up. "No, thanks. I just need the bill."

"Okay," she said with a shrug, irritation once again flashing in her eyes. "You don't know what you're missing."

When she tore off his bill and slapped it down on the table, Max merely picked it up, checked the total, and pulled out his wallet. Leaving her a respectable tip, along with the money for the total for his meal, he walked out. The second he climbed on his bike and drove away, however, his thoughts once again turned to Natalie.

He was, he decided grimly, acting like his father, mooning over a woman, and that scared the hell out of him. He wasn't going to do this. Not now. Not ever. He couldn't very well deny that he was seriously attracted to Natalie, but that was all it was—sexual attraction. He wasn't in love with her, he assured himself. Oh, he liked her a hell of a lot, and there was no question that she could get him stirred up, but that didn't add up to love. And he wasn't going to start letting himself think it might.

Despite the happiness his father and Becky seemed to share, he couldn't believe that he'd been wrong all these years. What most people mistook for love was nothing more than an incredibly strong chemistry that didn't last. Time and again he'd seen his father, friends, associates, throw caution to the wind and rush headlong into marriage because they made the mistake of getting involved with women who had marriage written all over them. Women like Natalie. Women who wanted home and hearth and husband and kids and huge Thanksgiving dinners every year, surrounded by children and grandchildren.

No, no, no! He wasn't getting caught up in the fantasy. He wasn't kissing Natalie ever again, he promised himself. He wasn't touching her. Hell, he wasn't even flirting with her! Maybe then, he wouldn't make a damn fool of himself over her.

Satisfied that he had his emotions well in hand, he stubbornly refused to let her intrude on his thoughts the rest of the drive home. And the second he walked in his front door, he went straight to his computer and spent the next two hours working on his book. And for the first time in what seemed like weeks, the words flowed.

Katherine would be pleased, he thought with a tight grin that held little humor. Giving in to impulse, he reached for the phone to call her. It wasn't until he heard the young male voice at the other end of the line, however, that he realized he had unwittingly called Natalie instead. "Tommy? Is that you?"

"Hi, Max," he said happily. "How did you know I wasn't Harry?"

Max frowned. That was a good question. The boys were the spitting image of each other and they loved playing tricks on him. Natalie could tell them apart, of course, but Max couldn't deny that he spent most of the time calling them by the wrong names. And when he did get their names right, he'd guessed. So how had he recognized Tommy's voice from his brother's? When had he gotten close enough to them to tell them apart?

"Max? Are you still there?"

He blinked, jerking his attention back to Tommy. "I'm here. I was just trying to figure out how I knew who you were. Lucky guess, I guess. So what have you guys been doing?"

"Fishing!" he said promptly. "Mommy took us fishing at the park after school. I caught a big perch!"

"No, kidding? I went fishing today, too."

"You should have come with us. Mommy almost fell in when I caught my big fish."

"Is she okay?"

"Yeah. She's right here." And before Max could stop him, he called out, "Mommy? It's Max. He wants to talk to you."

She came on the line almost immediately. "Hi, Max. Is everything okay? You don't usually call this late."

"I just got in and was checking to see what your schedule was for tomorrow," he lied. "We've only got a week left, and there's still a lot to do."

"Tomorrow I thought I'd start buying the nonperishable food," she replied. "What about you?"

"I've got to go finalize the contract with the charter bus company."

"So you've decided against the vans?"

"I was never really comfortable having students drive. This is safer."

"And more convenient," she added. "Everyone can relax and enjoy the trip."

Max should have been pleased—she was keeping the conversation strictly business, which was what he'd wanted. So why did he want to ask her about the fishing trip and the boys and what they'd had for supper and if she ever planned to trust a man again? What the hell was wrong with him?

He should have told her he was just checking to make sure they were on the same page and then found an excuse to hang up, but the words just wouldn't come. Instead he heard himself say gruffly, "Are the boys packed for their trip yet?"

She laughed softly. "They didn't care that they weren't

leaving until the Friday after Thanksgiving—they packed last week."

"They're going camping, too, aren't they? With their babysitter and her husband and her kids?"

"They're going to Rocky Mountain National Park."

"Are you having second thoughts about letting them go?"

"Second and third and fourth thoughts." She laughed ruefully. "I know they'll have a good time—Susan's brother works there and he knows all the best places to see the animals—but I'm going to miss them like crazy. They've never been away from me...."

"*Never?* Not even to spend the night with one of their friends?"

"They're only five," she replied. "They've had a couple of sleepovers with Susan's kids, but those were at my house. I just like knowing where they are at night."

"But you won't be home yourself," he pointed out.

"I know." she said, sighing. "It doesn't make sense, does it? But I'm their mother. I don't have to make sense. If something happens while they're gone—"

"Nothing's going to happen, Natalie," he assured her huskily. "Obviously, Susan's a responsible person or you wouldn't trust her to take care of the boys while you're working. And with her husband and brother both there, it sounds like there'll be plenty of adults to watch the kids. They'll be fine. Anyway, you're not going to have time to worry about them. You're going to be pretty busy. Remember?"

"How could I forget? It seems like I've been waiting for this forever. It's going to be so much fun!"

Max knew exactly how she felt. He'd lost track of the number of digs he'd been on over the years. He always enjoyed them, but it had been a long time since he'd looked forward to one as much as he did this one. And the reason was obvious. Natalie. He would have three full days with her. If just the two of them had been going, he would have been worried about his resolve to be just friends, but with forty-nine chaperones taking every step they did, he didn't think he had a thing to worry about.

The days that led up to the dig were wild, frantic, crazy. And Natalie had never been so excited in her life. It seemed as if she was constantly running…to school, to work, to get something for the dig or for the boys for their trip or both. When she fell into bed at night, she was so exhausted that she was asleep almost as soon as she closed her eyes. Still, she dreamed of Max, though she only had fleeting memories of her dreams the next morning. And there was no time to worry about that, because with the rising of the sun the madness started all over again. She couldn't complain, though. She loved the pressure, loved working with Max. They had become a team, and every time she turned around, they were on the phone to each other.

Three nights before they were supposed to leave for the dig, she didn't see how they could possibly have everything ready in time for the trip. With every passing hour, Natalie's to-do list seemed to grow by leaps and bounds—there were last-minute glitches, things that had slipped her mind, perishable groceries and dry ice to buy, but somehow she managed to get it all done. Then suddenly it was Thanksgiving and the dig was scheduled to begin the next morning. She was so excited, she could hardly sleep. She wasn't the only one. Before her alarm even went off, the boys were standing on either side of her bed, nudging her awake.

Groggy, she squinted at them in the light that streamed across her bed through the open door to the hallway. "What's wrong? What time is it? What are you doing up so early?"

"We're going camping," Harry crowed, grinning as he bounced on the bed. "C'mon, Mom, we gotta get going!"

"We can't be late!" Tommy added, trying to tug her into a sitting position. "And we still gotta eat breakfast and brush our teeth and—"

"Okay, okay!" she groaned, laughing. "I'll get up, but it's only five o'clock. You can sleep another hour if you want to. Why don't you just crawl in bed with me and go back to sleep? I'll wake you up when the alarm goes off."

"Mom!"

"You're going back to sleep!"

Jerking herself awake, she forced herself out of bed. "I'm up," she promised. "See? I'm up."

Delighted, the boys let out a whoop and raced down the hall to get dressed. Rolling out of bed, she had to admit she was glad the boys woke her early. She had plenty of time for a shower, and she intended to use every second of it. It was the only real shower she'd get for the next few days. Grabbing her clothes, she rushed into the master bath.

She'd made herself a list of everything that needed to be done before she locked the house and walked away from it for four days, but it seemed as if she'd hardly done half the things on the list when the doorbell rang a short while later, announcing Susan's arrival. "She's here, Mom! She's here!"

"I know. Do you have your toothbrushes and toothpaste? What about jackets? Make sure you bundle up when you're outside. I don't want you coming home sick," she told them as she hurried to the front door. Sudden panic squeezing her heart, she opened the door and announced, "I don't know about this, Susan. Maybe this is a mistake. You've got your kids to watch over—you don't need mine, too."

Far from shocked by her last-minute about-face, Susan only grinned. "Why did I know you were going to do this? Will you relax? The boys are going to do fine. I promise I'll take good care of them."

"But—"

"No buts," she said firmly. "You've been dying to do this for years. Go and have a good time and don't worry about the kids. I'll watch them like they were my own."

"I know that," Natalie replied, smiling. "I'm sorry. I know I sound like a nut—"

"No, you don't." She chuckled. "You just sound like a mom who's never been away from her kids before. Will it help if I promise to call you if they so much as get a sniffle?"

"How are you going to call me? The cell phones don't work in the mountains."

"If there's a real emergency, I know where you are. I'll call the sheriff and he'll find you. Okay?"

Hesitating, Natalie knew she was being paranoid, but she hadn't realized it was going to be this hard to let them go. They were growing up so fast—before she knew it, they'd be grown and gone. Did Derek ever think about them, ever think about what he was missing? She almost felt sorry for him…until she remembered that when he'd walked out, he hadn't given a damn that she was seven months pregnant with his sons.

Bracing for the old, familiar bitterness that always came rushing back whenever she thought of Derek, she was surprised to discover that it wasn't nearly as fierce as it had once been. And she knew it was because she'd gone on with her life.

"I'm not really worried about something happening. I'm not," she insisted when Susan gave her a skeptical look. "This is just their first trip without me, and the next thing you know, they're going to be going on school trips, then off to college and…" Suddenly realizing what she was saying, she laughed at herself. "Okay, so I'm a little nuts this morning. Give me a hug, boys, and have a good trip. Make sure you mind Aunt Susan and Uncle Joe."

"We will. Bye, Mom."

"Last one to the car's a rotten egg!"

They were gone in a flash, leaving Natalie with a smile on her lips and tears in her eyes. Clicking her tongue, Susan gave her a quick hug. "None of that. You're going off on an adventure of your own, remember? Go have fun. We'll see you Sunday."

With a wink and a smile she was gone. Staring after Susan's Suburban as it disappeared around the corner, Natalie shook off her melancholy. This was no time to get sentimental and weepy. Susan was right. She had a fantastic adventure of her own she was going on…with Max!

Her tears instantly vanished, and suddenly she couldn't stop smiling. How long had she been waiting for this? It seemed like a lifetime. From the moment she read Max's first book, she'd been fascinated with archeology and, she readily admitted, him. She couldn't wait to see him in action on a dig. After loading her backpack into the car, she did a quick tour of the house to make sure everything was in order, then headed for campus. Since she had the responsibility of getting her sons off that morning, too, Max had arranged for several of the other students to help him load all the equipment and supplies into the bus an hour before everyone else was scheduled to arrive. So when she arrived at the pickup spot on campus, the bus was loaded and the only things left to be dealt with were the students' personal items.

Almost everyone was there when she arrived, and Max was at the center of what looked like controlled chaos. In the process of checking each new arrival off his roster, he looked up the second she started toward him. The smile that started in his eyes and spread to his mouth warmed her all the way to her toes. "There you are. Did you get the boys off okay?"

"They couldn't get away from me fast enough," she answered, chuckling. "In fact, they woke me up before the alarm went off. I don't think they slept all night."

"I know the feeling. I'm always that way before a dig." Cocking an eyebrow at her, he grinned. "You ready for your first dig?"

"Now that all the planning's over with, yes! I can't wait!"

"Good. Because now we're going to have some fun."

The bus driver needed to talk to him about how some of the equipment was packed in the bus's luggage area, and as he hurried to take care of the situation, Natalie was left to wonder exactly what he'd meant by "we're going to have fun". Had he meant the entire class? Or the two of them personally?

With her heart skipping a beat at the thought, she swallowed a groan. She was not going to do this! She wasn't going to analyze everything Max said and try to read hidden meaning into his every word, or she would drive herself crazy. This was probably the only chance she'd ever have to go on a dig, and Max had made that possible for her. She was going to take him at his word and have fun.

Satisfied that she had her emotions well in hand, she and

the rest of the students helped load the last of the personal items on the bus, then it was time to board. The majority of the group moved to the back of the bus as Max conferred with the driver on the route they would take, but she wanted to be at the front, so she could see where they were going. So she sank into a window seat in the second row and pulled her camera from her purse. She'd brought far more film than any reasonable shutterbug would need, but she didn't care. She wanted pictures of everything!

In the process of loading film into her camera, she didn't realize that Max intended to sit with her until he was in the seat next to her. Surprised, she glanced up...and found him within touching distance. In the time it took to draw in a quick breath, her resolve to keep her heart under lock and key went up in smoke.

Max saw the surprise in her eyes and only just then noticed that he'd chosen the seat next to her without even thinking about sitting anywhere else. There was just something so right about being with her. When the dig was over and he regained his sanity, he was, no doubt, going to regret the fact that he just couldn't summon up any resistance where she was concerned, but he'd just have to worry about that later. They had four days together. He intended to enjoy every one of them.

Giving in to impulse, he reached for her hand and grinned. "Excited?"

"Stop that!" she hissed, trying to tug her hand free. "Everybody will see."

"Relax." He chuckled. "Steven Tucker and Lisa Green are the closest ones to us, and they're six rows back. They can't even see the tops of our heads over the backs of the seats."

"But what if they walk up here to talk to you for some reason? They'll see—"

"Two people who like each other holding hands," he said simply, twining his fingers with hers. "What's wrong with that?"

"Max!"

"I love it when you say my name that way. Do it again."

"Max!"

"Yeah, like that. There's just something about the sound of my name on your lips that makes me feel all warm and fuzzy inside."

She laughed at his outrageousness, just as he'd hoped she would, but she didn't pull her hand away. Instead, her fingers curled around his. It was a simple gesture, innocent, sweet. And nothing had ever felt quite so right before. Alarm bells should have been clanging in his head, but they didn't make so much as a peep. And he didn't care.

Chapter 10

The Broken Arrow Ranch was twenty thousand acres of prime Colorado ranchland that backed up into the Rockies and held centuries of secrets. Creeks and streams flowed through its canyons and pastures. Hundreds of years before the Pilgrims ever stepped foot on Plymouth Rock, the rugged wilderness was the home of a band of Ute Indians. The Spanish had been there, too, leaving behind abandoned mines throughout the mountains and rumors of a rich vein of gold that was lost long ago in a landslide.

It was the perfect place for a dig, but Max had known nothing about the ranch until its present owner, Buck Maverick, had contacted him. A lover of history and mysteries, Buck was the last of the Mavericks, but unlike the six generations of Mavericks who'd come before him, he hadn't been born on the ranch and knew nothing of its rich history.

His great-grandfather had gone to England as a diplomat at the turn of the twentieth century and married there. He'd never come back to the ranch, and over the decades, the two sides of the family had lost touch with each other…until the last American-born Maverick had died. Now it was Buck's and his sisters', and he wanted to know everything there was to know about the people who had called the place home long before he'd come on the scene. He'd read Max's last book and loved the idea of the Broken Arrow being the setting for one of his books.

When Buck called him and suggested that he not only investigate the summer campgrounds of the Indians but also look for the lost mine, Max had jumped at the idea. He'd been looking for a site where he could take his students, without success. The few available sites were either too far away or had been so picked over by other archeologists that there was little left to find. The Broken Arrow, a three-hour drive from the university, was uncharted territory and available to him without restriction. All Buck required of him was a report once a semester of what he and his students had found.

Buck was as excited as Max and his students and was waiting for them at the drop-off site with a handful of men and a team of packhorses when they arrived. "The hike into the mountains isn't terribly difficult," he told Max as he stepped off the bus, "but I knew you would have a great deal of gear. My men will help you load the horses and escort you to the dig site, then they'll return on Sunday when you're ready to hike back out."

"You didn't have to go to all this trouble," Max said, grinning. "But I know the students will appreciate it. They weren't looking forward to carrying everything in on their backs."

Natalie had stepped off the bus right behind him, and he turned to introduce her to Buck. "Natalie's helped me with all the planning," he said as the two of them shook hands.

"Max told me about the problems with the tour group," he said with a smile. "I hear you've been a godsend. Welcome to the Broken Arrow."

"Thank you," she replied. "I'm thrilled to finally be here."

"Max told me he'd be bringing fifty students, but I hadn't realized what an undertaking that would be until now. This is going to be quite an expedition. I almost wish I was back at university again."

"You're welcome to join us as much as you like," Max said. "It's your land."

"I know." He chuckled. "I still have a difficult time believing that." Smiling ruefully at the oddities of fate, he held out his hand once more to Max. "It's wonderful to have you here. Unfortunately, I'll have to wait until next time to join you. My sisters have flown in from England and we're recovering from our first American Thanksgiving. So I'll get out of your way and let you get started. If you need anything, just let one of my men know. John's my head wrangler. He's going to go with you and take care of the horses."

True to his word, he gave them the space, driving off with a wave as his men helped load everything onto the pack horses, and less than thirty minutes later it was time to head for their base-camp site. No one had been looking forward to packing everything in on foot to the camp, but that all changed, thanks to Buck Maverick's generous offer of horses. With the head wrangler leading the way, they made the three-mile trip in record time.

As Max divided everyone into groups and began setting

up camp, Natalie couldn't help but appreciate how efficient he was. He was always so laid back and charming that it was easy to overlook the fact that he was a scholar and teacher who definitely knew what he was doing. Within two hours of arriving at the site he'd chosen to set up camp, all the tents were assembled and he'd begun laying out the grid for the excavation of a grassy area near a bubbling creek where a band of Utes had reportedly camped every summer for hundreds of years. Once half the students were working on that, he had Natalie and the rest of the group accompany him to a steep hillside where the lost Spanish mine was rumored to have been located.

Surveying the area with a frown, Natalie didn't think it looked any different from any other hillside in the foothills of the mountains. And she wasn't the only one who thought so.

"How do you know this is the spot?" a tall, gangly eighteen-year-old with wire-rimmed glasses asked.

Max grinned. "We don't. Since the Mavericks have owned the property for a century and a half, we know from family history that the other site is definitely the location of the Ute's summer camp, but the mine is purely speculation."

"In other words, we're doing this one just for fun?" Natalie said. "Hoping we'll get lucky?"

"Got it in one," he said with a grin. "From historical records, we do know that the mine was on a hill within sight of the Utes' camp. Unfortunately, if you stand in the center of the valley and do a 360, all the mountains look the same."

"But wasn't there written documentation somewhere that said the mine was near a huge bolder that sat on the edge of a cliff?" another student pointed out. "That shouldn't be hard to find."

"True," Max agreed. "But you're forgetting another important bit of documentation. Just months after the mine was discovered, there was a major landslide that wiped out half the mountainside...and all landmarks. All the Spaniards working the mine were killed, and when the next supply train arrived, it was impossible to tell where the entrance to the mine was. The Spanish had detailed descriptions of where the mine was, but the landscape had completely changed."

"And no one looked for the mine since?" one of the girls at the back of the group asked incredulously. "Are they nuts? It could be worth millions of dollars!"

"Maybe." Max laughed. "Maybe not. There's never been a significant amount of gold mined in this area of the state, though that doesn't mean it's not out there."

"So we're not really looking for gold?" another female student asked, disappointed. "I wanted a nugget!"

"We're archeologists," he reminded her. "We're looking for Spanish and Indian artifacts. And even if we did happen to stumble across some gold, everything on the ranch belongs to Mr. Maverick. We're just here to experience a real dig. So let's get started."

Ruefully accepting the fact that they weren't going home at the end of the long weekend with their pockets filled with gold, they immediately went to work. Eagerly following Max's instructions, they staked out an area near a small mountain stream that would have been an ideal location for the miners to camp. Then they began the delicate job of shifting through the dirt, looking for anything that might indicate the Spaniards had been there.

It was tedious, detailed work—and Natalie loved it. Watching Max, seeing the excitement in his eyes, she could now see why he loved archeology. They were chasing a mystery. Who were the Spaniards who'd walked these same mountains four hundred years ago? Where had they camped? What had they brought with them and left forever in these mountains? There would, of course, be tools, clothing, cooking utensils. But what about more personal items like jewelry and religious items and journals? Only the mountains knew for sure.

Max moved between the two sites, answering questions, instructing, getting right down in the dirt with everyone else, and no one noticed the passage of time until it was nearly dark. Suddenly glancing at his watch, he swore softly. "Where'd the time go? Okay, everybody, that's it for today. Let's wrap it up and get back to camp. Is anybody hungry?"

The roar that went up from the group was all the answer he needed. Chuckling, he made sure everything was secure for the night, then found himself falling into step with Natalie as the rest of the class surged past them as if they were standing still.

He lifted a dark, teasing brow at Natalie. "Was it something I said?"

"Now you know how to start a stampede," she said, chuckling.

"Speaking of dinner, what are we having?"

"Not macaroni and cheese and hot dogs."

"Darn! I suppose chocolate-chip pancakes are out of the question, too."

She grinned. "I'm afraid so. How about liver and onions?"

Shocked, he stopped in his tracks. "Please tell me you're kidding."

"It would serve you right if I wasn't," she retorted,

amused. "Do you realize you never once asked me about the meals? You just told me to take care of it."

He grinned sheepishly. "You're a mom. I figured you would know how to feed fifty teenagers."

She just rolled her eyes. "Lucky for you I didn't take the boys shopping with me and buy fifty cans of ravioli—that's their idea of heaven. Just out of curiosity, who usually cooks when you go on digs?"

"Someone who doesn't have a clue what they're doing."

"Ahh. So even if I've never cooked for a crowd—on a campfire, no less—and the food is mediocre, it's going to be the best you ever had on a dig?"

Grinning, he winked at her. "Again, you got it in one."

"And if I'm more than mediocre?"

"Sweetheart, I knew that the first moment I laid eyes on you." And uncaring who might see, he took her hand and kissed it.

Just that easily he made her laugh and stole her breath at one and the same time. "Max, you're such a flirt! Stop that!"

"Make me."

Unable to stop smiling, she tugged her hand free and tried to look stern. "Keep this up and I'll tell one of Maverick's men we need some liver for dinner."

"No, no! Anything but that. I'll be good. I promise."

He was already good—that was the problem—but she had no intention of telling him that. "Then how does grilled sirloin burgers, baked potatoes and salad sound for dinner?"

"Are you kidding me? Do we have the makings for all that?"

She grinned. "I did the grocery shopping, remember? That's nothing. Before the trip's over, I'm making peach cobbler!"

"You are not!"

"I'll need some help, of course. Cooking for this many people, we're going to need at least five campfires going at one time so we won't be eating at midnight."

"You got it," he said promptly, and called a few of the guys over to help him.

Fifteen minutes later the fires were going and the students had gathered enough firewood to last a week or longer. As the fires burned down, Natalie organized a makeshift kitchen on two folding tables and had some of the girls wash the potatoes and wrap them in aluminum foil. As soon as the fires had burned down to mostly embers, she and Max placed the potatoes in the hot ashes.

"Now what?" he asked her, dusting his hands.

"We have a while before we need to start the burgers, so we can get everything else ready. I brought instant tea, so we can add that to four of the gallon jugs of water, and then put a salad together. Everyone has their own camp kits to eat from, but we'll need to put out napkins and salt and pepper. Oh, and there's steak sauce for the burgers and butter and sour cream for the potatoes."

"You brought butter and sour cream on a dig?" Max asked, amazed.

"It's not the real thing," she admitted, "but I was able to find some of the individual containers like they have at fast-food restaurants at a grocery warehouse. They were cheap, didn't require a lot of ice to keep cool and didn't weigh much. They might not be the real thing, but I figured they'd taste pretty good out in the middle of nowhere."

Max laughed. "Sweetheart, with everything that went wrong with this dig from the beginning, I thought we'd be lucky if we had bologna sandwiches for lunch and dinner and Pop-Tarts for breakfast. This is fantastic! How'd you do this and manage to stay within the budget?"

"I'm a single mom with two growing monsters who love to eat," she replied, smiling. "I learned how to shop for bargains a long time ago. And I saved a ton of money on the tents."

"Remind me to hire you for all my digs from now on. What's for breakfast?"

"You're going to have to wait and find out, just like everyone else." She laughed. "Right now the only meal that's important is this one. It's time to put the burgers on."

Max had brought some metal grills he'd used on previous digs, and he quickly laid those over the coals, supporting them on the rocks that ringed each campfire. Natalie retrieved preformed sirloin burgers from the ice chests, seasoned them and set ten patties on each grill. Within minutes the smell of grilling burgers wafted on the evening breeze, drawing sighs of appreciation from all around the camp. By the time the food was ready, the students had their camp kits in hand and were lined up ready to eat.

Just about all the students had brought folding stools to sit on and they soon circled the campfires and dug into their food as if they hadn't eaten in a week. One of the last to serve herself, Natalie remembered too late that the lightweight aluminum folding chair she'd meant to bring was still hanging on a hook in her garage.

Sighing—it had been a long day and she'd really been looking forward to a nice relaxing meal—she hesitated, looking around for a place to sit. Her choices were either the ground or a rock.

"The cook deserves the best seat in the house," Max said, surprising her as he came up behind her and reached around to take her plate from her. "Follow me."

"But I forgot my chair—"

"Don't worry—I always bring an extra." Leading her to a spot on the far side, he grinned. "Alone at last. Have a seat, sweetheart."

He'd set up two chairs under a tree twenty feet back from the circle of students around the campfires, allowing him to keep an eye on things without being in the direct line of sight of anyone but the students on the far side of the fire. And even they wouldn't be able to see him very well as it grew darker with the setting of the sun.

Hesitating, she tried not to smile at the romantic setting he'd somehow arranged despite the fact that there were forty-nine students twenty feet away from them. "You don't think we should sit with everyone else?"

"We are," he said with a grin. "We're just giving them their space."

"Max..."

"I love it when you say my name that way."

"Stop it!" She laughed. "You can't do this."

"I won't do anything," he promised, grinning, "if you'll just sit down and eat. You just cooked the most incredible meal in the middle of nowhere! Please...sit down and enjoy it."

How could she resist him when he was so darn charming? "Okay," she said, smiling. "But you have to behave yourself."

"I'll have you know I behave very well. I can prove it to you any time you like."

"Max!"

"Okay, okay." He chuckled, and relented. "Eat."

Sinking down into one of the chairs he'd set up for them, she sighed in contentment. As they both dug into their food as though they hadn't eaten in a week, she couldn't remember the last time she'd been this happy. And that should have worried her. This was just a holiday weekend stolen out of time. She was Cinderella at the ball, and the magic would all be over once she went home.

But home—and the real world—seemed very far away at that moment. Max was within touching distance, and she was falling in love with him.

The thought came out of nowhere, stealing the air right out of her lungs.

She shouldn't have been surprised. She'd known for weeks that this crazy attraction she had for him was growing deeper, stronger, with every passing day, and she'd thought she could handle it. She couldn't have been more wrong.

Torn between sudden tears and an inexplicable happiness, she wanted to take his hand and tell him, to kiss him, to spend the rest of her life with him. There was just one tiny little problem…she didn't doubt that he was attracted to her and liked her, but she couldn't fool herself into thinking that he had any intention of making a commitment to her. And that hurt.

You can't change the man, her heart warned her. *He is who he is and he's not going to change. Accept it or move on.*

There was no question in her mind of what she would do. She'd already had one man who hadn't been willing to stand up to his commitment to her and the boys—she couldn't have another. Just thinking about it brought tears to her eyes, but she quickly blinked them away. There was no point in crying. She had this time with him, and she was grateful for it. She would enjoy it, enjoy him and, for the moment, pretend it was never going to end. It would, of course. Not only was the clock ticking on the dig, but also on the class. There were only two weeks left of class when they returned to the real world. She had her term paper to finish and exams to study for. There would be no time to spend with Max—the only time she would see him was when she was in class. And when the semester was over, they would be, too.

Lost in her thoughts, she didn't realize he was studying her in the growing darkness until he said gruffly, "You okay? You got awfully quiet all of a sudden."

"I was just thinking how fast the semester's flown by. There are only two weeks left after we get home, and most of that will be spent finishing projects and studying for exams."

"Hey, none of that," he teased. "This might be a school-sponsored trip, but it's also a minivacation, and we're not going back to the real world until we're absolutely forced to. Okay? Worrying about exams and school projects and everything you've got to do when you get home isn't allowed."

It wasn't the exams she was worried about—it was having to walk away from him—but he was right. She would have to deal with reality soon enough. For now she was going to enjoy every second she had with him, and not worry about anything else.

"You're the teacher," she quipped with a grin. "Whatever you say."

His blue eyes sparkled with mischief. "I'll remind you of that later."

Heat stole into her cheeks, but they sat in the shadows, and as darkness stole over the camp, the only light was that of the campfires. Max had brought lanterns, but he didn't seemed inclined to light them, and no one else did, either. One of the guys had brought his guitar and was softly playing in the firelight. A quiet peace settled over the group, and everyone just settled back and enjoyed the music and the night.

More content than she'd been in a long time, Natalie could have sat next to Max in the darkness for hours. Mother Nature, however, had other ideas. One song changed to another, and suddenly, from out of nowhere, lighting streaked across the night sky. Startled, everyone glanced up…just as thunder boomed and the dark clouds opened up.

In the time it took to gasp, it was pouring. Muttering an oath, Max jumped to his feet and grabbed Natalie's hand. "C'mon!"

Instantly soaked, her wet hair streaming in her eyes, she could hardly see as he pulled her after him farther into the trees. Lightning cracked almost directly overhead, and the ground seemed to shake beneath their feet. Her heart pounding, Natalie instinctively ducked her head, but Max never checked his pace. Just as the downpour threatened to turn into a real gully washer, he ducked into his tent and pulled her in after him.

Breathless, she fell against him in relief. "Thank God! Where did that come from? I thought we were supposed to have nice weather all weekend!"

"Me, too." Pushing her streaming-wet hair back from her face, he peered down at her in the darkness. "Are you all right?"

"You mean other than being soaked to the skin?" she retorted, chuckling. "Nothing like a little thunderstorm to get the blood pounding."

"I can think of something else that gets the blood pounding," he murmured, and leaned down to kiss the side of her neck.

Need shuddering through her, she melted against him. "We can't do this."

"I know. Just let me hold you a little longer."

She should have stopped him right then. There were forty-nine students out there in the darkness, holed up in tents that couldn't have been twenty or thirty feet away. They'd all scattered when the rain hit, but that didn't mean they hadn't seen Max pull her into his tent. What would they think? She tried to tell herself she didn't care, but she did. She was a mother—she worried about people talking about her. Not that she could stop them now, she silently acknowledged. The entire group had seen her and Max cooking together, then later, sitting slightly apart from everyone else as they ate dinner. Like it or not, they were going to think the obvious.

"The second the rain hit, everyone ran for cover," he said quietly, reading her mind as his arms tightened around her. "Trust me, they didn't have time to pay attention to what we were doing. They were too worried about getting soaked."

"I know. And it's not like someone's going to come looking for you. It's pouring."

"Exactly," he murmured. "And from the looks of things, it's not going to let up anytime soon."

Outside, lightning flashed again, followed by an explosion of thunder that had her burying her face against his chest. All she had to do was breathe to draw in the damp, utterly male scent of him. Intoxicated, seduced, she sighed in pleasure. "Did I happen to mention how good you smell?"

He chuckled softly in the darkness. "No, as a matter of fact, you didn't. You smell pretty damn good yourself."

"It's the rain."

"No, it's you," he said thickly. "I noticed it before…it drives me crazy."

He dropped slow, easy kisses at her temple, the curve of her cheek, the tip of her nose, scrambling her thoughts, making it impossible to remember why she shouldn't be doing this. "Max…"

"You're trembling. Are you cold? There must be a front coming through—the temperature feels like it's dropped twenty degrees in the last half hour. Here, sweetheart, let me warm you up."

Dazed, dizzy, her head in a cloud, she expected him to reach for the buttons of her blouse to get her out of her damp clothes. Instead, he grabbed his sleeping bag and wrapped it around her, then pulled her back into his arms. "Better?" he asked gruffly.

Touched, love squeezing her heart, she suddenly found herself fighting tears. "Yes."

She would have sworn her voice was perfectly normal, but something in her tone had him pulling back slightly to peer down at her in the darkness. "Are you crying? What is it? What's wrong? Did I hurt you?"

"No," she sniffed. "It's just…"

When she hesitated, he cupped her cheek in his palm. "What, sweetheart?" he asked quietly. "Talk to me. What's wrong?"

How could she tell him what his tenderness and caring did to her? Derek had never been a gentle man—she was the one who'd been the caring one in their marriage, and she'd come to believe that all men were the same. "You just surprised me with your gentleness," she admitted honestly. "I thought you were going to pull my wet clothes off."

He grinned in the darkness. “I can do that, too. Just say the word.”

Laughing, she slipped her arms around his neck. “And what word would that be?”

His smile faded, and in the continuing flash of lightning, his eyes searched hers. “I’ve wanted you from the moment I met you, Natalie. All you have to say is yes.”

So they’d finally reached it, the moment they’d been racing toward from the moment he’d stopped to help her change a flat the very first day of class. And right or wrong, she couldn’t deny herself this time with him. “Yes,” she said simply, and stood on tiptoe to kiss him.

With a groan that seemed to come from the depth of his being, he started to return her kiss, only to pull back abruptly, frowning. “Are you sure, Natalie? I know it’s been a long time. If you’re not ready…”

She didn’t say a word. Instead she shrugged off the sleeping bag from around her shoulders, then reached for his hand. Bringing it to the buttons of her blouse, she pressed his hand to her breast and once again leaned up on tiptoe to kiss him gently, sweetly, on the lips.

Just that easily she completely unraveled him. He knew he was going to have to deal with that later, but for now he couldn’t think of anything but her and the way she seduced him with the soft, wet heat of her mouth and the giving fullness of her breasts beneath his fingers. She crowded closer, her hands sliding into his hair as she slowly, inexorably, took the kiss deeper, and he forgot his own name.

With a will of their own, his hands made short work of her buttons. Peeling her blouse from her, he reminded himself that he couldn’t take her like a wild man. She hadn’t let anyone this close to her in years, since her jackass of a husband had walked out on her. And she deserved a hell of a lot more than wham, bam, thank you, ma'am. And he was going to try his damnedest to give it to her.

She didn't make it easy for him. Trailing kisses along his jaw and down the side of his neck, she reached for the hem of his sweatshirt and nearly turned him inside out. "Whoa!" he groaned, grabbing her hands and holding them still at his waist. "Not so fast. Let's take this slow and easy."

"Do we have to?"

"Yes." He chuckled. "Or it's going to be over before it's begun." Cautiously he released her hands. "Don't move. Okay? Just give me a second to smooth out the sleeping bag so we can get comfortable."

She moved, but only to help him, and she had no idea how tempting she looked, kneeling in nothing but her jeans and a plain cotton bra as she smoothed the sleeping bag. Just looking at her made him ache. "Sweetheart, you're killing me," he groaned.

Glancing up in surprise, she smiled, delighted. "Really?"

"Really," he rasped and reached for her.

She came to him willingly, sinking down to the sleeping bag like it was a feather bed, her arms already closing around him as he moved to join her. Once again, her hands moved to the hem of his sweatshirt, and this time, his were there to help. She pulled it over his head and he tossed it aside, and a heartbeat later he reached behind her to the snap of her bra. With a whisper-soft movement that stole her breath, he whisked it away and sent it in the direction of his sweatshirt. Then his hands were closing around her, stroking, caressing, trailing liquid fire.

A cool, damp wind drifted under the closed flap of the tent, but the only notice either of them gave it was to slip inside the sleeping bag together. The rest of their clothes melted away, and in the dark of the night, their legs tangled, their hands stroked and teased, and it was nearly impossible to tell where she ended and he began.

Given the chance, Max would have sworn he knew what it felt like to make love to a woman he cared about. But as he moved over her, in her, and she arched to meet him, he realized that he knew nothing…nothing about women, nothing about need, nothing about making love. She moved, and his every nerve ending hummed in expectation. His name a soft moan on her lips, she called to him, gave to him, with an unselfishness that totally destroyed him.

A wise man would have known then that he was in trouble. But he couldn't think. His brain clouded, the need burning in his gut tightened like a fist, and when she cried out his name like he was the answer to all her dreams, he lost all chance of resisting her. With a groan that came from the depths of his being, he lost himself in her.

With the rising of the sun, Natalie came awake slowly. Sprawled on her stomach, her face buried in her folded arms, she shifted in her sleep, and the sleeping bag slid off her shoulder, exposing her bare skin to the cool touch of the morning air. Startled, she came awake with a gasp and realized she was naked. Just that quickly the memories of the night came rushing back.

Her heart pounding, she saw in an instant that the tent was empty, but she'd known that before she even opened her eyes. After what she and Max had shared during the night, she was intimately acquainted with the sound and feel and whisper of his every breath. If he'd been in the tent with her, she would have known it instantly.

Just days ago that would have shaken her to the core. But she couldn't regret what they'd shared, couldn't regret Max. He'd been so careful with her, so gentle, that if she hadn't already loved him, she would have fallen head over heels last night for no other reason than that. He was wonderful. With nothing more than the touch of his hands and the hunger of his kisses, he'd made her feel beautiful and wanted. And she told herself it didn't matter that he might not love her back. She almost believed it.

Sometime while she'd slept, Max had slipped her backpack into the tent, and she gratefully pulled on clean clothes and brushed her hair. Finding herself smiling over nothing, she realized she was as giddy as a schoolgirl. She couldn't remember the last time she'd been this happy. And it was all because of Max.

Laughing at herself, she debated the idea of putting on makeup, only to immediately reject it. She would be digging in the mud, cooking again over the campfire, and Max would hardly be expecting her to look like some kind of fashion model on a dig. If he was, then he'd obviously made love to the wrong woman last night.

Checking her hair once more in the small mirror she'd packed, she hurried outside and immediately spied Max working on the campfires, trying to relight them after last night's rain. He must have been watching for her. The second she stepped out of the tent, he looked up and his eyes locked with hers—and for a long, timeless moment, all she could think of was last night. Her heart slamming against her ribs, she wanted to go to him, to touch him, to kiss him like she had last night, but that was impossible. A handful of students were milling around the campfire, helping him, and others were poking their heads out of their tents, obviously sniffing for breakfast.

From fifty feet away her gaze met his, and the rueful frustration she saw in his eyes made her heart soar. He grimaced, and his shrug said it all. Later. He never said the word, but he didn't have to. She heard him, and suddenly she couldn't stop smiling.

There was, however, no chance of a private conversation, not when the students who were helping him clean out the wet fire pits were well within hearing distance. Crossing to him, all she could say was, "That was some storm we had last night."

"You're not kidding," he said gruffly, mischief glinting in his eyes. "I thought it was going to blow us right off the mountain."

"Me, too. I've never been caught up in something like that before. It was pretty incredible."

"Yeah, I was checking the weather on my cell phone earlier. Tonight we could have more of the same."

Fighting a smile, she raised a delicately arched brow. "Really? Good. I slept great last night."

The glint in his eyes promised her she would sleep just as well every night of the dig, but there was no time for any more innuendo. Last night's storm was long gone, the sun was rising above the treetops, and it was time to eat breakfast and get on with the day. "I'll keep you posted on those coming storms," he promised with a wink. "What's for breakfast?"

Chapter 11

Word spread through the camp like wildfire. Natalie and Beverly, a student in one of Max's other classes, had found a beaded pouch in the northwest quadrant of the dig. Before Natalie could even pick it up, Max came running with the rest of the students. "You found a hide pouch?"

Her heart pounding, Natalie held up the small bag that she and Beverly hadn't even realized was there when they first started trying to sift the damp dirt through a screen. Made of deer hide and sinew, it was intricately decorated with tiny blue- and rose-colored beads. "I didn't even think there was anything here," she told him.

He grinned. "That's why we screen everything—there's no way to know when we start what's hidden in the dirt. Okay, everybody," he told the students that surrounded them, "we're digging in the right spot. Let's see what else we can find."

He didn't have to tell them twice. Grabbing trowels and screens, they went back to work with renewed enthusiasm. Turning to Natalie, his blue eyes glinting, he grinned. "Good work. So what's the next step?"

"Label it, bag it and record it."

"Good. Glad you came?"

"Oh, Lord, yes! I feel like I just found a diamond."

"That's why I love it," he retorted. One of the other students at the opposite end of the grid called out to him, and he said, "Duty calls. See if you and Beverly can find the moccasins that probably match that."

Natalie would have liked nothing more, but excavating a dig wasn't something that was done quickly. Everything from the dirt to the smallest shard of pottery to pieces of bone that appeared to have been used as utensils were painstakingly collected and recorded. The sun had dried much of mud that was a result of the rain two nights ago, but it was still messy. Later, she knew she would probably be desperate for a bath, but she didn't complain, and neither did anyone else. This was what they'd been preparing for all semester.

As they diligently worked, small treasures were uncovered one by one, and Max moved around, helping, giving suggestions, getting down in the mud with everyone else. He was in his element and it showed. Every time her eyes connected with his, he was smiling, laughing, and there was a sparkle in his eye that said more clearly than words that he was having the time of his life.

And it was his enthusiasm that made the dig so much fun for everyone else. With any other professor in charge, the trip could have been a tedious exercise in excavation, but Max was like a kid going to the circus for the first time. He threw himself into the work and when anyone found something, he couldn't have been more thrilled if he'd single-handedly found the secrets to the pyramids. Excitement whipped through the dig site, and students that Natalie had never seen participate in class were eagerly asking for Max's help.

She could have spent the entire dig just watching him, but she couldn't, of course…not without him and most of the class noticing. So she forced herself to concentrate on her own task, but even when her back was turned to him and he was at the opposite end of the site and totally wrapped up in helping other students, on one level or another she was somehow aware of everything he did.

She'd thought she knew what it was like to be in love. She'd fallen in love with Derek when she was seventeen and had spent every waking and sleeping moment thinking of him. But this was different. That had been an innocent love that she'd naively thought would last forever. This was passion and love and a need that seemed to pull at her very soul…and all she would ever have of Max was this moment in time. She wanted to touch him, to kiss him, to disappear into the woods with him for hours at a time. Instead, she couldn't do anything but act as if the last two nights she'd spent in his arms had never happened and she was nothing more to him than another one of his students.

Preparing meals, however, was another matter. The minute she headed for the camp kitchen area, he was always there. "What's for lunch?" he asked Saturday as he joined her at the hand wash area.

"Actually, I thought we'd just have some subs. No, we're not having bologna sandwiches," she said when he started to grin, "or Pop-Tarts for breakfast. I was thinking of something a little more expensive than that."

"Are we going to Quiznos?"

"Cute," she retorted.

"My mother thinks so."

She tried not to laugh and failed miserably. "You're outrageous, do you know that? I bought deli meats and cheeses and some great hard rolls. If someone wants Quiznos, you can heat up one of the campfires and they can stick their subs on the grill. Okay?"

He lifted a masculine brow over twinkling eyes. "Are you saying you want me to light your fire?"

"Max—"

At her warning tone, he only chuckled and began helping her set out everything for lunch. Within a matter of minutes, it was time to eat. Max grabbed the dinner bell and held it out to her with a grin. "Would you like to do the honors?"

For an answer, she took the bell and rang it like a schoolmarm. "How's that?" she asked with twinkling eyes.

"You can ring my bell anytime you like, sweetheart," he murmured, playfully leering at her as the rest of the students came running. "Just knock on my tent."

Laughing, she could feel the heat climbing in her cheeks and prayed that the other students wouldn't notice. She needn't have worried. All they cared about was eating. Shooting Max a look that promised payback, she turned away to make her own sandwich.

With her back turned, she didn't notice that he'd moved to join her until he reached past her for a hard roll and his hip bumped hers. When her eyes flew to his, he gave her an innocent look that made her laugh all over again. What was she going to do with the man?

You can ring my bell anytime you like, sweetheart...just knock on my tent.

Long after Natalie retired to her tent after supper that night, Max's teasing words echoed in her head. The rest of the camp was quiet—everyone had called it a night with the setting of the sun—but she was wide-awake. And it was all Max's fault. She couldn't forget the look in his eyes when she'd quietly wished him good-night. It was the same look he'd given her last night when she'd retreated to her own tent when everyone else had turned in. She knew Max probably thought she was being foolish—they were both adults and could certainly share a tent if they chose—but she couldn't just blatantly walk into his tent with all of his students watching. So she'd slipped into her own tent—there were an odd number of girls, so she had a tent to herself—and waited for the camp to grow quiet.

Last night he'd come to her. Tonight it was her turn. He probably thought she didn't have the guts. He just didn't know.

The decision made, she waited for the camp to grow quiet, then peeked outside. A crescent moon hung low in the night sky, giving just enough light to see Max's tent in the trees. Her heart beating like a drum in her chest, Natalie soundlessly made her way through the camp and was amazed that no one woke up. Surely someone in one of the tents had to hear the crazy beating of her heart.

But she made it to Max's tent without mishap, only to hesitate just outside. How did you knock on a tent? Was he still awake? How would he feel if she just slipped inside and woke him up?

She was trying to decide when she thought she heard a sound inside the tent. Suddenly weak at the knees, she whispered, "Max? Is that you?"

"No, it's the big bad wolf," he growled softly. Pulling back the tent flap, he reached for her hand and tugged her inside. A heartbeat later she was in his arms. "I didn't think you would come," he rasped, and kissed her hungrily.

When he finally let her up for air, her head was swimming, her body was humming, and all she could think of was how short her time was with him. How was she going to bear to walk away from him? Fighting the need to cry, she buried her face against his neck. "I wanted to go with you the second everyone called it a night, but this isn't easy for me," she said quietly. "I guess I'm more old-fashioned than I thought. I just can't be as bold as the kids are today."

"You're bold, sweetheart." He chuckled as she planted a soft kiss just below his ear and set his heart tumbling into a free fall. "You just do it behind closed doors. Or maybe I should say closed tent flaps." His chuckle turned into a groan as she slipped her hands over his bare chest, heating his skin with just the brush of her fingers. "Did I happen to mention that I like a woman who knows what she wants and goes after it?"

"Then you're going to be a very happy man tonight," she replied, and pulled her sweatshirt over her head. A heartbeat later, the zipper of her jeans growled softly in the darkness. Before the rest of her clothes even hit the ground, she was reaching for the waistband of the flannel pajama bottoms he slept in. He sucked in a sharp breath, and in the darkness her eyes met his and she asked, "Do you mind?"

When her fingers slid lower, taking the rest of his clothes before he could manage a single word, his low laugh changed to a strangled groan. "Not at all," he rasped, spreading his arms wide. "I'm totally at your mercy, sweetheart. Do whatever you like."

What she liked was kissing him until they were both breathless, caressing every hard male inch of him until he was mindless and shuddering with need. And then, when she didn't think either one of them could stand the pleasure another second, something in him seemed to snap. Growling her name, he kissed her fiercely, desperately, wonderfully and stripped what was left of her clothes from her. Then he was rolling her under him and his hands and mouth were rushing over her.

Gasping, her heart slamming against her ribs, every nerve ending in her body attuned to him, she was the one who was at his mercy, and she loved it. With his hands alone, he brought her to one peak, and she'd hardly caught her breath before he surged into her and his kiss caught her cry of surprise. Moaning, she tried to tell herself that she had to remember this, that when she was old and gray and he'd long since disappeared from her life, she was going to remember what it was like to make love with a man she absolutely adored, but he moved with her, in her, driving her crazy from the inside out, and she couldn't think. Her brain fogged, her senses blurred, and there was only Max. Kissing her. Loving her. Driving her over the edge, making her shatter.

What was left of the weekend passed in a blur. The lost mine was still buried somewhere in the mountains, but Max couldn't have been more pleased with the artifacts the students had found in the dirt that had once been the Utes' summer camp. There were dozens of bags of pottery pieces, arrowheads, cooking utensils and beadwork to take back to the university lab to be analyzed, and that was just scraping the surface. He would bring students back next semester, then have an extensive dig in the summer, and there was no telling what they would find as they dug deeper.

Max couldn't remember the last time he'd been so pleased with a dig. He tried to convince himself it was because he'd spent years trying to convince the powers that be at the university to let him take his students on a dig, and the final report that would eventually be published as a result of his students' finds was going to be damned impressive. But it was more than that, and he knew it. The real reason he couldn't stop smiling was pure and simple. Natalie.

He didn't have a clue how she'd done it, but she'd somehow found a way to slip past his guard and grab a place for herself in his heart. And for the first time in his adult life, he understood how his father felt when he lost his head and heart to a woman. It was wild, crazy, exhilarating...and scary as hell. The problem now was...what the devil was he going to do about it?

The question nagged him all day Sunday, but he had no ready answers. And long before he was ready to say goodbye, it was time to break everything down, pack, and head back to Eagle Creek. Everyone helped, and for the next hour, the dig site was a beehive of activity. Doing his share of the work, Max hardly noticed. Staying within touching distance of Natalie, he couldn't take his eyes off her. He'd seen his father do the same thing with every single woman he'd married.

Alarm bells didn't just ring in his head—they blared like

a thousand sirens all going off at once. For no other reason than that, he should have put some distance between them until he could get his head on straight. But she needed help with the kitchen stuff, and he was right there. And she knew how to pack the bus in a way the other students just didn't understand. It was a mother thing, he told himself, but he was the teacher and he had to supervise. And then when everything was loaded and they were the last two to climb on the bus, it just seemed natural to sit together as they had on the trip up.

Yeah, right, that irritating voice in his head drawled. *You sat with her because you couldn't stop yourself, because it's the only place on the whole damn bus where you want to sit. At least be honest about it, dammit!*

Okay, so he wanted to sit next to her. He wanted to make her laugh, make her sigh, make her call his name in the dark with a longing that set him on fire. But most of all, he wanted her.

He was in a hell of a mess.

They hardly spoke all the way back to Eagle Creek, but there was a quiet contentment between them that he'd never felt with another woman. And then all too soon the bus was pulling into the parking lot where they'd all left their cars and it was time to unload. Troubled, Max could literally feel time slipping through his fingers, and he didn't like it one little bit.

Natalie and the other students were laughing and joking as they helped transfer the treasures they'd collected from the bus to a van Max had left there to transport their finds to the climate-controlled storage units where they would be stored until they were examined in the archeological lab. He was usually in a great frame of mind after a dig, but he could find little to smile about this time, and it was all Natalie's fault. And she didn't even seem to notice.

Irritated with himself—he was acting like a two-year-old!—he tried to shake off the blue funk that had fallen over him, but without much success. Needing some time to himself, he retreated to the bus so that he could deal with his emotions in private. Checking for items left behind, collecting trash, he didn't realize he was no longer alone until Natalie said quietly, "We finished transferring everything to the van, Max, and all the camping gear's in the storage unit. Does anything else need to be done? Beverly and some of the others were wondering if it's okay to leave now."

"If it's all cleared out, then they're free to go," he said gruffly. "I'm just making sure everything's picked up in here. The bus company will give us a break on the cleanup fee if we return the bus in good order."

"I'll help you," she said. "Just give me a second to tell everyone it's okay to leave."

She was back almost immediately and started picking up the front of the bus while he started at the back. Aware of her every move as they both worked toward the center, he asked, "Well? What'd you think of your first dig?"

"It was incredible," she said simply, her eyes unusually somber as she faced him. "I hate that it's over."

"Coming home is always the hard part," he said ruefully. "It doesn't have to end immediately, you know. We could go back to my place and have something to eat, maybe figure out a way we could have done some things better while it's still fresh in our minds."

He'd never asked a woman back to his home. Afraid of making the same mistakes his father had made and letting a woman get too close, he had, over the years, been very careful not to cross that line with the women he dated. Natalie, however, was different. She had been from the first moment he'd met her, and he couldn't let her go—not yet. He wanted her with him, in his arms, in his home, in his bed.

"I'm sorry. I can't," she said regretfully. "The boys will be home in thirty minutes from their trip. Susan's going to bring them straight home, so I have to be there."

Disappointed, he understood. "I'm sure they've missed you. We can get together another time. I need to get these samples over to the lab, anyway. So I guess I'll see you in class."

Her eyes searching his, Natalie couldn't believe the most incredible holiday weekend of her life was ending this way. Had the time they'd spent in his tent, making love, meant so little to him that he was willing to just let her walk away without so much as a "Take care"? He hadn't mentioned the future or how he felt about her, and she had no reason to believe he ever would. Pain squeezed her heart, but she knew she had no one to blame but herself. She'd known from the beginning that he was a man who wanted nothing to do with commitment, so she'd gone into their relationship—or whatever it was they shared—with her eyes wide-open. She couldn't complain now because he wasn't the kind of man she wanted and needed him to be.

Fiercely holding back the tears that burned her eyes, she forced a grimace of a smile. "I guess I'll see you on Tuesday then," she said stiffly. "Good night."

Later, she didn't remember making her way off the bus…or loading her things into her car. She turned right, out of the parking lot, and was three miles down the road before she wiped away her tears enough to see that she was going the wrong way. With a soft sob she turned at the next corner and headed back in the direction she had come.

Long after she'd disappeared down the street, Max stood in the parking lot, fighting the need to go after her. The boys would be home soon, he reminded himself, and it had been three days since they'd seen her. They would need some time with her. And it wasn't like he wasn't ever going to see her again. In less than thirty-six hours she'd be walking into his classroom. He should have been able to find some satisfaction in that, but he already missed her.

Natalie had just enough time to carry her things inside and wash her face with cold water before Susan pulled into the driveway and the boys burst out of her minivan with huge grins stretching across their freckled faces. "There're my baby boys! Did you have a good time?"

With a screech of pure joy, they launched themselves at her. "Mom! We saw a bear!"

"And an eagle. It flew right over our heads!"

"I caught a fish—and Tommy fell in the water."

Instantly concerned, she glanced sharply at Tommy. "Are you okay? What happened?"

"It was an accident," Susan said with an easy smile as she, too, hugged Natalie. "He wanted to see the fish Harry caught, but the grass along the bank of the stream where we were fishing was wet. The next thing we knew, he slipped and he was in the water. It couldn't have been more than ten inches deep. His pants and shoes got wet, but he was fine."

"Susan dried my clothes by the campfire," Tommy said, beaming. "I smelled like smoke all day!"

"I'll bet you did, sweetheart." She laughed, ruffling his hair. "So you had a good time, even with the dunking?"

"The best! Wait'll you see what we brought you!"

"I picked it out!"

So excited they could hardly stand still, they jerked open one of their bags and pulled out a beautiful crocheted poncho that glistened with beadwork. "Do you like it, Mom? Huh? Susan said you would!"

Stunned, she touched it with fingers that weren't quite steady. "Where did you get the money for this? All you had was your allowance, and that was your spending money for the trip in case you went somewhere fun or you ate out."

"They were really tight-fisted with it," Susan said, grinning. "They only spent what they had to until this morning, when they pooled everything and bought you the poncho. Tommy was sure pink was your color. I think he was right."

Tears welled in her eyes as she scooped them both up for a fierce hug. "You guys are so sweet! Thank you!"

"We really wanted to get you a stuffed porcupine," Harry added, hugging her back. "But it costed too much. It was cool!"

"Thank God for that!" She laughed, and hugged them again.

Wound up like clocks, they were still talking long after Susan left, and Natalie found herself wishing time and again that Max was there to hear their wild stories. Why couldn't he be the man she needed him to be? she wondered as she finally got them to bed. It had been over five years since Derek had walked out, and in all that time she hadn't even looked at another man. Until Max. She wanted to share her life with him, her children, all the ups and downs of their future that made life such a roller coaster…and he wanted nothing to do with that kind of commitment. What was she supposed to do now?

She had no answers for that. Her heart numb with pain, she lay in bed long after the boys had gone to sleep, fighting the need to cry. It had been a long time since she'd felt so empty.

When the phone suddenly rang in the darkness, her heart jumped into her throat. Who would be calling at ten-thirty at night? She wanted to believe it was Max, but she was afraid to let herself hope. *Idiot!* she told herself. *If you want to know who it is, answer it!*

Leaning over to the nightstand, she snatched up the phone with fingers that weren't quite steady. "Hello?"

"Natalie?"

She almost dropped the receiver. She hadn't heard Derek's voice in five years, but she would have known it on the far side of the moon. And in the time it took to blink, sudden, inexplicable fear was twisting like a snake in her stomach. Why, after all this time, was he calling? "What do you want, Derek?" she asked coldly.

"I'm sorry to be calling so late," he said stiffly. "I tried calling all weekend but couldn't get anyone, and I didn't want to leave a message on the machine."

"What do you want?" she repeated. "I haven't heard a word from you in almost six years. Why are you calling now?"

He hesitated, only to blurt out, "I'm in town. I'd like to see you and the boys."

Horrified, she felt her blood turn cold. This couldn't be happening! How many times had she dreamed of this? Dreamed of him showing up on her doorstep with no warning, wanting the only thing in the world she cared about—her sons. No! she cried silently. She wasn't going to let him do this!

"People in Hell want ice water," she said flatly. "It's not going to happen!"

Furious, she slammed the receiver down on its base and only then realized she was shaking. How dare he! He'd walked out on her, on his unborn sons, to be with another woman and hadn't cared if they were alive or dead. It'd been over five years. Five damn years, for God's sake! And not once in all that time had he called to see if they were all right, let alone sent some money for their support. Damn him! Where was he when they were sick or needed clothes or had to stay with Susan while she worked every available hour she could at Finn's just so she could keep the lights on? She'd never felt so alone in her life as the day she'd come home from the hospital with her newborn twins and there'd been no one to help her. And now he wanted to see the three of them? Like hell!

Livid, she paced the confines of her bedroom like an angry lioness, years of pent-up resentment over his abandonment fueling her rage. But when she walked off the anger, the fear set in. What if he didn't just want to see the boys? What if he wanted to take them? He was a lawyer. He knew judges…

Panicking at the thought, she reached for the phone. She had to call Max! She just needed to talk to him. He would know what to do.…

But even as her fingers closed around the phone, she dropped it back onto the base. No! She couldn't call him, she thought with a sob. There wasn't any kind of commitment between them. They weren't even dating! How could she put this on his shoulders when he wasn't really a part of her life and didn't want to be? This was her problem, her nightmare to deal with. And she had to handle it alone.

* * *

Max lost track of the number of times he reached for her during the night. Frustrated, missing her more than he thought possible, he couldn't wait for class Tuesday just so he could see her.

"You've got it bad, Sullivan," he muttered as he headed toward campus on his motorcycle. "So what the hell are you going to do about it?"

He didn't have a clue. At that particular moment all he cared about was seeing Natalie.

She didn't, however, show up for class on Tuesday. Surprised, he frowned when the bell rang, then checked his watch, but it was eight o'clock on the dot. So where was she? She'd only missed class once before, and that was the week she was sick. Concerned, he assured himself she was fine. She'd been perfectly healthy when she helped him clean the bus on Sunday—she couldn't have gotten sick that quickly. And if she had, she would have called him. She was just running late. She'd probably come rushing in any second.

But an hour and a half later when the bell rang again, signaling the end of class, there was no sign of Natalie. Maybe she wasn't the one who was sick—it could be the boys. They could have picked up some kind of flu bug while they were gone. Concerned, he pulled out his cell phone as the class filed out and quickly punched in her number, but all he got was the answering machine. Then he really started to worry. If the boys weren't sick, was she? Was that why she wasn't answering her phone? Or was she really not home? She could have had car trouble on the way to school. If she'd had a cell phone, he would have called her just to make sure she was all right. As it was, all he could do was leave a message on her answering machine and ask her to call him. He was, he decided grimly as he hung up, getting her a cell phone for Christmas.

His next class started, but he still couldn't shake the feeling that something was wrong. He'd felt the same way the last time she'd missed class—when she'd been sick. This time, though, he wasn't waiting nearly a week to check on her. He'd drop by to see her between his second and third class.

Keeping the blinds drawn and the television off, Natalie flinched when someone suddenly pounded in the front door. If it was Derek, he was wasting his time. She'd kept the boys out of school yesterday and today, sent them to Susan's and then waited. She might not have seen Derek in five years, but she hadn't forgotten what kind of man he was. When he wanted something, he didn't let anything get in his way. And he'd decided he wanted her sons. Oh, he hadn't said the words, but he hadn't fooled her when he'd claimed he just wanted to see her and the boys. He never did anything without a reason. He wanted the boys. Well, he damn well wasn't getting them, not as long as she had anything to say about the matter.

"Natalie? Are you in there? It's me…Max."

For a second all she heard was a male voice—then his words registered. Her heart thundered, but she couldn't throw open the door and fall into his arms as she longed to. As much as she loved him, he couldn't help her, not with this. And that hurt. All these years she'd thought she could never trust another man enough to let herself fall in love, and now that she had, she couldn't turn to him in a crisis.

"I'm okay," she called huskily through the door. "You don't need to worry about me."

"Then open the door, sweetheart, and let me see that for myself."

She almost didn't, but she knew he wouldn't go away until he saw with his own eyes that she was all right. Quickly wiping the tears from her eyes, she smoothed her hair, pinched her cheeks and reached for the dead bolt. "See, I'm fine."

Max took one look at her drawn, pale face and knew that something was terribly wrong. Without a word he reached for her and pulled her into his arms. "What is it?" he asked gruffly, holding her tight. "What's wrong? And don't you dare tell me you're fine! Your face is an open book, sweetheart. You're as white as a sheet. Is it the boys? Tell me."

For a minute he didn't think she was going to. She stood as stiff as a board in his arms, holding on to her control with everything she had in her. But she couldn't stop the sob that welled up in her throat or the tears that spilled into her eyes. "It's Derek," she choked, burying her face against his neck. "He's in town and wants to see the boys."

Whatever Max had been expecting, it wasn't that. Relief hit him first—no one was dead. Then he was surprised to discover he was hurt. "You should have called me. You don't have to go through something like this all by yourself."

"I couldn't put my troubles on you," she said simply. "That's not fair to you. He's my ex. I'm the one who has to deal with him."

"Not alone you don't," he retorted. "Dammit, Natalie, I care about you and the boys! You're not going through life alone anymore. Okay? I expect you to call me when you need me."

She wanted to believe him, wanted to believe that he was always going to be there for her, but how could she? Even if he had been willing to make a commitment, Derek had taught her the hard way that there were no guarantees in life when it came to love. "I wanted to call you," she said huskily. "I've just handled everything on my own for so long that it didn't seem right to pull you into this."

"But I am in it, sweetheart, because I care about you." Following her into the living room, he frowned as she prowled restlessly from window to window. "Where are the boys? Do they know about this?"

"No, and they're not going to."

"He's their father, Natalie," he said quietly. "You're going to open up a whole can of worms if you don't let him see them."

"He abandoned them!"

"I know, sweetheart, and I'll be the first to agree that the man's a slimeball. But he's still their father…and an attorney."

"If he wants to fight, then fine. I'll hire my own damn attorney, and I'll win. He walked out on us and never paid a dime in child support. How do you think the courts are going to look at that?"

"Not well," he agreed. "But is that what you really want? A knock-down, drag-out fight in the courts? Because if it is, you have to know that nobody wins in that situation, least of all the boys."

In a world of panic, his was the voice of reason, and she knew it. But tears welled up in her eyes just at the thought of Derek hurting her sons the way he'd hurt her. "I can't let him come into their lives, then walk right back out again. I won't let him hurt them the way he hurt me."

Crossing the room to her, he pulled her into his arms. "I understand, honey. I don't want the boys—or you—hurt, either. But you don't even know why Derek wants to see you and the boys. Until you do, you're boxing in the dark. Call him. Find out what's going on, then decide what you want to do about it."

She knew he was right, but she was afraid. Terror gripping her heart, she hugged him fiercely. "I can't lose them, Max."

"You're not going to," he promised huskily. "No judge in his right mind would take them away from you, Natalie. You've done a wonderful job with them, and all on your own, so don't tear yourself up this way. Call Derek and find out what the devil he wants. It's the only way you're going to be able to deal with this."

She knew he was right, but just thinking about seeing him, talking to him, made her sick to her stomach. "All right," she said with a sigh. "I'll do it. But if he gives me any kind of trouble, the deal's off. I won't even talk to him, let alone let him see the boys."

Snatching up the phone, she punched in the number he had left when he'd called Sunday night. "I can meet you tomorrow afternoon at two at McCormick Park," she said flatly the second he answered the phone. "I'll be at the pavilion, but I won't bring the boys. Not yet."

"I understand," he replied. "I'll see you then."

There was no idle chit-chat, nothing else to say. She hung up, then turned to Max. "All right, I did the right thing. So why do I feel so lousy?"

"Because you're a mother and you're worried about your kids," he retorted. "I'd be worried about you if you *weren't* worried. I can go with you tomorrow, if you like," he added. "You don't have to go through this alone."

He didn't have a clue how much he tempted her. She would have liked nothing more than to cling to him and let him fight her battles for her, but she couldn't take advantage of him that way. Derek was her problem, and she was the one who had to deal with him.

"I appreciate that," she said, "but I need to do this alone, Max. I'll be all right. It's not like he's violent or anything. He's not going to hurt me, if that's what you're worried about."

There were other ways to hurt someone besides physically, but this was her call. "If you change your mind, you know where I am." Giving her a fierce hug, he growled, "I've got to get back to my next class. Call me if you need me." Feeling as if she was shutting him out, he walked out.

Chapter 12

Later Max couldn't have said how he found the resolve to walk away from her. If she'd just given some indication that she wanted him to stay, he would have skipped his last class and spent the rest of the day with her. She hadn't, however, said a single word to stop him from leaving.

That ate at him all afternoon.

He'd thought she would call after his last class, but his cell phone never rang. There was nothing waiting for him on his answering machine at home, either, but he got her message loud and clear. She didn't need his help dealing with Derek. Oh, she'd gone into his arms when he'd shown up on her doorstep earlier that morning, Max readily acknowledged, but he hadn't spoken to her since.

Frustrated, irritated with himself and her, he tried to distract himself with work, but he didn't get very far. All he could think of was Natalie…and Derek. Had he called her again? Is that why she hadn't called? Was the jackass trying to convince her to let him come back to her?

She wouldn't do that, Max assured himself. She might find a way to forgive and forget what her ex had done to her, but her sons were another matter. She loved those boys with all her heart and she was extremely protective of them. Derek could talk until he was blue in the face, but it wasn't going to change anything. He'd turned his back on his sons before they were even born. Natalie would never be able to get past that, and he couldn't blame her.

He couldn't begin to imagine how difficult the last five years had been for her. Who was with her when she had given birth to the boys? Had her mother come into town to be with her? Or had she been alone, with no one but her doctor and the nurses there to help her through the pain of childbirth, not once, but twice?

No, he thought grimly. After everything Derek had done to her, Natalie wouldn't be interested in taking the jerk back. And if he had any brains at all, he had to know that. So why *was* he back in town? What the hell did the bastard want?

Natalie had to be wondering the same thing. His frustration evaporating at the thought of the hell Max knew she was going through, he reached for the phone. If she wasn't going to call him, then, by God, he'd call her!

But just as he started to punch in her number, the doorbell rang. He wanted to believe it was Natalie, but she'd never been to his place and he didn't think she would just show up without calling. It was probably one of the neighborhood kids selling something for a school fund-raiser—they all knew he was an easy mark.

But when he opened the door, it wasn't a kid standing on his front porch—it was his father. "Dad! What are you doing here?"

"I was in the neighborhood and thought I'd drop by, if that's okay."

"You know you're welcome here anytime, Dad. C'mon in." Opening the door wider, he stepped back, then frowned as his father meandered around his living room as though he didn't quite know what to do with himself. "What's up? You all right?"

John Sullivan grinned sheepishly. "Becky had to go to Denver on business, and I'm feeling kind of lonely. You want to go play some pool or something? We haven't done that in years."

At any other time he would gladly have taken his father up on the invitation—they didn't spend nearly enough time together—but the timing couldn't have been worse. "Maybe another time," he said with a grimace. "I just got back from the dig and I'd really rather stay home tonight."

Surprised, his father studied him through narrowed eyes. "You're not usually a homebody, even after a dig. What's going on? What's her name?"

"I don't know what you're talking about."

"Yes, you do," his father retorted with a broad grin. "You're not the type to sit home and brood and you know it. There's got to be a woman involved. Don't try to deny it," he warned when Max scowled and started to protest. "I know the signs, remember? I've been there eight different times, son, and I know how a man acts when a woman knocks him out of his shoes. So…who is she?"

Irritated that he'd seen right through him, Max reluctantly grinned. "You're worse than an old woman gossiping. You know that?"

"Quit trying to change the subject and tell me about her. How long have you known her?"

He hadn't intended to tell him anything, but he couldn't seem to stop himself. "A couple of months. Her name's Natalie. She's one of my students."

"I thought you didn't date your students," his father said, surprised.

"I don't," he said defensively. "But she's different. She's thirty-six. She's got kids…twin boys. They're five."

Images flashed before his eyes of the boys at the football game and Natalie on the back of his bike and in the mud at the dig, marveling over the beaded pouch she and Barbara had found. And just that easily, words came pouring out of him. He told John Sullivan about how she'd raised her boys alone, how independent she was, how frustrating it was for him when she wouldn't let him help her. "Her ex is back in town and wants to see her and the boys, and she's worried sick about it. She's not the only one. What if he wants her back?"

"Don't torture yourself with what-ifs," his father said. "How long have you been in love with her?"

"I'm not in love—"

When his father just looked at him, daring him to argue further, he swore softly. "I don't know…maybe from the first moment I laid eyes on her."

Delighted, John Sullivan grinned like a Cheshire cat. "There's hope for you yet. I was beginning to worry about you."

"Are you kidding me? I'm in love with a woman with two five-year-olds, and her ex-husband has just come back into the picture, and you think there's hope for me? Dad, what the hell am I going to do? She's all I can think about. I want to protect her and take care of her and do whatever I have to to make her happy, and she won't let me!"

"Does she love you?"

Frustrated, Max shrugged. "I don't know. I hope so."

"You mean you haven't told her how you feel about her? Dammit, Max, are you trying to lose her? A woman has to be told these things!"

"Well, I just found out myself," he retorted. "How the heck was I supposed to tell her when I didn't know myself?"

"You've got to tell her, son," he said grimly. "Especially if she's going to see her ex again. They've got a history…and children! That makes him dangerous. You have to let her know how you feel about her."

"She's got a lot on her mind right now, Dad."

"Which is all the more reason why she needs to know that you love her," he replied. "Just think about it. Going through a crisis alone is tough. She needs to know you're in her corner and why."

He made sense, but telling her he loved her when he'd never let himself love a woman before wasn't something he was going to rush into. "I'll think about it," he said roughly. "That's all I can promise."

Satisfied, his father squeezed his shoulder and grinned. "Quit fighting it, son. C'mon in. The water's fine."

Long after his father left, Max couldn't get his father's words—or grin—out of his head. He couldn't blame his father for being so amused. How many times over the years had he claimed he was never going to fall in love, never make the mistakes his old man had? And now here he was, up to his neck in love. The joke was on him, and he couldn't complain. He was crazy about the woman.

* * *

Her stomach twisted in painful knots, Natalie approached the pavilion at McCormick Park on legs that were far from steady. Every instinct she had told her to turn around and get the hell out of there. She didn't care what Derek wanted. She didn't want to see him, didn't want to talk to him, didn't want to dredge up all the old anger and hurt from the past. She was in love with Max, and even if there was no future in that, she'd moved on with her life and left Derek far behind. She wanted nothing to do with him.

He's their father...you're going to open up a whole can of worms if you don't let him see them.... Find out what's going on, then decide what you want to do about it... It's the only way you're going to be able to deal with this....

Max's words echoed over and over in her head, but even though she knew he was right, she readily admitted that she was still terrified. She didn't have the money to fight him if he wanted to fight for custody. And he had to know that.

Run! Not for the first time, the thought blinked like a neon light in her head, but she couldn't avoid Derek forever. The sooner she got this over with, the better. Straightening her shoulders, she picked up her pace and wasn't surprised to find him waiting for her at the pavilion. He'd always been irritatingly early for appointments. Seated at one of the cement picnic tables, he rose to his feet as she drew near.

She saw in an instant that time had been good to him since she'd seen him last. Tall and slender, his blond hair and mustache neatly trimmed, he looked fantastic. She wasn't surprised—he'd always been a good-looking man. She could appreciate that...and the fact that her heart didn't lurch—not even once!—at the sight of him, vastly relieved her mind. The old feelings she'd once had for him were completely gone. Instead all she felt was wariness.

"You wanted to see me," she said by way of a greeting. "Here I am."

She wasn't going to make it easy for him, and he knew it. "You're looking good, Natalie."

"What do you want, Derek? You didn't come all this way to comment on my looks."

"No, I didn't," he agreed. "I came to apologize."

Surprised, she blinked. He didn't throw the words around lightly—apologies had never come easily for him. "There was a time when I'd have killed to hear those words from you just so I could throw them back in your face," she said, studying him suspiciously. "I've gotten past that, thank God. So why now? Why, after all this time, have you decided to apologize?"

"Debbie and I got married—"

Insulted, she glared at him. "If you're waiting for me to congratulate you, you've got a long wait."

"Damn it, Natalie, I didn't say that to hurt you," he snapped. Swearing, he sighed. "Would you just listen to me, please? We got married four years ago. What I'm trying to say, and apparently not very well, is that we're married and we had a baby last month. A little girl. Her name is Jessica."

Natalie stopped dead in her tracks, pain squeezing her heart. They had a baby? Her sons had a sister? "The last I heard, you didn't want children," she said coldly.

His shoulders slumped. "You have every right to hate me," he told her quietly. "What I did to you and our sons was outrageous. There's nothing I can say, no apology I can give you, that can make up for that. Debbie and I never argue…except about you. She never agreed with the way I left you and the boys. She's hounded me for years to make amends."

"But you didn't."

To his credit he didn't try to make excuses. "I was a jackass, okay? A stubborn, stupid jackass. Then I held Jessica in my arms, and everything changed."

He was a man who seldom showed emotion, but his entire expression softened at the mention of his daughter. "She's the most amazing baby. And I know you're probably not going to believe this, but the first time I held her, I was haunted by what I had done to my sons and their mother. I want my children to know and love each other—"

"You're not taking them, Derek!"

"I wasn't suggesting that," he assured her. "After what I did, I lost any right to ask anything of you where they're concerned. I just hope that at some point, you can find it in your heart to forgive me. That's why I'm really here. As much as I'd love for the kids to grow up knowing each other, I know that's never going to happen until I make peace with you."

He'd hurt her so much. Did he really think he could say I'm sorry and everything would be all right again? "You made me hate you," she said huskily. "Do you have a clue what you're asking of me?"

"You can't hate me any more than I hate myself," he replied grimly. "I know this isn't something that's going to happen overnight, if ever. I just want you to think about it. That's all."

Long after he left, Natalie sat at one of the nearby picnic tables, staring blindly at the park. Her sons had a baby sister. For some reason she'd never considered the possibility that Derek would have other children, not after he'd walked away from his sons before they were even born. And now he wanted her to forgive him? To act as if he'd never walked out on her? To forget that in the past five years, he'd never once called her about the boys to see if they were all right or needed anything?

"Are you okay?"

Lost in her thoughts, she glanced up to find Max standing at the edge of the pavilion, watching her in concern. Tears welled in her eyes. "Oh, Max!"

He took a step toward her, and just that quickly she was in his arms. "I'm so glad you came!"

Holding her close, he chuckled. "You didn't really think I was going to let you go through this all by yourself, did you? I know you wanted to handle it on your own, but I had to be close, just in case." Pulling back slightly, he cupped her face in his hands. "I couldn't hear what the two of you were saying, but you looked like you were holding your own. What happened?"

Up until then, she'd held it together fairly well, but now that she was safe in his arms, she couldn't hold back the emotions threatening to tear her apart. "He has a baby girl," she choked. "He wants her to know her twin brothers."

The tears spilled over her lashes then, and there was nothing she could do to stop them. "I'm sorry," she sniffed, burying her face against his chest. "I just wasn't expecting this."

"Don't you dare apologize for being upset," he said huskily. "This has got to be like a kick in the heart for you. All this time he completely ignored the boys like they didn't even exist and now he wants to make amends just because he has a daughter? That stinks. What about for his sons' sake? Does he realize what he did to them for five lousy years? Does he know what he did to *you?* Does he care?"

"He admitted he'd been a stubborn jackass." Pulling back,

she gave a watery smile. "And Debbie, apparently, has been giving him grief about the boys for years. I have to admit, that made me feel good."

Grinning, he chuckled. "Tacky, tacky, sweetheart."

"Okay, so I'm human." She shrugged. "I admit it. What he did to me is one thing. But he walked out on his children, Max. He wasn't even there when they were born. I called his mother because I felt like she deserved to know that she had twin grandsons, and she called him. I don't know what they said to each other, but I never heard a word from him."

"At least he seems to realize what a mistake he made," he replied. "If he was sincere."

"Oh, no, he was sincere," she said, remembering the look on Derek's face when he'd talked about his daughter. "He regrets what he did—there's no question of that."

"So how did you leave it? Did you accept his apology?"

"He told me to think about it," she replied, "but there's really nothing to think about. This isn't about me and Derek anymore. It's about the boys and their sister. It's very important that the three of them have a relationship as they grow up, and they can't do that if Derek and I are at each other's throats. So I have to find a way to bury the hatchet someplace other than in his head."

"That's a tall order, sweetheart. Think you can do it?"

"I have to," she said simply. "For the boys. My only concern is them and seeing that this is done right. They can't be rushed into a relationship with their father and sister—they're going to be confused and have a lot of questions. We have to give them time."

Taking her hand, Max kissed it. "Did I ever tell you how much you amaze me? You're a great mother. The boys are lucky to have you."

She smiled slightly. "Thank you, but I don't think I'm anything out of the ordinary. I bet your mother did the same thing for you."

"Actually, she did." He laughed. "How did you know?"

"Because you wouldn't be so concerned for the boys if your mother hadn't made sure that your feelings were protected all those times your dad got married and divorced." Smiling up into his eyes, she said, "Did I say thank you?"

Surprised, he blinked. "For what?"

"For being here for me. I don't know what I would have done if you hadn't shown up on my doorstep yesterday. I was in a full-blown panic, and suddenly there you were." Tears glistened in her eyes. "And you came again today—"

"Even though you didn't want me to," he said.

"Only because this isn't your problem and I hated to drag you into it. You've been so wonderful—"

"Sweetheart, don't you get it?" he cut in. "This *is* my problem. Anything to do with you and the boys is my problem…because I love you."

He watched stunned surprise bloom in her eyes and grinned ruefully. "I guess I sort of caught you off guard, huh? I hadn't meant to tell you this way—you deserve candlelight and romance—but I can't wait for that. You need to know how I feel now. I love you."

Not giving her time to say a word, he pulled her into his arms and kissed her until her head was spinning, her heart was pounding and her feet no longer seemed to touch the ground. Dizzy, convinced she was dreaming, she wanted to laugh, to cry, to never let him go. But first she had to be sure.

"Don't do this if you're not positive," she told him, pulling back to study his face with searching eyes. "I love you too much to just want the words, Max. You know I'm a package deal. I don't play around. I don't have affairs, not when I have kids to consider and an example to set. If you don't love me enough to go the whole nine yards, then tell me now."

Over the last few months, she'd seen him grin and laugh and flash his dimples, but she'd never seen him smile at her as he did then, with his heart shining in his eyes and a love that was so tender it made her want to cry. "Sweetheart, do you think I don't know that? I've never been more sure of anything in my life. I love you! Do you know how incredible that is? I've never said those words to a woman before. All these years, I thought my father was crazy, that he was confusing lust with love, and it turns out he was right all along."

"Oh, Max!"

"I want to spend the rest of my life with you. And just so there's no misunderstanding, I'm talking marriage. And you don't have to worry about the boys. You know I'm crazy about them. Regardless of what happens with their father, I'll love and protect and cherish them just like I will you. So… will you marry me?"

Tears glistening in her eyes, there was only one thing left to say. "Yes."

Epilogue

Her heart in her throat, Natalie saw Derek's car pull into her driveway and had to fight the urge to bar the door. "He's here," she told the boys. "It's going to be okay, guys. There's nothing to be afraid of."

Her sons stood at Max's side, each one clinging to his pant leg, staring up at her with identical expressions of uneasiness. And Max wasn't much better. Oh, he seemed relaxed enough, with an arm around each boy's shoulder, but she wasn't fooled. There was a don't-mess-with-us look in his eyes that Derek would see in a heartbeat. "This is going to be nice and easy and nonthreatening. Remember?" she said, shooting Max a pointed look. "We're just going to visit and get to know each other."

"Of course," he said, amazed she would think he had any other agenda. "The boys don't have to worry about anything.

They know we're here for them and we always will be. Isn't that right, boys?"

"Yeah, Mom," Harry said eagerly. "Max says we're all one big happy family now, and family looks after family. Is our daddy part of our family?"

"Yes, he is, sweetheart, though I don't know how often you're going to see him since he doesn't live here. Right now, we just want to see how this meeting goes. Okay? Everything takes time."

The doorbell rang, and Natalie frowned at the boys worriedly. They stepped behind Max, using him as cover, and Natalie couldn't really blame them. This had to be as unsettling for them as it was for her. "It's okay, boys. Nothing's going to happen that you don't want to."

"Do we have to hug him, Mom?"

Her heart broke at Harry's plaintive question. "Your daddy's not going to force you to do anything you don't want to do," she promised him. *I'll make sure of it.* She didn't say the words, but she didn't have to. Her eyes met Max's, and she knew they were both on the same page.

She went to answer the door and was surprised to see Derek standing there alone. "I thought you were bringing Debbie."

"The baby was fussy—she seems to be coming down with a cold. Is that a problem?"

"No, not at all," she said easily. "The boys were just looking forward to seeing her." Pulling the door wider, she said, "Come in."

A few seconds later he followed her into the den, where the three men in her life were waiting. Not surprisingly, Derek stopped short at the sight of Max. She hadn't told him anyone else would be there—or that she was engaged. For now she was holding that news close to her heart. Today was about the boys.

Quickly introducing the two men, she went to stand by Max and smile down at the boys as they moved between the two of them. "This is Harry and Tommy," she told Derek quietly. "Boys, this is your daddy."

To his credit, he didn't try to rush them. Sinking down into a chair halfway across the room from them, he said, "Hi, guys. Wow, you really are identical! You even dress alike and everything. Do you like being twins?"

He couldn't have said anything that would have pleased them more—they *loved* being twins!—but they were still wary. Not budging from where they stood, one latched on to her and the other grabbed on to Max. Tommy did, however, volunteer, "We're mirror twins."

When Derek looked at her in confusion, she explained, "Tommy's left-handed and Harry's right."

"No kidding? You know, my grandpa and his brother were twins, too," he told Tommy. "And I think one of them was left-handed. Maybe that's where you get it from."

"Max is left-handed, too," Harry said, smiling shyly. "Just like Tommy."

Encouraged, Derek grinned. "So that means you're like me—right-handed."

As far as starts went, it wasn't a great one, but some of the tension seemed to drain out of the boys. Tommy was the first to bring up the baby. "Do we really have a sister?"

"Yes, you do," he said, pleased. "Her name's Jessica. She's just a month old, but when she's older, you guys can all play together."

"Maybe you could send them some pictures," Natalie said

quietly. "Then they can put them on their wall in their room with Grandma's picture and Uncle Steve's and their best friends from school."

"I'll do that," he promised. "Just as soon as I get home."

They had agreed to limit the first meeting to ten minutes, and that was just about over. Glancing at her watch, Natalie said, "You guys need to get ready for Larry Drake's birthday party, don't you? Why don't you tell your dad 'bye and go change? Your clean clothes are laid out on your bed."

"Okay!"

"'Bye, Daddy!"

Relieved, they rushed down the hall to their room, leaving behind a silence that was tense and awkward. Derek was the first to break it. "Well, I suppose I shouldn't complain. At least they talked to me."

"It's going to take time," Natalie told him. "You knew that."

He forced a smile that was little more than a grimace of disappointment. "I have no one to blame but myself. I lost my chance to be a father to them when I walked away."

"They're good kids," Max told him gruffly. "This is just strange for them."

"That's right," Natalie said. "They didn't know you existed until I told them about you this morning. I couldn't tell them about you and not be able to produce you," she added stiffly. "That wouldn't have been fair to them."

"You've done everything right with them, Natalie. I'm the bad guy in this, not you, and I know it." Shrugging off the grimness that had settled over him, he sighed wryly. "Would you mind if I called them once a week? Maybe on Wednesday nights?"

"Not if you're serious about being a part of their lives,"

she replied bluntly. "If this is just a passing urge, then leave them alone, Derek. They don't deserve that."

"I wouldn't be here now if I wasn't serious," he told her. Reaching into his pocket, he handed her an envelope. "That's a child support check. I know it should go through the courts—and I will set that up so you'll know you can depend on it—but for now, I want you to have it."

Stunned, Natalie took the check. "Thank you."

"Don't," he said gruffly. "You have nothing to thank me for."

Long after he left, Natalie stared at the check as if she'd never seen one before. The amount was exceedingly generous, but she hardly noticed it. Over the years she would have given anything for a tenth of what he'd just handed her—that's how desperate she'd been. "Why couldn't he have done the right thing when we divorced?" she asked Max, more confused than ever. "Why did it take him so long?"

"Some men are slower than others," Max retorted. "Look how long it took me to come to my senses about marriage. I'm smarter than Derek, though," he added with a grin. "I know a good thing when I see it." Pulling her into his arms, he grinned down at her. "Did I tell you today that I love you?"

Smiling, she pretended to consider. "Actually, I believe you did mention it a few times."

He grinned. "I thought I did. While we're talking about love, what do you think about New Year's Eve?"

"That depends. What's New Year's Eve got to do with love?"

"Oh, I don't know," he said casually. "It's the beginning of a new year, a new life, new beginnings. I thought it might be a nice time to get married."

Her heart jumped into her throat. Fighting a grin, she said just as casually, "You know, I think you may be right. Were you planning on marrying anyone in particular?"

Chuckling, he snatched her close. "Minx! I thought I might marry you."

"Good," she laughed, "because I'm certainly planning on marrying you. For a moment I thought we had a problem on our hands."

"The only thing I have my hands on is you, sweetheart," he growled. "For the rest of our lives."

* * * * *

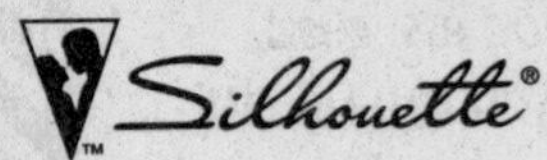

COMING NEXT MONTH

INTIMATE MOMENTS®

#1427 SOMEBODY'S HERO—Marilyn Pappano

Recently divorced Jayne Miller moves to the small town of Sweetwater, where she plans to revive her career as a romance author…and it doesn't hurt to have a handsome, brooding neighbor for inspiration. Tyler Lewis isn't happy to have neighbors, but no matter how much he refutes his desires, Jayne makes him want what he can't have…not with the secrets in his past.

#1428 MORE THAN A MISSION—Caridad Piñeiro

Capturing the Crown

When undercover agent Aidan Spaulding is asked to investigate the murder of Prince Reginald, he is given the chance to identify the Sparrow—the infamous female assassin who killed his best friend. All signs point to Elizabeth Moore, a local restaurant owner, but as Aidan gets to know the refreshingly kind woman, he realizes there is no way she is the assassin. But if Elizabeth isn't the Sparrow, who is?

#1429 BAPTISM IN FIRE—Elizabeth Sinclair

Two years ago, arson investigator Rachel Sutherland's home went up in flames, followed by her marriage to Detective Luke Sutherland when they were unable to find either their daughter or the fire starter. Now divorced, they must join forces against a serial arsonist—the same one who destroyed their dreams. Could they rebuild in time to find the firebug—and possibly their child?

#1430 DEADLY MEMORIES—Susan Vaughan

Sophie Rinaldi is researching her ancestors in Italy when she overhears plans of a terrorist attack in her host's mansion. Barely escaping death, she turns to U.S. Marshal Jack Thorne for help and finds comfort in his steady gaze. They get swept up in a dangerous attraction, which Jack tries to temper during his investigation. Can Jack keep his vow to capture his enemy without jeopardizing the life of the only woman he will ever love?

SIMCNM0706